59372083325509   WFR

D0049188

WITHDRAWN

The HIDDEN

ALSO BY JESSICA VERDAY

The Hollow
The Haunted

The HIDDEN

Jessica Verday

SIMON PULSE

NEW YORK   LONDON   TORONTO   SYDNEY

SIMON PULSE
An imprint of Simon & Schuster Children's Publishing Division
1230 Avenue of the Americas, New York, NY 10020
First Simon Pulse hardcover edition September 2011
Copyright © 2011 by Jessica Miller
All rights reserved, including the right of reproduction in whole or in part in any form.
SIMON PULSE and colophon are registered trademarks of Simon & Schuster, Inc.
For information about special discounts for bulk purchases,
please contact Simon & Schuster Special Sales at 1-866-506-1949
or business@simonandschuster.com.
The Simon & Schuster Speakers Bureau can bring authors to your live event. For more information or to book an event contact the Simon & Schuster Speakers Bureau at 1-866-248-3049 or visit our website at www.simonspeakers.com.
Designed by Paul Weil
The text of this book was set in Caslon.
Manufactured in the United States of America
2 4 6 8 10 9 7 5 3 1
Library of Congress Cataloging-in-Publication Data
Verday, Jessica.
The hidden / Jessica Verday. — 1st Simon Pulse hardcover ed.
p. cm.
Summary: Seventeen-year-old Abbey knows that Caspian is her destiny and theirs is a bond that transcends even death, but as Abbey finally learns the full truth about the dark fate that links her to Caspian and ties them both to the town of Sleepy Hollow, she suddenly has some very difficult choices to make.
ISBN 978-1-4169-7897-8 (hardcover)
[1. Ghosts—Fiction. 2. Supernatural—Fiction. 3. Death—Fiction. 4. High schools—Fiction. 5. Schools—Fiction. 6. Irving, Washington, 1783-1859. Legend of Sleepy Hollow—Fiction. 7. Sleepy Hollow (N.Y.)—Fiction.] I. Title.
PZ7.V5828Hid 2011
[Fic]—dc22
2011013704
ISBN 978-1-4169-8543-3 (eBook)

To Lee. You know why.

Preface

❧❀❧

My name is Abbey. And I'm in love with a ghost.

Chapter One

BROKEN

"If I can but reach that bridge," thought Ichabod, "I am safe."

—"The Legend of Sleepy Hollow" by Washington Irving

All I could hear was my heart beating. And all I could see were the Revenants looking down at me. As I stared up into Kame's colorless eyes, I kept thinking, *This can't be happening. This isn't real.* It was going to happen like *this*?

"Will it happen now?" I asked Kame. "Are you here to help me . . . die?"

He didn't answer my question.

"Is she okay?" Cacey whispered. "She doesn't look good."

Hysteria bubbled over, and I glanced down at myself. Blood covered my knees in dark, jagged lines, and my arm burned from where Vincent had tried to yank it out of the socket. My bedroom was in shambles. "I don't look good?" I said. "I don't *look good?*" Then I put my head down as tears covered my cheeks. *This is it. Sophie, Kame, Uri, and Cacey are here to collect me. To help me pass over.*

I was never going to see my parents again. Or Ben. I'd never have my own perfume shop, or graduate from high school. I'd never buy a house and get a dog.

I'd always wanted a dog.

But that didn't matter anymore. My time was up. Besides, Kristen was already dead. And *I* was the reason for that. At least I'd get to be with Caspian.

"Caspian . . . ," I said desperately, and sat straight up. "Caspian!"

The floor was covered in glass and bits of broken wood— what was left of my perfume cabinet—but I didn't care. Vincent had thrown Caspian. Hurt him. And he needed me.

I tried to crawl. Tried to get to him, but strong arms held me still. A wave of nausea swept over me, and the room spun crazily. My hands were slick from gripping the floor. Little pools of blood surrounded me in squiggly lines and half-shaped circles, forming a macabre version of a child's painting.

"Easy, easy," Kame said, his voice smooth and melodic, like the rush of soft spring air after a long-closed window has been opened. "Let's look you over, Abbey."

He glanced at my hands and my knees, gently moved my head from side to side to check for other wounds. Beside me Cacey was blowing out the candles that Vincent had lit, before gathering them into a small pile. Uri and Sophie were removing the flowers from the bed. Tossing them into a garbage can.

"Caspian!" I said, seeing his still form by the fireplace mantel. "Please . . . check Caspian . . ."

Cacey crouched down next to him and pulled up one of his eyelids. "That's the trouble with Shades," she complained. "Should I feel for a pulse? He's already *dead*."

"Cacey!" Uri reprimanded her, pausing from tying a knot in the trash bag to look over at me. "Tact? She's been through a lot."

"Sorry, sorry. I'm just saying." She looked into his other eye and gave him a shake. "I think he's still here."

"Go check the bathroom for a first aid kit," Kame instructed Cacey. "Sophie, find a phone. Call 911. We need to finish cleaning this up and get her to the hospital before—"

The sound of the front door banging open echoed beneath us, and Mom's voice drifted up. "Abbey? Are you home yet? We got the strangest note that said there was an emergency town council meeting, and . . ."

Her voice got closer as she climbed the stairs and moved toward my room.

"Well, shit," Cacey said. "Parents. What are we supposed to do about them?"

Kame sprang into action, directing Uri to toss the trash bag out the window, and then he scooped me up without even a second's hesitation. Sophie grabbed the phone and punched in 911. Then she said loudly, "I'm so glad we got here in time! Just hold on, Abbey. Hold on. Help is coming."

Mom burst into the room, and panic spread across her face. "What *happened*?" she screamed, seeing the blood and broken glass. "Abbey!"

She rushed over and tried to pry me free from Kame's grip. "What's wrong? What *happened*?" she asked, over and over again.

I couldn't answer.

"She's okay," Kame said calmly, catching her eye. "Abbey will be fine and everything will be back to normal soon." His tone was soothing. Mom started nodding at him, but the concern didn't leave her face.

In the distance I could hear sirens. They sounded odd. Both loud and blaring, and then quiet and almost muted. Kame's words started to fade in and out, with Mom's voice in the background.

"... paramedics coming? I ... don't understand. Why would ... Could have been killed! ... Thank God you were ..."

My head felt funny. My tongue was thick, and I tried to say something. Tried to say anything, but it wouldn't come out. Dark spots crept into the edges of my vision, and my chest tightened. *I think I'm ...*

But even that thought drifted away. So I did the only thing I could do.

I closed my eyes and slept.

The next time my eyelids opened, I saw a blue plastic chair with Cacey slumped over in it, asleep. I looked down, and there was tubing sticking out of my hand. I was lying in a hospital bed.

My throat ached fiercely, and I tried to clear it. "Cace—," I croaked. "Cac ... ey ... water ..."

She shifted, then sat up. Completely alert. "Oh. You're awake."

"Water?" I tried to look for a glass or pitcher, but the only thing sitting on the stand next to me was a TV remote and a small bowl.

Cacey came over and picked up the bowl. "Here. Ice chips. They don't want you to drink any water yet. Something about a test they want to run."

I greedily sucked down the chip of ice, and the tiny bit of cold relief that spread down my throat was blissful. She fed me four more pieces before she pulled the bowl back.

I laid my head down on the pillow and tried to remember what had happened as Cacey returned to her seat. "How are you feeling?" she asked. "You were pretty out of it."

Suddenly everything came rushing back.

Vincent in my room, lying on the bed, surrounded by rose petals. Him breaking my perfume cabinet and hurting my arm. The glass . . .

The blood . . .

I glanced down at the sheets, and then over at the beeping machine by my side. "How long have I been here?"

"A couple of hours. They're going to release you tomorrow." She picked up a Coke can from the floor next to the chair and took a long sip. "They didn't want to keep you overnight, but your mom pushed them into it. It was pretty impressive. She and your dad have been in and out the whole time."

I stared at the Coke can.

"I told them we were friends from summer school. Your mom totally bought it. Well, after she calmed down, I mean. She was crying and yelling. I—" Cacey finally noticed that I was ogling her beverage. "What? You want some of this?" She tipped the can back and drank down the last of it. "Sorry, all gone," she said with a smile that was just a tiny bit cruel. "So anyway . . . since you've been in here, Kame and Sophie made up this killer cover story about an intruder breaking into your house. You *didn't* get a good look at him, by the way."

She waited for my nod before she continued. "So he broke into your house, smashed up all your stuff looking for drugs or stuff to steal or something like that, and when you interrupted him he got physical before taking off. We came and saved the day."

She paused again, and I took it all in. Then she made me repeat it back to her. "Intruder. Didn't get a good look. Smash and grab. You saved the day."

Cacey nodded, looking pleased. "That about covers it." She leaned forward. "Oh, and get this, Uri and I are 'interns' for Kame and Sophie. That's how we know them. You should know that too."

My head was starting to hurt. Normally Cacey's voice was smooth and comforting, but now it was starting to grate on my nerves. And she had a weird habit of not blinking. It was like staring into the eyes of a fish.

She came to stand next to me, and stared at me as she said, "Remember what I told you, Abbey. You remember, don't you?"

A funny feeling prickled the back of my scalp, and suddenly

I felt much calmer. And happier. She was right. Everything had happened exactly the way she'd said it had.

"So tell me," I said, reaching up to fluff my ragged curls. "On a scale of one to ten, how bad do I look?"

She cocked her head to one side and looked me up and down. "You're a solid five. Maybe a five and a half. I've seen worse. But I've seen better, too."

I laughed. The sound was raw against my throat, so I tried again. It came out funny and high-pitched. I opened my mouth to say something, and caught a whiff of burning leaves. "What's . . ."

The question died in my throat as Cacey looked at me strangely. "What's what?"

I sniffed again. But the odor was gone. "Nothing. I thought I smelled . . . nothing."

She leaned over and fluffed up my pillow, then pulled the sheets higher. "I'm going to watch some TV. Your parents should be back soon."

Her words made something in my brain click. "Caspian," I said. "What about Caspian?"

"Oh, you finally bring up lover boy now, do you? You know, for being all fated to be together and whatnot, you took long enough to ask about—"

"Cacey. Please," I said softly. "I need to see him."

She sighed. "He's safe right now with Nikolas and Katy. He should stay there until we can figure out what Vincent wants."

"Please?" My eyelids were drooping, and she started swimming before my eyes. Sleep was pressing down, hard and heavy. "I really need to ..."

"I know, I know. You need him. Blah, blah, blah."

I felt blindly for her hand. "Have to make sure he's ... okay. ... Tell him I ..."

The last thing I heard her say before I drifted away was, "I know. I will. I'll tell him that you love him."

There were words. Soft words. Words I didn't understand but knew I would follow anywhere because he was speaking them.

"Astrid."

I turned my head to follow the voice but kept my eyes closed just in case it might not be real. In case it was a dream. The words came again, intermingling with ones I recognized.

"Astrid, can you hear me? *Tu sei una stella ... la mia stella.* You're my star, Abbey."

I opened my eyes slowly. His face came into focus. Tears stung the backs of my eyes, and my throat burned. "I'm so happy to see you. I thought you were ..."

He shook his head and glanced back at the door behind

him. "I'm fine, and you're fine, and we'll talk later. You just concentrate on getting better. You're going home tomorrow, right?"

I nodded.

"Get some sleep. I'll be right here when you wake up. But remember, other people will be here too. Don't talk to me if anyone else is in the room."

I nodded again and closed my eyes. A shiver came over me as he spoke into my ear. "I love you, Astrid."

"Love you, too," I mumbled. "Caspian . . ."

I spread my left hand wide on the covers, palm-side up. And fell asleep to the sensation of a faint tingle against my arm.

When I woke up the next morning, Caspian was there just like he'd said he would be, sitting in the chair on the other side of the bed. But Cacey was gone. I shot him a grateful smile, glad that he was with me and I wouldn't have to be alone when a couple of police officers came in to ask me some questions about the "break-in." I just kept repeating what Cacey had told me. Once it became obvious that my answers weren't going to change, they decided to leave.

"If you think of anything else, give us a call," one of them said. He pulled a business card from his pocket and handed it to me.

"I will," I promised.

The one who handed me his card shook my hand before they left the room. An instant later a huge balloon bouquet squeezed through the door, being carried by Mom. Dad was right behind her with a fistful of flowers.

"Hi, sweetie! How are you feeling?" She nodded toward the door. "How did that go?"

She set the balloon weight on the empty bed beside me, then leaned down and brushed some hair away from my face and kissed my cheek.

"It was okay," I replied. "I don't really remember much."

Mom shot Dad a look and busied herself with rearranging the balloons. Dad put the flowers he had on my nightstand and came over to my other side. "Hey, honey. It's good to see those baby blues again."

I beamed up at him. "Good to see you, too, Dad." I shifted my elbow underneath me so that I could sit up. Suddenly I noticed the flower bouquets that filled a table in front of a large window. Daisies, carnations, lilies, roses . . . even a baby tree.

"Are those all for me?" I asked, stunned at how many there were.

"They sure are," Mom said proudly. She flitted over to some pink daisies in a polka-dotted pot. "These are from the Maxwells." White lilies were next. "And these are from Mrs. Walker, the librarian." She fussed with a carnation stem. "Word spread pretty quickly about what happened . . ." She stopped and bit her lip.

"Who's the tree from?" I asked as a distraction.

Caspian surreptitiously moved out of Mom's way as she came closer to it. I flashed him a quick smile.

Mom picked up the card. "Oh! It's from Ben. Isn't that nice of him?"

I had to hold back a snort of laughter at the "matchmaker" tone in her voice. She had no idea that Ben was in love with my dead best friend, and I was in love with a ghost. My eyes found Caspian's. He gave me an exasperated look, and I quickly raised one eyebrow. "Yeah, Mom," I said. "He's very . . . nice."

"We're going to have a fun time dealing with them on the way home," Caspian said as soon as Mom and Dad left the room again.

"*We?* Are you planning on hitching a ride with us?"

"As long as Vincent's still out there, consider me rabbit skin."

"Rabbit skin? Do I even *want* to know what that is?"

"It's glue. Sorry. Obscure artist term."

A thrill raced through me at the thought of having him so close. "What if I just call you Elmer's?"

He snorted. "I guess that's better than Casper."

"Hey! I happen to like—"

A knock sounded on the outside door frame, and immediately I grew silent. A second later a nurse stuck her head in. "You have a visitor. Feeling up to some company?"

It's probably Uncle Bob. "Sure. Send him in."

The nurse disappeared. And Ben walked in.

"Hey, Abbey. How are you?"

He had a small bunch of flowers with him, and his curly brown hair was messy. His face clearly showed that he was nervous.

"I'm good." I glanced down at the IV tubing still in my arm. "Well, as good as I can be, stuck here."

The nurse peeked back in. "I hope I can trust you two alone in here. She needs her rest, mister." She directed a steely gaze at Ben.

"Oh, we're not—," I said at the same time as Ben said, "I'm not—"

"Mmm-hmm." She looked back and forth between us. "That's what they all say."

I rolled my eyes at Ben when she left, and he laughed. "Awkward."

"Yeah."

He shifted from foot to foot, then hastily laid the flowers on the edge of the bed.

"Thanks," I said. "And thanks for coming to see me." My

eyes landed on the baby tree. "And thanks for the other gift too."

He followed my gaze. "It's from my dad's farm. He just bought some new seedlings. It's supposed to flower."

I could tell that Caspian was trying *very* hard not to look at Ben, and it made me want to tease him. "Why don't you sit down?" I said, pointing to the open seat next to Caspian.

Ben sat. Glancing back at the door, he volunteered, "Hospitals really freak me out."

Caspian slowly inched away from him, and said, "They're starting to make me pretty uncomfortable too."

I tried not to laugh, and just replied, "You should try being on this end."

Ben's expression suddenly changed from nervousness to anger. "I can't *believe* that someone broke into your house, Abbey. I should have walked you in. Made sure everything was okay before just driving off like that."

"It wouldn't have made a difference," Caspian said to Ben, even though he knew his words would go unheard. Then he turned to me and said, "There's no telling what Vincent would have done to him."

I nodded solemnly, but spoke to Ben. "It's not your fault. You couldn't have known what was going to happen."

"But I feel so bad. And now there's this crazy guy out there who hurt you, and if I had just been able to stop him, you wouldn't be here."

"There was nothing you could have done," I told him. "It's not your fault. End of story."

"Are you sure?"

"Yes, I'm sure. Now, can we talk about something else? Like what happens if we end up as science fair partners again this year?"

Ben laughed. "I'm counting on it, Browning. In fact, I think I'm going to slip Mr. Knickerbocker a twenty to make sure it happens. Since you bailed on me last year, you have a lot to make up for."

The nurse knocked on the door again, then entered. "Your parents are on their way, dear. You're being discharged."

Ben stood up.

"I'll see you at school, right?" I said to him.

"Yup. Seniors, baby."

He left right before Mom came back in, but I could see the gleam in her eye even though I was halfway across the room. "Ben came to visit?" she said.

I nodded.

"Well, isn't that nice of him."

Chapter Two

STUCK LIKE GLUE

...for it is in such little retired Dutch valleys, found here and there embosomed in the great State of New York...

—"The Legend of Sleepy Hollow"

Dad drove twenty miles per hour under the speed limit on the way home and constantly kept looking back at me in the rearview mirror. It was making me crazy.

"It's okay, Dad," I called from the backseat. "You actually *can* drive, you know."

He gave me a worried look in the mirror again. "I know, honey, but I just want to make sure I don't jostle you."

I sighed. "I'm fine, Dad. Driving at the speed limit so we can get home at a decent hour isn't going to kill me."

His face paled.

"Sorry," I said. "Bad choice of words."

Caspian was next to me, and I leaned my head back against the seat. *This is going to be worse than when I came home from Dr. Pendleton's. At least then everyone just thought I was crazy.* Now they were treating me like I was as fragile as glass.

Dad turned onto a side road, and our house came into view. A giant banner that said WELCOME HOME, ABBEY! was hanging over the front door.

"Oh, jeez," I muttered.

"Party time," Caspian said. "I hope they have those little blower things that make noise."

His comment made me laugh, and I had to cover it with a fake cough. Dad came to a stop, and Mom opened my door for me. "Let me help you," she insisted. "You could still be woozy and not even know it until you stand up."

The doctors had put my arm in a sling because of a sprain. Since I wasn't used to not being able to use my hand, I put my free arm around her neck, and Caspian slipped out behind me.

"I'm so glad you're home," Mom said, steering me into the house. "I'm taking a few days off work so I can be here with you."

I wanted to argue that I was seventeen, not five, but I didn't have the heart. "I should probably go up to my room and rest for a while," I said. She nodded, and then escorted me up the stairs. Caspian followed us.

As soon as we entered my bedroom, I noticed that it was different. Gone were the spilled perfumes and broken glass bottles that Vincent Drake had strewn across the floor, yet a smell still clung faintly to the air. I could tell that Mom had probably sprayed some cleaner, because a lemony scent was there too—the unmistakable odor of wood furniture polish—but it didn't mask the reminder of destruction entirely. A burgundy wingback chair sat in the corner where my perfume cabinet had been. I recognized it as a remnant from the attic.

The red roses that Vincent had placed around the room were cleaned up by Uri and Sophie, but all I had to do was close my eyes to see them again. And to see Vincent lying on my bed, dressed in a black funeral suit, his hair white-blond like Caspian's, even down to the black streak . . .

Mom put a hand on my shoulder. "Is everything okay?" she asked. "You don't have to sleep in here if you don't want to. I can make up the guest room."

"It's okay, Mom. I'll be fine." I purposefully went over to my bed and sat down on it. I didn't want the memory of Vincent to drive me away from here. *This is my room. Not his.*

Mom came over too, and moved the pillows around, stacking them one on top of the other. Then she turned back one edge of the covers, folding it and unfolding it again.

I caught her hand and held it. "I'm *fine*, Mom." I forced a brave smile. She had no idea what had really happened here, and I wasn't going to let on.

"Is there anything that I can get you?" she said. "Anything you need?"

"Nope. But thanks for the offer."

She looked at me for a long time without saying anything, her eyes wide and kind of glassy. Then she leaned forward and kissed my forehead before standing up. "Try to get some sleep. I'll wake you when dinner's ready."

"Okay, Mom." I kept the smile on my face until she left the room, then I slumped against the bed and let out a little sigh. My arm ached, and I lifted the sling with a sad little wave at Caspian. He sat down beside me.

"Hurt myself," I said.

"I see. Looks like you're going to need an extra hand."

"Know any takers?"

"By your side like glue." He grinned at me, but his eyes were sad.

I wanted to take away the sadness that was there. Make it disappear and have it never return. "What I told Ben goes *double* for you, you know. It's not your fault."

He ran a hand through his hair and looked away. "Yeah, but

unlike Ben, it *is* my job to protect you. Or at least . . . to do the best that I can. I can't believe I let that happen." He smacked his fist against his open palm as he spoke. "Vincent attacked you, and now you're here, like this, and I'm . . ."

"Stuck like glue?"

"That's right," he said softly, catching my eye. "Stuck like glue."

"Lucky for you I happen to like glue." I kicked off my sandals and unzipped my hoodie. It was hard to pull my injured hand through the sleeve, but once it was out, I was able to shrug the shirt off the rest of the way and tossed it on the floor.

Caspian reached down and picked it up. Then he walked over to the closet door and hung it on the knob. "Is this okay here?"

"Yeah, it's fine. You know, you're going to be handy to have around. You can put away *all* of my laundry."

He made a short bow, then came back to the bed and stretched out beside me. "If laundry duty is what milady wants, then laundry duty is what she will get."

He turned to face me, and his black streak of hair covered one eye. My heart fluttered.

"That's the picture of domestic bliss," I said. "Add in a big fan and an exotic drink, and you have every girl's dream fantasy."

"Domestic bliss, huh? You wanna play house with me, Abbey?"

I felt my cheeks heating up. "I, um . . . You know what I mean. Servant. Fantasy. That sort of thing."

"Right. Right. Every girl's fantasy. But I'm only interested in one girl's fantasy." He leaned forward. *"Yours."*

I thought back to our recent hotel stay in West Virginia. Where we'd shared a bed . . . and a towel. Then something else struck me. "Hey, who did the laundry at your house?" I asked softly.

His face grew serious, and he looked away. "We went to the Laundromat. There was a lady there who washed it for us. Eventually she showed me how to do it. She even made me a cheat sheet so I wouldn't forget. Only took a couple loads of pink shorts and one overflowing washer, but then I taught Dad."

I watched his face move as he spoke, and was struck once again by how beautiful he was. And by something more . . . How *mine* he was.

"So you did all of your own laundry? What else did you do?"

"I got myself up for school and made my own lunches."

I pictured a younger version of Caspian trying to put together peanut butter and jelly sandwiches every morning, and my heart felt sad. Mom had *always* made my lunches for me when I was little. She'd even taken special requests, like when I wanted egg salad for three months straight. "I would have made your lunch for you," I said softly.

He went to squeeze my hand, but pulled back as he remembered he couldn't. "I know, Abbey," he replied instead. "I know."

We lay there in silence until finally I said, "You know what's going to be the best thing about having you here with me?"

"Having a manservant at your beck and call?"

"Nope. But that's a close second." I moved my free hand closer to his until that faint tingle of almost touching buzzed through me, and I gazed up at the constellations covering my bedroom ceiling. "The best thing is having someone to look at the stars with."

A couple hours later Mom called me down for dinner, while Caspian stayed up in my room. The whole time we ate, I kept thinking about what it was going to be like to have him there without my parents realizing it. *I'll have to be careful. Have to watch that I don't let anything slip in front of them, that they don't hear me talking to him.*

"You're awfully quiet over there," Dad said. "What are you thinking about?"

"The fact that we should get an alarm system."

Okay, so that wasn't really what I'd been thinking about, but it sounded good.

Mom and Dad exchanged uncomfortable glances. "Your mother and I have someone coming over this week to talk about our options," Dad replied.

I forked a piece of broccoli and kept eating. "Okay."

They both just looked at me, dumbfounded.

"So . . . you're okay with that?" Dad asked.

"Yeah. Why wouldn't I be?"

"Well, we wouldn't want you to be uncomfortable with the idea of needing to have one, to feel safe here."

I put my fork down. "Dad, someone broke into our house. I think an alarm system would be okay."

Mom put her hand on the table with a loud bang. "Enough! Enough of this conversation! I don't want to discuss it anymore."

"I think we should *all* discuss this," Dad said.

"Yeah. It's only an alarm system, Mom. No big deal . . ."

Mom's face was stricken. "*I* don't want to discuss this. We've lived in this town our entire lives and nothing like this has *ever* happened before. I don't want to know that we're getting an alarm system put in because there's some crazy person breaking into homes and hurting people's children and . . . *and* . . ."

 25

Her voice grew louder with every word until she was practically screaming.

Then she shut down.

"I can't deal with this. I need a pill."

She suddenly left the room, and I waited for some type of explanation from Dad.

But he didn't give me one.

"What was *that* all about?" I prodded him. "'I need a pill'?"

"Your mother is just upset by everything that happened. The doctor prescribed her some pills to calm her nerves."

"Calm *her* nerves? You'd think she was the one who'd been attacked."

Dad sucked in a sharp breath of air.

"I didn't mean it like that. It's just—"

He shook his head. "I know what you meant. But it's going to be tough for a while. We all need to . . . adjust. Your mother and I love you very much, Abbey."

"I know, Dad. I guess I just need some time to adjust too." Time to adjust to the fact that they didn't know what had happened, and I could never tell them.

My broccoli was cold now, but I didn't feel like heating it up. Pushing my plate away, I maneuvered my sling out from under the table and stood up. I turned toward the stairs, but stopped short.

"Hey, Dad? What would you and Mom do if I died? Or if I had already been dead when you guys came home and found me?"

All of the emotion bled from his face. "What kind of a question is that?"

"Just a question."

"It may be 'just a question,' but it's certainly not something you need to worry about." He patted my arm. "You have a very long life ahead of you."

When I made it back to my bedroom, Caspian was lying on the bed, looking up at the stars. "You know they're much better in the dark," I said.

"I know. But I was waiting for you." He propped himself up on one arm, and I sat down beside him. "How did things go down there? I heard yelling."

I sighed. "Yeah. It was Mom. She's freaking out because they have a security system guy coming to put an alarm in."

"And she doesn't want that?"

"Oh, she wants it. Or doesn't. Or doesn't want to want it . . . I don't know. It's confusing. She's confusing. It's not like it's going to stop Vincent if he comes here again anyway, but they don't know that. I think she's just mad about the fact that she feels like she has to get one."

I shrugged. Or tried to. The sling on my arm pulled tight and hurt. "I can't wait to get this stupid thing off," I said, lifting it up.

"Aw, poor baby. I can't even rub it or anything."

I gave a mock sigh, but my arm was really hurting now. "Can you grab me that pill bottle on the desk?" I asked him. "The tall one with a yellow lid."

He obliged and dropped it next to me on the covers. I popped the top open and reached for the glass of water sitting on my nightstand. After washing down two pills, I recapped the bottle and rolled it back across the covers to him.

Caspian scooped it up and put it back on the desk. Then he walked over to the closet. A moment later, a blanket was placed next to me. I looked at it in surprise.

"I figured you'd want that," he said.

He'd figured right. I was already pulling it on top of me and snuggling underneath. He sat down beside me without a word.

"Can I ask you something?" I said. "About . . . Vincent?"

"What do you want to know?"

"After I went to the hospital, what happened?"

He looked like he was thinking about it. Then he said, "The last thing I remember was seeing him in your room. All I could think about was getting him out of here. Then it's just a blank.

When I woke up, I was with Nikolas and Katy. At their house."
He put his head down, right next to my ear. "I said that I needed
to find you. Sophie and Kame were there, and they told me
what had happened. Then they brought me to the hospital."

"Did they tell you why Vincent came after me?" I asked.

"What do you mean?"

"He came after me because he got the wrong girl," I said
sadly. "He thought Kristen was me. I'm the reason why she's
dead, Caspian."

"That's not true," he said. "It's *not* your fault. You're not the
reason she's dead. *He* is. Don't put that on yourself."

"But if I had just known . . . had done something to warn
her . . ."

"Warn her how? You couldn't have changed anything, and if
you had—" He stopped.

"You know we're going to have to talk about it sooner or
later," I said. "The reason why the Revenants are here. Because
I'm going to d—"

"Don't say it, Abbey," he begged. "Please don't. I can't think
about that. About you . . . I just can't."

"Everyone has to die sometime."

"You think I don't know that?" He put his hand out, and it
went through mine. "I know better than anyone."

He turned away from me, obviously upset.

"I'm sorry," I said. "Don't be angry."

"I'm sorry too. I didn't mean for it to come out like that. I just can't . . . I can't picture you dead, Astrid." Caspian held out both hands and spread them wide.

"I won't bring it up again," I promised, desperate to make everything better. "I swear."

He exhaled a shaky sigh and closed his eyes, leaning his head next to mine. We would have been touching . . . if we could.

I closed my eyes too. The pain pill was making me sleepy. "Will you stay?" I asked, burrowing deeper into my covers, closer to him and yet still so far away. "Stay with me."

"Forever," he whispered. "I'm staying forever."

Chapter Three

STRAIGHT CORNERS
AND BAD ANGLES

In this way matters went on for some time . . .

—"The Legend of Sleepy Hollow"

When I woke up the next morning, I noticed two things. The first was that my sling was stuck underneath me at an impossible angle, and second . . . I had a hot guy in my bed.

Ignoring the dead weight sensation that I knew would lead to pins and needles when my trapped arm woke up, I lay very still and took in the sight before me. Caspian was on his side, one arm thrown up above his head. His T-shirt twisted slightly so that I could just barely make out the bare flesh above his jeans.

My eyes traced a path down the stripe of black hair that lay across his cheekbones. Then to his nose, his lips . . . Lips that I wanted to kiss again. *How many days until November first?*

How many days until the anniversary of his death day, when we can touch?

Two weeks until school started, and then thirty-one days in October . . .

Too long. *Much* too long.

My gaze slipped lower. To his skin. I couldn't help myself. Couldn't stop myself from reaching out to try to feel that piece of him I wanted so badly. I'd never realized, never *dreamt,* that a relationship without something as simple as a touch could be so hard.

Caspian's eyes flickered open, and I knew he felt the same tingle that I did.

"Hi," I said softly.

He just looked at me. Then a slow smile came across his face. "Were you ogling me?"

"Drawing a mental picture," I said, with a wicked grin of my own. "Remembering that night last Christmas when you took off your sweater and showed me your tattoos."

With one swift movement he reached down and twisted up the shirt. It slid off, and my pulse skyrocketed. "Better?" he asked.

"Much." I sighed. My heart beat like a drum in my ears, and the air around us felt heavy and thick. I couldn't stop staring at him. Couldn't stop looking at his skin. So different from mine, yet the same. It was fascinating. Little bumps and ridges made up the hollows of his collarbone, while smooth, taught flesh stretched all the way down . . .

He looked at me and raised his eyebrows. "Are you going to return the favor?"

"No." I swallowed hard.

"No? That's not really fair."

"Oh, yes. It is. I'm the injured one here, so you have to indulge me a little."

Caspian nodded. "All right. Have you indulged enough yet?"

I shook my head.

He rolled over and stretched out on his stomach, arms crossed in front of him, back fully exposed. The edges and lines of the tattoos on his shoulder blades blurred a little. The interlocking chain of small black circles and triangles all ran into one another. I realized I was staring too hard. And possibly drooling.

I shifted and pulled my arm out from under me, turning so that I was on my side, facing him. "You aren't . . . I can't even . . . Does it ever bother you that we can't touch?" I asked desperately.

"Every day."

His tone was soft. Simple. But a whole different world lay behind those words. *His* world. A world that I couldn't be a part of. Not yet, at least. We were miles apart.

"What were you thinking about when you got your tattoos?"

I said, changing the subject to something easier. Something with answers. "What was your inspiration?"

He shifted too. "The stop sign outside my old house was graffitied. Someone painted big circles on it. Then someone else overlapped it with a triangle. It wasn't the same pattern I have on me now, they were two distinct designs, but my mind just put them together in this weird way."

"That's cool."

"It may sound hippieish," he said, "but when I saw the circles, I felt this . . . connection. To the earth. Or Mother Nature. Or whatever 'it' is. I've always had this feeling that I was connected to something. Or someone."

"Maybe it was me." His eyes held mine, and I would have given *anything* to be able to reach out and touch him. "We're connected. Maybe we—"

"Morning, sweetie!" Mom called from right outside the door. She came in holding a laundry basket, and I bolted upright. I'd never even heard her come up the stairs.

My gaze flew to Caspian. Even though I *knew* she couldn't see the half-naked shirtless boy on the bed, I still had a moment of panic. "Hey, Mom," I said awkwardly.

She crossed the room and pulled back the curtains. "What do you want for breakfast today?"

"I'm, uh, not really hungry."

"But you have to eat. Why don't I make chocolate chip pancakes?" She went to the closet, opening up drawers and putting away socks.

"Yeah. Fine. Good. Sounds great. I'll get dres—"

"Or Belgian waffles? You love those."

"Yeah, Mom. Okay." I mentally willed her to leave the room. "I'll be down as soon as I get dressed."

She came out of the closet and smiled at me. "I was thinking that maybe after breakfast we could do a movie day. I rented a bunch of them."

I got to my feet and opened the bathroom door, hopefully sending the message that I needed to get in there. "Okay. But first waffles, right?"

Looking way too excited, she said, "You got it," and headed out the door.

A breath I didn't even realize I'd been holding escaped me, and I turned back to Caspian. He reached under the sheet and pulled out his shirt. I was sad to see his bare skin get covered up. "Well, great," I said. "Now I have to go do breakfast. Want to come with?"

"I'd say yes, but since she can't see me *and* I don't eat, I think I'll just hang out here." He blew me a kiss as I padded into the bathroom, and I returned the favor.

Already I was regretting Mom's terrible timing, and wondered just how fast I could get back to him.

Half an hour later I entered the kitchen and glanced at the plate stacked ten waffles high, wondering how Mom had made so many so quickly. Then I took a seat at the table. "Did you make some for the neighbors, too?"

She grinned and brought them over to me. "I just wanted to make sure you had enough to eat."

I neatly slid two waffles onto my plate. Mom came over with apple *and* orange juice, and plunked them both down next to me. Then she put a couple of waffles on her own plate and sat down.

"We should go get another mani-pedi once your sling is off," she said, pausing in between bites. "I think I want to go red on my toenails."

"Bright red? Or dark red?"

"I think dark red. Maybe maroon."

I looked down and pushed the waffle around on my plate. *Kristen's casket was dark red . . .* Then I said, "Hey, Mom, if someone else is spending a lot of money, but it's a purchase for you, would you get to decide the details?"

"I don't know what you mean. Like a car?"

"Yeah. Like a car. If someone bought a car but it was actually *for* someone else, could that person make the decision about the details? Like what paint color it is?"

Mom laughed. "Is this some kind of graduation gift hint, Abbey?"

I moved my waffle around again. I wasn't sure how to say what I wanted to say. After all, how exactly do you blurt out, *I'm going to die soon, and I'd like to make sure that my casket is red,* without sounding like a crazy person?

"What's your favorite flower?" I asked instead.

"Daylilies. White ones. I know they can be sort of Easter-ish, but I think they make such a beautiful display."

Not exactly my first pick, but it wasn't that bad.

"What about your favorite church song? Like a hymnal?"

Mom leaned back and thought about it for a minute. "I guess I'd go with 'Oh, When the Saints Go Marching In.'"

"Really? I wouldn't have guessed that one. 'Oh, When the Saints Go Marching In' is kind of peppy for a funeral."

"A funer—?" Mom stared at me. "What did you just say?"

"Funerals have songs and flowers. I just wanted to know which ones you like."

"Why are you talking about this, Abigail?" Mom's voice had that high-pitched hysterical note in it again.

"Well, since Kristen died really young, it made me realize

anything could happen. For my funeral I want a red casket. Like she had. White lilies are okay. I don't really mind those. But pick a better song than 'Oh, When the Saints Go Marching In,' okay?"

Her fork clattered to the floor. Pushing back her chair, Mom stood up abruptly. "That's not funny. This conversation is over. I'm not in the mood to watch any movies today. You'll have to find something else to keep yourself occupied."

She left the kitchen without saying another word, but her footsteps were angry as she stomped into the living room.

I stared down at my plate. Why was everyone around me so sensitive about death all of a sudden?

I went back upstairs to Caspian and threw myself down onto the bed. Groaning, I said, "You're so lucky you don't have a mother to deal with anymore."

He didn't respond.

I looked up, regretting the words already. He was sitting at my desk, hands folded. "Sorry. I didn't mean . . ." I sighed loudly. "I keep doing this. Keep saying the wrong things. I don't know what it is, but it's like I'm all straight corners and bad angles."

He came over and reached for my face. I sat still, unsure if he was actually going to try to touch me, or was going to keep some space between us. I felt the faint buzz on my cheek, and I turned my face toward him. "Is it November first yet?" I whispered.

Caspian shook his head and mouthed a silent *No*. But he held his hand there a bit longer. "Just let her get over everything, Abbey, okay? Give her some extra time. And space. She's going to need it."

"I know, I know. When did you get so smart?"

"I've always been this smart. Wait, are you into smart guys?"

"*Definitely* into smart guys." I smiled at him, then looked away. I didn't know how much more of this not-touching I could take. It felt like this invisible wall was between us every time we got close, and I couldn't tear it down. I got up and walked over to the window.

The window Vincent Drake had escaped from.

I traced a line down the glass. It made a soft rubbing noise as my finger slipped down it. An invisible trail left behind.

"Don't you think it's kind of messed up that the Revenants want me dead, while Vincent wants me alive?" I mused, keeping my fingertip on the glass pane.

Caspian came up behind me. "What did you say?"

"Vincent doesn't want to kill me. In fact, he even told me not to do anything stupid."

"What *does* he want, then?" he asked.

"Me. Alive. Why? I don't know."

I stared out the window, lost in my thoughts. I couldn't stop the scene with Vincent from playing out again and again in my head. If I'd only done something different . . . defended myself somehow, or made him pay for what he'd done to Kristen . . . If only I could make it all go away . . .

I turned, and my eyes landed on an old perfume notebook gathering dust on the corner of my desk. I couldn't even distract myself with a project; all of my perfuming supplies had been inside the cabinet Vincent had destroyed.

"I wish I had something new to work on," I said. "Maybe it's time to take Mom on a little shopping trip for some perfume stuff. Spend some *quality time* together. That should make her happy." I crossed over to the chair and rested my sling on the desk.

"You could always learn to draw," he replied.

"I could? Know anyone who would teach me?"

"As a matter of fact, I do." He picked up his drawing pad and a charcoal, then sat down on the bed. "Come here."

Quickly abandoning the desk, I went to go sit beside him. Caspian flipped to a new page and pointed to it. "Draw a tree," he instructed.

"I can't. It's not going to be any good. I can barely hold a pencil, let alone draw anything."

"So? Just try."

I sighed, then grasped the charcoal carefully. It left black streaks on my fingers. Conjuring up all of the things my elementary school art teacher had once said about basic shapes and "becoming one with the object," I tried to sketch the barest outline of a tree.

It looked like a squiggle.

My hand shook as I tried to smooth it out, tried to press the charcoal down harder and make the branches take shape, the trunk appear, the limbs extend outward.

It still looked like a squiggle. Only . . . worse.

"Yeah, I got nothing."

Caspian looked down at it. "That's not true."

"I have some black smears. Hardly anything to get excited about." I turned the page sideways and studied it, putting the charcoal down. "Hey, if you look at it this way, it kind of looks like a giant monster hand or something."

He laughed. "Let's see what we can do with this." Picking up the charcoal again, he set it to the page and started making quick, short strokes. Dark magic seemed to flow from his hands and settle right onto the paper. Long, smooth lines were next, and I could see something taking shape.

"Is that a forest?"

He nodded and kept working, transforming my pathetic, spindly attempts at a tree into a dark, twisted stump. The background came together, and trees started springing up, gathering around the edges in a wild dance of abandon. Some of the trees had spiky, forked branches, a stern warning to pay attention to what they had to say—while others pointed whimsically this way and that, their arched spines and flowing limbs swaying in time to some unheard beat.

"That's amazing," I breathed. "You're making it all so real. I can see the story there."

He kept working, smoothing and shading, until the edges were perfect. The lines sharp where they needed to be sharp, and soft where they needed to be soft. I didn't speak, barely breathed, not wanting to interrupt him.

Finally he finished.

When he looked up at me, his eyes were bright and happy. He nudged back the sweep of hair that had fallen into one eye, leaving a charcoal smear on his forehead. Overwhelming gratitude filled me to have this chance, this perfect moment, to witness his happiness.

His passion.

"What should we call it?" he asked.

Without hesitation the words flew out of me. "Dance of the Forest."

"Perfect." He scrawled the name on the bottom of the paper, and then ripped the page out of the art pad, placing it on the covers beside me. "For you. See what a good team we make?"

I snorted. "Yeah, right. Without my terrible tree you *totally* couldn't have made that brilliant drawing."

"I wouldn't have had anything to start with," he corrected. "So, I wouldn't have ended up with that." He began another piece as he spoke, this one just a simple river. It was finished quickly, and he flipped the page again. Next a garden came to life, and he filled it with flowers.

I could have watched him draw all morning, but eventually he broke the stillness. "You know, you're not completely out of perfume supplies, if you want to make something."

"Yes, I am. Vincent broke everything."

"What about your supply briefcase?"

My briefcase? I got up and went to check under my desk. "It's still here! You're right! I can make something with the supplies I have in here."

I propped it up on the desk and opened the latches. Delight filled me as I ran my uninjured hand over the rows and rows of shiny amber glass bottles. I grabbed vanilla essential oil, butter CO_2, basil essential oil, and oakmoss absolute to start with. Then I plucked up a handful of transfer pipettes and a mixing glass, and sat in the chair.

After pulling out a bottle of jojoba oil, I poured twenty

 43

drops into the mixing glass and flipped open the nearby perfumer's notebook to write down which oils I was using.

"Did you know that the art of perfume is one that goes back to ancient times?" I said to Caspian. "Perfume was commonly found in the Bible. Cypress, sandalwood, myrrh, frankincense, cinnamon, and Balsam essential oils were used in the preparation of anointing oils and were burned as incense for sacrificial offerings." I carefully measured out ten drops of basil oil and mixed it with the jojoba carrier oil. Five drops of oakmoss came after that. And then five of vanilla.

Caspian watched over my shoulder.

"There was even a bunch of perfume on the *Titanic*," I said. "Adolphe Saalfeld was a perfumer who lived in England but wanted to market his scents in the United States. So he booked passage on the ship and took sixty-five test tubes of concentrated perfume scents with him. He survived the sinking, but left the perfumes behind. When they made that big discovery over the crash site a couple of years ago, they found his perfume samples and brought them up. Almost all of them had been perfectly preserved and they were able to re-create them."

Using one of the transfer pipettes, I stirred the mixture awkwardly, not used to having to work around a sling, and then put the lid on. "Can you even imagine that? Being able to re-create a perfume that sat for all that time buried under the depths of the ocean? God, what a find." I opened the bottle a couple of seconds later and inhaled deeply.

He watched in rapt fascination as I kept writing and mixing, adding more drops of this and that, then recapping and smelling.

"Needs more woodsy tone," I muttered to myself after the fifth try. "Something . . ." I searched my supply case, eyeing what I had left. Spotting the Balsam oil, I grabbed for it. "Like *that*."

Caspian read the label. "Isn't that a Christmas tree?"

I nodded. "But you're thinking of Balsam fir. That's the pine-needle-smelling kind. This is Balsam from the Balsam bush. It smells spicy. A little bit like cinnamon. Unless it gets old. Then it smells like vanilla." I added a couple of drops and made a note. "Some people believed that Balsam was harvested by a group of people called the Essenes who lived in Egypt and were known for their healing practices using essential oils. They lived where there were Balsam bushes and became cultivators of it, collecting it to sell and using it to support their way of life."

He put his hand next to mine on the desk, and I paused, looking up.

"You are amazing," he said softly. "Smart and beautiful and talented. Where did you learn all of this?"

Embarrassment filled me, and I looked away. "Research,

mostly. I'm just some dork who needs to get another hobby."

"No, you're not. You're—" He suddenly paused and glanced back at the door. Like he had heard something I hadn't.

And then I heard it too.

Someone was right outside my room.

A halfhearted knock came, and the door opened. I leaned back, getting ready to say something to Mom, and then I saw Beth, from school.

Here.

At my house.

In short shorts and a bikini.

"Hey, Abbey," she said brightly, all smiles. Her skin glowed like she'd just been airbrushed to perfection, and the toned gap of skin between her bathing suit top and shorts made me all too conscious of the fact that I hadn't exactly spent my summer running track like *she* obviously had. "I totally called first, you know."

Caspian moved to the closet. I watched him go, trying not to notice if *he* was noticing the short shorts.

"Hey, Beth," I said slowly, getting to my feet. "This is . . . unexpected."

She wandered over to the bed and sat down by the pile of drawings. Flipping past the top one, she stared at the garden of flowers. "Yeah, I'm on my way to the family beach house and thought you might want to come." Her gaze flitted over to my sling and then swung away. "I, uh, heard about the whole hospital thing. How bad was it?"

"It's fine. This is just overkill, really. The doctor insisted."

"I hate when doctors do all this bullshit stuff just to tell you you're fine. My mom works for an insurance company, and I swear, the things she says hospitals can get away with . . ."

Her fingers idly traced paths down the page in front of her. I could tell she wanted to ask me more about the attack, and I groaned inwardly at the thought. Beth was really nice, and I liked her, I did, but I totally wasn't in the mood to go through it again.

"Thanks for the invitation," I said, steering the conversation off that track. "I wish I could go, but . . ." I held up the sling as explanation.

Beth looked down again. She'd found the drawing of the forest. "Hey." She sat straight up. "Hey, Abbey, these are really good. I didn't know you were an artist."

"I'm not. I didn't. I mean, they're not mine. They're someone else's."

Beth smiled. I groaned inwardly again because I knew that smile. And it was not one I wanted to see. "Ohhhh," she said. "Someone drew them for you? Who are you dating, girl?"

"No one," I said weakly, trying to laugh it off. *Technically, not true. But easier than the real answer* . . . "Hey, what ever happened to Lewis? Are you guys still together?"

"Ugh, no." She blew her bangs out of her face with a disgusted breath. "He got too serious for me. He kept wanting to make plans for our future, and discuss what we'd do at college. And then! Then he brought up moving in together at some, like, halfway point if we went to different schools, so we could see each other on weekends. *Seriously?* I mean, dude, you're a great lay and all, but I need some variety."

"Um, yeah. I totally get it." *No, I don't. I'm going to be with my boyfriend for all eternity. Talk about a commitment.*

I tried *very* hard not to glance at Caspian, but I couldn't help a quick peek. His face was blank, unreadable. I couldn't tell if he was purposely keeping it that way or if he truly didn't have any interest in what Beth was saying.

Or wearing.

"So, how'd he take it?"

"He was heartbroken, of course," Beth said, drawing my attention back to her. She walked over to my desk and picked up the bottle of oakmoss oil. Her face wrinkled as she sniffed it. "Ew. Gross. That smells like dead plants or something."

I laughed and took it from her. "Here." I handed her vanilla. "Try this one."

Her face lit up with a blissful smile as she inhaled. "Mmmmm. Could you make me a perfume like this?"

And just like that, my thoughts were spinning. Already working. *I could add Madagascar vanilla with just a hint of butter crème, and some brown sugar to spice it up.* "Yeah. Sure. No problem."

Suddenly she hugged me. "Come to the beach with me," she urged before pulling away. "We'll find some lifeguard hotties and get drunk under the moon at midnight. I don't care what Lewis says. I'm *young*. I need to live life. Look at you, right? You don't have some high school boyfriend hanging around your neck like a chain, and you're fine."

I didn't even know what to say. "I . . . Beth . . . I . . ." I shook my head.

"Puh-*lease*? Come on, Abbey. It's just for one day. Just come hang out with me for *one day*. That's all I ask."

The problem was that, in a normal world, it was something I might have agreed to do. But now Vincent was here, and so were the Revenants, and I didn't know what to tell Caspian . . . and *Mom*. Plus, how could I act like I was single? It wouldn't feel right flirting with some hunky boy. I had my *own* hunky boy right here.

The only trouble was, no one could see him but me.

"I can't, Beth," I said firmly, shaking my head. "I'd just feel awkward with my sling, and I'm not really up to finding some guys right now, after everything that happened. Maybe next time?"

She gave me a pouty look, but I could tell she saw that I was serious. "Okay, fine. Whatever. Just don't go all moldy being cooped up in here, okay? Get some air."

"I will."

"And you better make me some of that vanilla perfume too."

I laughed. "I will. I will. I'll bring it to you on the first day of school."

Beth blew me a kiss as she went out the door. "'Kay. Later, *chica*. I'm on my way to go find some beach hotties on my own."

I waited until the coast was clear, and then I shook my head as I closed the door behind her. But I couldn't stop the smile from spreading across my face.

"She seems nice," Caspian said, a teasing lilt to his voice. "Why didn't you tell her about me?"

"Riiiiiight. What was I supposed to say? 'Yeah, sure, Beth. I'll go with you. But there's just this one teeny, tiny thing. See, I don't need to find a boyfriend because I already have one. He's just dead and therefore invisible.'"

Caspian laughed, and I pinched the bridge of my nose. Why was my life so complicated?

Chapter Four

MIND MOJO

❧❀❧

Such is the general purport of this legendary superstition, which has furnished materials for many a wild story . . .

—"The Legend of Sleepy Hollow"

The next week and a half passed by quickly, and I was just getting used to having the sling on when it was time to take it off. Caspian went with me to the doctor's office, but it was when we got home that the real surprise of the day came. Cacey and Uri were waiting there for us, standing by a car parked at the end of our driveway as Mom pulled up.

They were both dressed in khaki pants and business shirts— outfits similar to what they'd been wearing when they'd come to my room right after Vincent had been there. But Cacey's blond hair was blue at the bottom.

"Surprise!" Cacey said when Mom turned the car off. "We thought we'd come see you."

Mom, of course, was thrilled to see my new friends. "Well, hi! How nice of you two to stop by. Aren't you working today?"

Cacey shook her head. "Kame suggested that we come talk to Abbey to see if she wants to join the intern program at the real estate office with us. It's such a fantastic experience. We're sure she'd be great at it. There's nothing more valuable than learning the lesson of hard work!"

Trying to keep a straight face through Cacey's BS was becoming a monumental task. Real estate interns . . . Yeah, right. How long was she going to keep this act up? It didn't help matters when she started winking at Caspian.

Mom must have noticed the winking, because she asked Cacey, "Are you okay?"

"I think I have something in my eye." Cacey winked again and then grinned unabashedly. "So, do you want to come with us, Abbey? We're heading over to the office now, and you can see what we do. Learn more about the program." She stretched out the word "program" into two long syllables.

Mom glanced at me, and out of the corner of my eye I saw Cacey nod her head once. I followed suit. "Okay . . ."

Mom's smile couldn't have gotten any bigger. Clearly she was pleased by my "initiative."

It's not real, I wanted to tell her. *They aren't really interns, and Kame and Sophie aren't real estate agents.*

But the less she knew, the better.

"We'll have her back by dinner, Mrs. Browning," Cacey called, directing me to the backseat of their car. Uri said something to Mom to distract her, and Cacey motioned for Caspian to get in too. He slid in next to me, and I shut the door.

"What are we getting ourselves into?" he asked.

"I have *no* idea. But it must be important for them to come get us like this."

Cacey got in the front passenger seat and pulled down the mirror, checking out her blue-tipped hair. "I know. I know," she said, almost to herself. "That was laying it on thick. 'The value of hard work.' Ha! But I get so caught up in this little drama. I just love it."

"What's up with the whole pretending to be an intern thing?" I asked. "And the outfits?"

"Just playing a role. It's better for us to fit in when we can." She smiled at me, and I had the distinct impression of a shark eyeing its prey. Her clear, gray eyes were wide and focused. The faintest scent of smoke, or burning leaves, filled the car, and then it was gone. I felt a rash of goose bumps run up and down my arms.

"Did anyone ever tell you that you're kind of creepy?" I said suddenly.

She burst out laughing. "Yeah. I am. Thanks for noticing." Preening, like I'd just offered her a compliment instead of an insult, she patted her hair and air-kissed the mirror.

Uri came over to the car and got in. "Hi, Abbey." His smile was genuine and friendly, his voice smooth like chocolate. He slammed the door shut. "Caspian."

Caspian nodded back, and I wondered if this was it. Were they here to take me to my everlasting reward in a . . . "Hey, is this a Jetta?" I asked.

"Yup." Uri kept his eyes on the road and pulled out of the driveway.

"Nice, right?" Cacey said. "Totally better than some of the other rides we've had. Do you have *any* idea how long a Volkswagen bus can continue to run? Even when the floorboards are rotting out and the dash is falling to pieces and the whole thing smells like a Sunday school nursery class?" She shuddered.

"Well, it's no sweet chariot," I replied, and grinned at Caspian. He didn't seem to get it.

Or maybe he did, because he frowned.

"Are we supposed to be impressed by your ability to remember church hymns?" Cacey asked. "Ooh, do you know one called 'Amazing Grace'?" she deadpanned.

Heat bloomed in my ears. "No. I meant 'swing low, sweet chariot.' Like the song? Aren't you guys 'coming forth to carry me home' and all that? Aren't we, you know . . . *Going?* To my next destination? A long drop and a short stop?"

Cacey laughed, and it rang through the car like the clear high-pitched peal of a bell. "Dramatic much, Abbey? We're just going to get some lunch."

I sat back and looked morosely out the window, feeling duly chastised. Highway blacktop rushed up to meet us, and the single lane became two. I felt a slow flare of sensation in my knee and looked down. Caspian was trying to nudge it.

He gave me a sympathetic smile. "I thought it was pretty clever," he leaned over to whisper. "The whole 'sweet chariot' thing."

"Good-looking *and* loyal," I whispered back. "You're a deadly combination."

"Deadly." . . . Good going there, Abbey.

But if he noticed my poor choice of words, he didn't let on.

"Hey, you two," Cacey said. "This isn't secret time. Do you want to share with the rest of the class?"

"No." I crossed my arms.

"Fine. It's rude, but whatever."

Cacey was calling *me* rude? The same person who had drunk all of her soda in front of me just so she wouldn't have to share any of it when I was in the hospital and practically dying of thirst, and who had a snarky reply whenever someone asked her something, was calling *me* rude?

I was about to launch into it, when all of a sudden Caspian leaned forward and said loudly, "So, Uri, about that Volkswagen bus . . ."

Instantly the tension in the car broke, and I laughed.

"Loyal, good-looking, and *smart*," I said to him. "But you already knew that."

Uri grinned and switched lanes. "It was a 1951 VW bus, and it was a beast. Already going on forty years old when we, uh, acquired it. It had some interesting history."

"It was a crap-mobile," Cacey said. "With pleather seats and orange shag carpeting. I swear it had to have once been a traveling sideshow circus car or something."

"Do you remember the mummified mouse?" Uri asked her.

"Yup. Stuck between the seats."

"*What?* Ew. No way," I said.

"True story," Cacey replied. "Someone had actually taken the time to mummify this thing."

"How could you tell?" Caspian interrupted. "Couldn't it just have been a really old dead mouse?"

Cacey tapped her mouth. "The lips. They were sewn shut."

"God, Cacey!" Nausea roiled through me, and I wanted to barf at the thought of seeing some poor little mouse that way. "That's just insane."

"Do mice even *have* lips?" Caspian mused. Uri laughed, and they shared a grin.

"Moving on," I said.

But Cacey obviously didn't want to move on. "Its little fingers had been pushed apart. Splayed open, instead of curled shut." She mimicked it with both hands. "And the eyeballs—"

"I'm not going to be able to eat lunch," I warned her.

"Then there was the tooth," she said.

"Do I even *want* to know about the tooth?" I groaned, and then promptly answered myself. "No. No, I do not."

"... on a key chain," Uri filled in.

"Lost baby tooth?" Caspian suggested. "A family memento?"

"Molar," Cacey and Uri both said at the same time.

"Must have been pried right out of someone's mouth with something blunt, because the ends were all damaged and jagged," Uri supplied. "The bus came from a junkyard in West Virginia. Crazy-ass place. Who knows what happened there."

Cacey laughed delightedly, and I shook my head at her. She saw me and stopped, but grinned at Uri. "Abbey thinks I'm creepy. She told me when she got into the car."

Something passed between them—more than just a look— and I got the impression there were silent words being spoken. "She's right," he said. And then he put a hand on her knee. "You *are* creepy."

Uri directed his next words to me and Caspian. "She totally gets off on this stuff. I don't know why." He shook his head bemusedly at her, someone who had obviously been putting up with his partner's peculiarities for a long time and didn't mind doing it.

"Why didn't you just get a new car if that one was so awful?" I asked.

"Ooh! We're here!" Cacey squealed. A restaurant called the Pink Peppercorn came into view, and we pulled into the parking lot. "First we go get a seat. Then I'll tell you why about the car. Deal?"

I nodded, but she was already climbing out.

"Wait until I've stopped the car," Uri admonished.

She did. But barely.

I got out and kept the door open long enough for Caspian to get out too. "Are we going to be okay going in?" I said softly to Uri, nodding my head at Caspian and then Cacey. "I mean, all of us?"

"It'll be fine," he said.

Cacey heard my question. "He doesn't eat much, right? Because it's going to be embarrassing trying to explain *his* order."

"I don't—," Caspian said.

"I know! I know!" She laughed. "I'm just teasing. Lighten up. It'll be fine. Come on."

I glanced at Uri. "It *will* be fine," he said again, ushering us to the door. "She'll behave."

Doubtfully, I followed behind them as Caspian brought up the rear. When we got inside, Cacey flagged down a waiter, and he seated us right away in a large booth. The interior of the restaurant was decorated in pale pinks and grays, with tiny hints of black. It had a smooth 1920s vibe to it.

"How'd you get service so fast?" I asked Cacey, settling in next to the space where Caspian was.

"It's the mind mojo," she said absentmindedly, poring over the menu. "Works every time."

"Mind mojo?" I asked. "What's that?"

She pointed to the extensive listing in front of her. "Choose what you want to eat. Then talk. When he comes back, I want to give him our order. I'm *starving*."

I perused the list. It looked like the Pink Peppercorn was strictly vegan fare. I'd never been to a vegan restaurant before. "Where's just plain breakfast?" I asked. "That should be safe enough."

Cacey flipped the menu and pointed to the back.

"I guess I'll take the tofu scramble," I said after a minute. "Spinach, soy cheese, asparagus, and shiitake mushrooms with home fries doesn't sound too bad."

"Yum! I'm going with the vegan hot tamale platter. And I want a Coke, like, *now*," Cacey replied. "What are you getting, Uri?"

"Tofu burrito."

"You don't mind if we eat in front of you, do you?" Cacey asked Caspian. She didn't seem to care that people might notice she was speaking to him.

"It's not like I have a choice, do I?" he said. "Be my guest."

The waiter glided over and took out a pen and pad. Cacey rattled off her order, and I could see that he was taken with her melodic voice, just like I'd been the first time I'd talked to her. He had a hard time paying attention to what he was writing as Uri and I told him what we wanted, and his gaze kept straying back to her colorless eyes.

"I would absolutely *love* a Coca-Cola to go with my meal,"

Cacey said, maintaining eye contact. "In fact, we all would."

A funny metallic taste filled my mouth, like burned toast, and I reached for the pitcher of ice water that was sitting on the table. After pouring a glass, I gulped some of it down quickly.

"I'll see to it," the waiter murmured. "And I'll get this order put in right away."

"Thank you!" Cacey called as he walked away.

"Is she always like this?" Caspian asked Uri.

"Every time. Worse when she really wants something."

"That's enough from *you.*" Cacey pointed to Uri. "And you, too, dead boy." She pointed to Caspian.

"Don't do that," I whispered.

"Do what?"

I made some abstract gesture with my hand. "Point to Caspian. Bring attention to him. People might see."

She looked around us at the half-empty room. "Honey, these people in here have better things to do with their time than pay attention to us. They're too busy discussing what will happen when they go home to their underground bunkers and assemble to conquer global hunger and world peace with hugs and teddy bears. They don't give two shits about what we say or do."

"*You're* eating here," I said to her. "Does that mean you go home to your bunker and hug teddy bears?"

Her smile turned sharp. "I don't hug anything."

Then she winked at me, and I laughed. "Okay, okay. Tell me about this car, then. Why couldn't you just get a new one if the bus was so crappy?"

She leaned back in her seat. "Um, duh. Because we're Revenants."

She left it at that, and I swear to *God* I could have strangled her. Instead I raised an eyebrow.

"Neat trick," she said.

I waited for her to continue, but she didn't. "Soooooo, are you going to give me the real reason?" I said.

She just stared blankly at me.

"Uri?" I pleaded, turning to him.

"We couldn't get a new car because that was the one given to us to use for our job duration," he explained. "You take what you can get."

"So, wait," I said. "Were you guys given the bus, or did you take it?"

They exchanged a look.

"A little of both," Uri said.

"Is that because of the mind mojo thing?"

Cacey nodded, but Uri frowned.

"How does it work?" Caspian asked.

"Like all things wise and mysterious beyond your grasp," Cacey said. "It just *is*. Accept it. Move on."

"Do I have it?" he persisted. "Can I do mind mojo too?"

The waiter suddenly appeared, holding three cans of Coke and three glasses of ice on a tray. He sat everything down on the table with a flourish, and Cacey beamed at him. "Thank you, good sir."

He stuttered a "Y-you're welcome" before fleeing.

Cacey didn't even bother with her glass, but chugged the soda straight from the can. "Deeeee-licious!" she crowed after a full minute's worth of swallowing. "This really is the best stuff on earth. Trust me. I've been around."

Caspian drummed his fingers on the table. "Cacey," he said. "Mind mojo? Do. I. Have. It?"

"Why don't you try?" she taunted. "Go ahead and lay one on me, big boy."

I couldn't help the snort of laughter that escaped me. Honestly, she was so ridiculous at times.

Caspian stared at her.

She stared back.

He screwed up his face and squinted his eyes. Nothing

happened. Finally he wiggled his fingers. "Abracadabra?" he said.

"Nope," Cacey replied. "You don't have it."

Uri leaned sideways and spoke to Caspian. "What were you trying to make her do?"

"I was trying to make her tell us that she's a pretty, pretty princess."

I laughed loudly. "*That* I would have paid to see."

"Hey!" Cacey said.

"*Paid*. Like, a hundred bucks."

"I am a pretty, pretty princess," Cacey said automatically. "Pay up."

"Doesn't count. You already told us he doesn't have it."

Uri, Caspian, and I burst into laughter while Cacey crossed her arms and acted all pissy.

"Oh, get over it," I told her. "Move on." She stuck her tongue out at me, and I rolled my eyes. "Seriously, though. Is there a reason why Caspian can't do the mind mojo thing?"

"Because he's a Shade, not a Revenant," Cacey said. "He's not like us."

"So only Revenants can do it?"

She shook her head. "Sorry. I can't tell you how everything works. That's the way it . . . works."

I glanced at Uri and opened my mouth to ask him, but he shook his head too. "Sorry, kiddo. She's right on that. No unfair advantages."

"But this whole thing is like an unfair advantage," I replied. "How many people know that they're going to die?"

"Technically, everyone knows they're going to die," Cacey said.

"I mean, how many people know they are going to die *soon*? As in having-lunch-with-the-people-that-will-take-their-souls-any-minute-now soon."

Cacey and Uri shared another look, and then Cacey shrugged. I was about to ask again, when she said, "Ooh! Here comes the food!"

The waiter made his way out of the kitchen with a loaded serving tray and then passed around the plates when he got to our table. My tofu scramble actually looked pretty good, and it smelled delicious. I felt bad that Caspian was going to have to just sit there and watch us eat, but he gave me a reassuring nod.

The food, as it turned out, *was* tasty.

Cacey barreled her way through her tamale while Uri demolished his burrito. "Wow," I said, only halfway through mine. "You guys were hungry."

 65

"We've just come to appreciate fine food," Uri replied.

Cacey sighed in happiness as she drained the last of her Coke and reached for Uri's. "Sleepy Hollow doesn't have *any* place like this," she said. He patiently nudged his glass over to her.

I cleared the rest of my plate as they discussed ordering something to go. Ultimately they decided against it, and the waiter came back with our check. Luckily, I'd pocketed some money before I'd gone to the doctor's that morning, and I pulled a ten from my back pocket.

"Don't worry about it," Uri said. "We've got it covered."

"That's okay. I don't mind. Really, I—"

"You can give me the ten if you want, Abbey," Cacey interrupted. "But I'd keep it if I were you. If Uri said he's gonna cover it, he's gonna cover it."

"Are you sure?" I lowered my voice. "I didn't know if you guys had any money."

Uri pulled out a wallet and opened it, flashing a billfold stuffed full of hundreds.

"Oh," I said meekly. "Sorry,"

"No big." He left enough money on the table to cover the tab, and we headed outside.

We climbed into the car and pulled out of the parking lot.

Cacey talked the whole way home about more weird stuff that they'd found in their circus mobile, but I couldn't shake the feeling that there was some important question I needed to be asking, or something I should know the answer to.

I just couldn't figure out what it was.

Chapter Five

REGRETS

❦

. . . he had various ways of rendering himself both useful and agreeable.
—"The Legend of Sleepy Hollow"

There were precious few days of summer vacation left, but Caspian and I settled into a routine that consisted of drawing lessons for me, perfume lessons for him (well, more like perfume *watching* sessions, where I made the scents and he told me stories from his childhood), and nights under the stars. It was an easy rhythm. Comfortable, and safe.

The little things were what surprised me the most. Like how awkward I thought it would be having him around all the time. How uncomfortable getting undressed every evening, or using the shower every morning with him in the next room, would be. But . . . it wasn't. He was a perfect gentleman.

And a surprisingly good roommate.

"You don't have to keep doing this, you know," I said, turning back the covers to get ready for bed one evening, and finding a pair of socks tucked by my pillow.

I *told* him he didn't have to do it, but a shiver of happiness went through me that he had.

"Your feet get cold at night. You're always getting up to go get another pair." He brought over an extra blanket, too, and placed it at the foot of the bed.

"You're going to spoil me," I said. "But while you're at it, could you turn off the overhead light?" I climbed into bed and pulled the sheets up over me.

He obliged, and flicked the light off. A second later the bed dipped slightly under him as he came to sit next to me.

"I still don't know how you can stay here with me when I fall asleep," I murmured, trying to get comfortable. "Don't you get bored?"

"Time passes quickly for me, remember?"

I closed my eyes and nodded, snuggling deeper into the pillows. "If you're sure."

"Don't you want me to stay? I can always leave—"

"Don't." I yawned. "Don't leave. I like it when you stay with me."

"Then, that's enough for me," he said. "Sweet dreams, Astrid."

And that was the last thing I heard before I drifted down into the dream.

Around me glass crunched, and sharp edges bit into my hands. I was on the floor, kneeling among the bits and pieces of my life. Scattered dreams surrounded me.

"Pay attention, Abbey. This might just save your life." Vincent Drake leered down at me, and I felt sick.

"No . . . Don't . . ."

He grabbed my arm and hauled me to my feet. My knees screamed as glass slivers ground deeper and deeper into my open skin.

I reached for a piece. Slid my fingers around that cool, sharp edge and held on. Then swung.

A spray of blood erupted from Vincent's cheek.

I looked down at my hands covered in blood. His blood. *"This isn't . . ." I dropped the glass to the floor. "This isn't how it goes. It didn't happen like this. I didn't stab you."*

My eyes turned red, and I realized that blood was dripping down into them. Hot and sticky, it stung as I tried to rub it away.

"Isn't this how you like them?" a voice whispered in my ear, and then he was pushing me toward the bed. Horrified, I tried to get up. Tried to see.

 70

The bed was surrounded with flowers. And candles.

Vincent appeared in front of me, a rose clenched between his teeth. "For you, a dance!" He crossed his arms in front of himself, and kicked his legs high. Around us the candles flickered. They looked strange, and I noticed that they were thick and heavy. Old-fashioned. And covered in cobwebs.

The stench of dying flowers overtook me. It's too much . . . I can't breathe . . . Can't . . . breathe . . .

All the while, Vincent danced. Crazy, jerking moves at first, but then his pattern changed and he acted like a puppet on a string. Stiff, and controlled. "Want to jerk my strings?" he taunted. "Oh, wait. I forgot. You like the dead ones."

He stooped. Head bowed, arms splayed wide. And waited for my applause.

"This didn't happen!" *I screamed inside my head.* "None of this happened. This isn't how it goes!"

He moved closer. In his teeth the rose was no longer a rose, and I stared at it before I realized what it was.

A bone.

Vincent brandished it like a prize, then tossed it away. "Too much?" he asked. "You didn't like my performance, I see. No clapping. I'm upset by this, Abbey."

He planted a hand on my back. Forced me toward the bed again.

His features changed. Eyes turned huge and black, as craggy, dark wings sprouted from his shoulders and his teeth grew long and sharp.

"And now, the pièce de résistance!" he shouted.

He threw back the covers. The candles swelled, the flowers were overwhelming, and there . . . was a body . . .

I sat straight up in bed, my blood racing and my face covered in sweat. My heart was thumping so hard, it felt like it was going to burst right out of my chest. The clock said 3:12 a.m., but that couldn't be right. I'd been asleep for only a couple of minutes.

I kept staring at it. Blinking. Trying to bring it into focus and force it to make sense.

"Abbey?"

I heard Caspian's voice, but I couldn't see him. My eyes weren't adjusted to the dark yet, and I had the strangest feeling that he was floating all around me.

"Are you okay?" he whispered.

My dream came flooding back, and suddenly the room seemed smaller. The air thinner. My chest tightened painfully, and I tried to suck in a breath. "Caspian? Where are you?"

A faint tingle on my arm flared, then died.

"I'm here," he said softly. "Right here. It was only a dream. Are you okay?"

"I don't know. . . . Stay with me."

"I will. I'm here." Moonlight filled the room, and I could see the worried look on his face. "Was it about Vincent?"

"Yes."

Caspian got up and turned on a small lamp. Instantly I felt better as the shadows receded and light flooded the room.

My T-shirt was clammy, and I pulled it away from me. Swinging my feet to one side of the bed, I stood up. "I'm going to change. I'll be right back," I said.

I padded over to the closet and pulled the door shut behind me. My stuffed animals were piled up in one corner, and I sat beside them, looking blankly at the wall. I must have been lost in my thoughts for a while, because a soft knock eventually came on the door, and then Caspian said, "Abbey? Is everything okay?"

I struggled to my feet and peeked out at him. "I'm okay. Just thinking about everything. I'm going to get changed right now. Be out in a minute."

He nodded and closed the door. I went over to the pajama section of my closet and reached for a pair that was light blue and covered in white fluffy clouds. I slid them on, and then returned to bed.

Caspian sat down beside me. "Want to talk about it?"

"Yes." I shivered. Then changed my mind. "No." Drawing my feet up under me, I hugged my legs to my chest. "I don't know." I wound the sheet around my fingers. "I don't even . . ." I shook my head.

"What?"

"It doesn't do any good to talk about it. It was just a stupid dream. It doesn't mean anything and it doesn't change anything."

"Sometimes it helps to talk things out."

"But my dream didn't make any *sense*." I told him what I could remember of it. "In real life I didn't cut Vincent with a piece of glass. Or even try to defend myself."

"Maybe that's *why* you had the dream," he said. "To act out a different course of action."

I laughed. "Yeah. Right. Because I have a hero complex."

"It's not a hero complex to want to defend yourself, Abbey. He came into your space and hurt you. You didn't get the chance to do anything about it then, so let yourself do something about it now. Even if it is only in your dreams."

"What I'd really like is to dream about saving Kristen," I mused. "To stop her from meeting Vincent. Or going to the river." I thought about it for a minute. "Actually, you know what's weird? I haven't dreamt about Kristen at all lately. Not in the hospital, or here at home. The only thing I've dreamt about so far is Vincent. Violence. And death."

"Maybe that's a good thing," he said.

"Dreaming about violence and death?"

"No. I meant not dreaming about Kristen."

"Why would that be a good thing?"

"Because aren't the dreams you have about her sad? They seem that way."

"Yeah. But I don't know . . ." I shrugged. "It's a way to keep her close to me, you know? I'd rather have sad dreams about her than not have any dreams at all. At least that way I still get to see her." Then I shuddered. "Although, I'd like to *not* have the dream about her dying again. That one I'll gladly skip."

Caspian nodded sympathetically.

"What was it like when you died?" I said suddenly. "I know you told me what happened right after your car crash, but did you feel any pain?"

He sat up straighter and glanced down at his hands. "Abbey, I—"

"Please? Please tell me? I want to know if . . . if I'm ready."

"You can't *be* ready," he said with an exasperated look on his face. "No one is."

"I know, but I can try to prepare. Right? At least be more

 75

ready than the average person who doesn't know it's coming."

"What are you going to do?" he asked. "Set your affairs in order? Write notes to your family?"

"Maybe I am," I said. "So?"

"So don't you think that might freak them out? If you start giving them 'Dear Mom and Dad, I won't be alive much longer' letters, they might think you're going crazy."

"It's not like I'm going to give it to them *now*. Just, you know . . . Get them ready. For after."

He shook his head. "It's not healthy, Abbey."

"Why? What's so unhealthy about it? How different is it from someone knowing that they have a terminal illness and getting everything ready for when they pass on?"

"It's just different. You're not sick," he said.

"But I am. I'm terminal."

"No. You're not. You have no idea when—"

"But I do!" I exploded. "I *do* know, Caspian. I know I'm going to die soon, and there's nothing that I can do to stop that. So why can't you just support me on this?"

"I can't," he said quietly. "I just can't." He let out a shaky breath. "If the situation were reversed, you'd feel the same way."

"*I* would support you in anything you wanted to do. I'd help you do it."

"Why?" he asked suddenly.

His question threw me off guard. "Because I love you. Because I want you to be happy. Because I want us to be together."

"You don't know what it's like to have the one person who makes everything around you come to life start talking about her death," he said. "It's just . . ." He spread his hands and looked at them. "I don't even know how to describe it. But to know that you're talking about being like me, like *this* . . ." He clenched a hand into a fist. "How can I want that for you? You're beauty and light and color and smell, and I'm darkness and ash and shadows and death. Cold and alone."

"But you won't *be* alone. Don't you see that? We'll be together. And then it won't matter about everything else, as long as we're together."

"Is that the only reason you want to be with me, Abbey? So I'm not alone? It's different. Different from anything you can ever imagine. What if it's not what you think it is? What if you come to regret losing the chance you had at life? The chance to be surrounded by the people you love?"

"*You're* the person I love," I insisted. "All I need."

"What about your shop? What about Abbey's Hollow? The opportunities you'll miss to go to Paris and study with the artists there. Or London, to go on shopping trips to buy new bottles or perfume supplies. Are you so ready to give up that dream?"

I didn't know what to say. Did he have a point? There was still so much I wanted to do. To accomplish. Could that change? Would *I* change? What if I came to resent him for not having had any of the things I'd wanted in life?

"That's not going to happen," I said.

"Are you sure?"

His eyes seemed to see straight into my soul, down to my deepest thoughts, and I squirmed uncomfortably.

"I'm not saying that I won't regret not having the chance to open Abbey's Hollow," I said slowly. "But how do you know what I will or won't be able to experience once I'm with you? Maybe there's a perfume shop somewhere on the other side that needs an owner." I made a halfhearted attempt at a smile.

"For your sake, I hope so." He smiled back. "But for now . . . just live the life you have, okay? Don't become fatalistic. Don't try to set everything up for your end days. Just enjoy the here and now."

"I will," I promised, and he looked relieved.

We sat in silence, the moon shining through the clouds and peeking into the bedroom as it played hide and seek behind them. "I don't want to go back to sleep," I finally murmured. "I don't want to dream."

"I can help with that." The bed shifted and he got up, moving toward my bookshelf. A moment later he returned. In his hand was my battered copy of *Jane Eyre*.

"A book?" I said happily, moving the pillows behind me so that I could be propped up.

"Something else to think about." He sat down and opened to the first page. "'Chapter One. There was no possibility of taking a walk that day. We had been wandering—'"

"You're going to *read* to me?" I asked, interrupting him. I couldn't help the giddy note that had crept into my voice.

"Yes, but be quiet now, my *bella*."

"What does that mean?"

"'Beautiful.'"

That word. The way he'd said it triggered a memory. "Did you speak to me in a different language? When I was in the hospital?"

Caspian nodded. "Something to keep the nightmares at bay. To let you know I was there. *Tu sei una stella . . . la mia stella*," he said. "It means 'You're a star. My star.'"

"What language is that?"

"Italian."

I leaned forward and propped my chin on my fist. "I didn't know that you knew Italian. Are you holding out on me?"

"It was just something I remembered from middle school. I took Italian from sixth grade through eighth." He looked at me sternly. "Now, are you going to let me finish?"

I zipped a finger across my lips and threw away the imaginary key.

"Chapter One," he said. And he began to read.

Chapter Six

LAST FIRST DAY

The schoolhouse stood in a rather lonely but pleasant situation, just at the foot of a woody hill . . .

—"The Legend of Sleepy Hollow"

I spent the next day working on Beth's perfume, while Caspian sat at my desk, drawing. Mom came in after dinner, asking if she should make me a lunch for tomorrow.

"What are you talking about, Mom?" I said. "What's tomorrow?"

She looked at me like I was crazy. "The first day of school, silly. Are you feeling okay?" She frowned and reached out a hand to feel my forehead.

School. *Crap.* I ducked out of her way. "I'm fine, Mom. I just forgot. Whatever you want to make is fine." I'd probably end up just buying something from the cafeteria, but if Mom wanted to make herself feel better by putting together a lunch, that was fine with me.

"I'll make you a hoagie," she decided. "Italian?"

"Sounds good." I gave her a wide grin and kept the smile on my face until she left. As soon as she was gone, I dragged over a giant stuffed beanbag chair from my closet and sat it next to Caspian. "I can't believe school starts tomorrow," I said, flopping into it. "Who starts school on a Friday? Why not wait until Monday?"

"Are you ready to go back?" he asked.

I shifted, and the chair made a squishy sound as the stuffing moved around. "I guess. I mean, I'm not exactly looking forward to it. Exams. Homework. Everyone trying to cram college stuff down my throat." I shrugged.

"It's the last first day of high school you'll ever have."

"In more ways than one." I glanced over at him, but he scowled.

"I meant because of the fact that you're a senior. Not because—"

"Because of the fact that I'll be dead?"

"God, Abbey." He pushed back his paper and stood up from the desk, looking upset. "Can't we have just one conversation where that doesn't come up?"

I looked down at my jeans. "I didn't mean to—"

"I know you didn't mean to. It just seems like that's all you can talk about lately."

"I'm sorry. I just want to be ready."

"I need to go for a walk," he said suddenly, moving to the door.

Panic shot through me. Why was he leaving? Should I tell him no, that I needed him to stay? Or would that make me look weak? I finally settled on, "How are you going to get out? You can't just open the front door and leave that way. My parents are down there."

Caspian stopped pacing and looked at the window. "Will you leave it open for me?" he asked, gesturing to it.

I nodded. And bit my lip, trying not to cry.

He went to open it, and hooked one leg outside. I turned back to my desk. *Everyone needs their space. Don't be a baby.*

"Abbey," Caspian said softly. So softly that I almost didn't hear him. "Love."

I turned my head.

"I'm not mad. I want you to know that, okay? I'll come back in a little bit, I swear. I'm just going for a walk. That's all."

I couldn't trust myself to speak, so I just nodded again, and then he left.

It was fine. No big deal.

When I woke to Mom's voice calling up the stairs that it was time for me to get up, I noticed immediately that Caspian was back. He was sitting there on the bed, next to me.

I sat up quickly and tried not to act too relieved.

"Good morning, beautiful," he said. "Sorry I didn't make it back before you fell asleep."

"That's okay. I'm just so glad you came back." The words spilled out of me, and I glanced down at the sheets, incredibly embarrassed that I'd just said that.

"I told you I would."

"What took so long?"

"I ran into Uri at the cemetery. We decided to see if Vincent might be hiding out there."

I got up and stretched my arms above my head, then went over to the bathroom. "No luck, huh?"

"None yet."

Grabbing a towel, I turned to shut the door behind me. "Going to take a shower," I said. "See you in twenty."

"Let me know if you need me to do any back scrubbing," he called through the door.

I just laughed. "You wish."

Thirty minutes later, I was clean and dressed. "Are you sure this looks okay?" I asked, turning to Caspian. "I don't want to look like I'm trying too hard."

I smoothed down the edges of my white shirt and readjusted the black vest I'd thrown over it. My four-leaf clover necklace was the last touch, and I re-knotted the ribbon at the back of my neck to make sure it stayed put.

"I'm not a fashion guy, but you look great to me."

I smiled at him and slid my book bag onto my shoulder. Mom yelled for me to hurry, that we were leaving in five minutes, but suddenly I was loathe to leave Caspian behind. "Who needs school?" I said. "I can just stay here. With you."

He pointed to the door. "*Go*. Have fun. I'll see you in a couple of hours."

I plodded slowly out of the room. He followed after me, and I turned back. Reaching out a hand, he cupped my face. Or as close to it as he could.

"I'll miss you," he said.

I nuzzled my cheek into the low buzz. "Me too."

I picked up my necklace and kissed one side of the smooth, cold plated glass, then held it up to him. He kissed the same spot, letting it linger at his lips for a moment. When he returned it to me, I touched it gently.

I pulled away from him after one last call from Mom, then reluctantly trudged down the stairs.

Senior year started off with a bang. Literally. Someone's car backfired in the parking lot right after Mom dropped me off, and half the students that had been milling around went running and screaming that someone was outside shooting. The whole school was put on lockdown, and we didn't get to homeroom until after lunch.

After the situation was settled, and our lockers were assigned (which is pretty much a joke since we all end up with the same locker year after year), I stood twirling my padlock and staring into the teeny, tiny space my stuff would call home for the next nine months, when someone tapped me on the shoulder.

"Excuse me," a voice said. "I need to get in there. I don't think the bell is going to hold off much longer. And while I'm normally cool with just hanging out, the hallway isn't my first choice of places to do that."

When I turned around to find bright green eyes, I paused in the middle of saying "Yeah?" to think about Caspian for a moment. *I wonder what he's doing. Is time going fast for him again? Or slowly, since he's awake? Or is he even awake? Maybe he's sleeping.*

Hair was the second thing I saw. Her hair was long, even longer than my own, but not quite as curly. And red. Impossibly red. I snapped back to reality. "Oh! Sorry. You need me to move?" I glanced around. "Where?"

She looked down at a piece of paper clutched in one hand. "I'm 9-C. So I need to get in right there. Beside you."

My stomach dropped to the floor, and my book bag slid out of my grip, spewing books everywhere. "Beside . . ." My throat seized up, and I coughed. "Beside me?"

She shifted her books, and something else she was holding. Something that I couldn't get a glimpse of. "Yeah. Beside you. That's how numbers work here, right? You're 9-B, so 9-C comes next, right?"

"But that's Kristen's locker."

"It's already taken? Shit."

I shook my head. And then found my voice. "It's not. Taken, I mean. Kristen's dead. It was just . . . It used to be her locker."

There was silence, and then the unmistakable sound of the bell buzzing overhead.

"Shit. Twice," she said, throwing one hand to point up. "There goes the bell."

Glancing around me at the scurrying students, I realized that I was going to be late for class too. And my books were still all over the floor. Dropping to my knees, I started to gather them.

The new girl bent to help me pick one up. "I'm Cyn, by the way. And before you ask, no, 'Cyn' isn't short for Cynthia, or

Cynder, or Alicyn, or any of those. It's just Cyn. Sweet. Short. *C-Y-N.* Got it?"

I glanced up. I think I liked her. "Abbey," I said. "Short for Abigail. And it's with an *e.*" She nodded, and just like that, we had an understanding.

Upon closer inspection, I could see that she had thin green highlights scattered throughout her hair. The color of new leaves. The effect was striking.

"I like your hair," I said.

"Thanks."

I stepped to one side and cleared a path for her to get to locker 9-C. As she slid the numbers around and then threw open the door, a wave of nostalgia overwhelmed me.

Kristen dropping notes into my locker after fifth period. Kristen letting me use her mirror because I was always forgetting to buy my own. Kristen waiting with a Cheshire cat smile and the latest study hall gossip. Kristen—

Cyn snapped her fingers. "Earth to Abbey. Are we losing you there? You're zoning out on me."

I shook my head and stuffed my books into my own locker. "Sorry. Just . . . lost in a memory."

"I get it. You knew Kristen, huh?"

"You could say that. We were best friends."

"Oh. Jesus. That sucks. How did she die?"

Such an innocent question. But it made my skin crawl. "She drowned," I said curtly. "I don't really want to talk about it."

"Got it. That memo is loud and clear." Cyn finally slid the other thing she'd been holding onto the little top shelf of the locker, and I couldn't help but steal a peek.

It was a dead plant.

She caught me looking. "I have to keep them here," she explained. "Otherwise my mom will throw them out."

Why would she want to keep a dead plant?

Apparently my question was written all over my face, because she said defensively, "It's a hobby, okay?"

I shrugged. "It's cool." *Weird, but whatever.*

Cyn slammed her locker door shut, then turned to head down the opposite hall. "Nice meeting you, Abbey," she said. "And don't worry, I never stay in one place for long. My mom is always moving me from school to school. It's such a pain in the ass. But that means you won't have to put up with me, or my *dead plant*, for long."

She said with such conviction the exact words that I'd been thinking, that I stared after her with my mouth hanging open long after she was gone. What was she, a mind reader?

~ ~ ~

With the lockdown in the morning, I had only two classes to get through before the end of the day, and when the final bell rang, I heaved a sigh of relief. I ran into Beth on the way back to my locker.

"Hey, girl," she said, stopping to give me a quick hug. "You totally missed out on the beach house. And the hotties."

I laughed. "I know, I know. But I made your perfume for you. Hopefully that counts for something?" I pulled out the little sample vial that was in my pocket, and gave it to her.

She opened it, and a look of sheer bliss crossed her face. "This is *so* awesome, Abbey. Thank you." She poured some of it onto her fingertip to rub across her wrists. "This is just what I needed after a day like today."

"What happened?"

"Lewis again. The boy can*not* get over our breakup. He's like this little puppy dog that follows me around, and it's just driving me cray-cray."

"Cray-cray?"

"Crazy? You know."

"Uh, yeah. Right." I entered the combination into my lock. "He'll get over it. Just tell him to give you . . ." The door swung open, and there was a folded-up note with a flower drawn on it sitting there. Immediately happiness filled me. Caspian had been here.

"I just need him to give me what, Abbey?" Beth said, interrupting my thoughts.

I glanced back at her, completely forgetting what I had been about to say. *Something about Lewis* . . . "Space!" I remembered. "Just ask him to give you some space. It'll give you room to breathe and him time to accept the truth."

"I know." She sighed and pulled out her phone. "Speaking of . . . Guess who just texted me?"

"Mmm-hmm." I smiled at her, but already I was turning my attention back to the note. Smoothing down the edges, I took a peek.

A quick hello for you, my dear Astrid, to let you know that I'm thinking of you. Hope your first day back was everything it should be. Meet me at my place when school is over.

—Caspian

His place. . . . *The mausoleum?*

Beth furiously texted away, then said, "I guess this is my cue to leave. I'll catch ya later, girl. Call me!"

I looked up from my note, confused as to why she was leaving. And then I saw Ben coming my way.

I'm going to have to set her straight on that *one again.*

"Hey, Abbey," Ben said, getting closer. "You aren't hiding any Funyuns in your locker, are you?"

I slid the note from Caspian into my bag and turned toward him, shaking my head. "Nope. No Funyuns here." Ben always knew how to make me smile.

"That sucks. If next Monday is anything like today, I'm going to need some serious snackage."

"'Snackage'?" I laughed. "Is that the technical term?"

"Totally."

Slamming the locker door shut, I hoisted my bag over one shoulder.

"Hey," he said. "Your arm is better."

I looked down at it, and then flexed it once. "Yup. The sling came off last week."

"So now you're all ready for basketball, right?"

"Maybe if I grow another six inches." I shook my head at him. "I think basketball is out. But bowling? That I can do. And it doesn't require any talent."

He scoffed. "No talent? I'll have you know that I'm a talented guy when it comes to shoving heavy balls down wooden lanes."

I stared at him, then started laughing.

Ben scratched his head and cocked it to one side. "Wait a minute. That didn't come out right."

"You're crazy," I said, grinning at him.

He grinned back. "Yeah, what else is new?"

"What did you think about that whole lockdown thing this morning?" I asked. "That was new. Talk about overreacting."

He held up his hands. "Anything that gets me out of classes for half the day, I do not question."

"Can't say I disagree with that. I skipped English today too because of the new girl that was assigned to Kristen's locker."

"New girl?" He looked intrigued.

"Down, boy."

Then he cast a glance at her locker and moved closer to it. "I guess they had to give it to somebody new sometime. But I thought . . ." He trailed off and looked sad.

I put out a hand and reached for his arm. "I know what you mean. I thought maybe it would stay empty this year too."

"Now she's really gone, you know?" His face darkened. "That's stupid to say, but it's true."

I shook my head. "It's not stupid. This was like one last piece of her, and now it's gone." We both looked at the locker, and a lump started to form in the back of my throat.

Ben cleared his throat, and I saw that his eyes were watery.

He looked embarrassed that I'd noticed, and he stepped away from me, cracking his knuckles as he went. I guess that was the manly thing to do to cover up embarrassment or something.

"I need to get to work," he said. "See you on Monday?"

"Yeah." I shifted my book bag again. "See you then."

Ben turned and started walking backward down the hall. "We need to hang out again soon," he called. "Maybe get something to eat?"

Always thinking about food. "You know where to find me," I said.

He raised one hand in a salute, and then disappeared around the corner. Smiling to myself, I headed to the main door and pushed my way out into the late afternoon sunshine. Cyn was standing on the curb outside, looking at something, with one hand shading her eyes from the sun. She let out a low whistle when I came near.

I followed her gaze across the street just in time to see a black Mustang turn slowly around the corner. A flash of white-blond hair glowed, and I could have sworn I saw a silver Rolex watch on the wrist hanging out the window.

Panic chased a ribbon down my spine, and I stood ramrod straight.

Vincent.

"Such a hot car," Cyn mused. "God, what I wouldn't give to take a ride in that."

"Looks dangerous," I said, stepping away from her. "I'd stay away from him—*it*," I corrected myself, "if I were you."

She didn't say anything, and I moved away from the curb. Angling myself firmly in the opposite direction, I started toward the cemetery.

"It was just a stupid car," I said to myself out loud as I kept walking. "You can't be positive that it was him. There's no reason to worry everybody. Let it go. Just drop it."

Nodding my head in self-affirmation, I tried not to think about Vincent anymore.

Or the fact that I wasn't going to tell Caspian he might be hanging around.

Chapter Seven

UNCERTAIN

It is said by some to be the ghost of a Hessian trooper, whose head had been carried away by a cannon-ball . . .

—"The Legend of Sleepy Hollow"

When I got to Caspian's mausoleum, he was inside reading a book by candlelight. I was so happy to see him that I couldn't stop a huge smile from taking over my face. It would be even better when I could finally touch him.

"Got your note," I said.

He put the book down onto the floor. "Hey, beautiful. How was school?"

I moved toward the wrought iron bench that sat against the wall nearest me. Shrugging off my book bag along the way, I replied, "It was fine."

He came and sat next to me.

"They put us all on lockdown for half the day because a car backfired outside and someone thought it was shots being fired. But other than that, nothing exciting."

I leaned forward and let my head hang down, hair cascading around my hands. Scrunching up my fingers, I gently massaged my scalp. "They reassigned Kristen's locker to a new girl," I said quietly. "Cyn."

"How was she?" he asked.

"She was nice, I guess. But she thought Kristen was still alive because I mentioned it being her locker."

"Awkward."

"Yeah."

Caspian got up for a minute, and when he returned, there was something behind his back. "Speaking of . . ."

He held out a drawing to me.

It was Kristen. A drawing of Kristen. In her favorite red corset shirt and hippie-style jeans.

"How did you . . . ?" I said.

"I saw you guys in the cemetery last year. This is what she wore, right?"

I nodded and took the drawing from him, stroking the outline of her face. Cheekbones, jawline, eyes . . . Everything was right. Even in her black-and-white world, he had captured

Kristen's vivacity. It was there, in the slight tilt of her chin, the excited look in her eyes, the way she stood. Happy and ready to experience anything.

"It's beautiful, Caspian," I said. "Absolutely beautiful. It's her. She's here. Now she's always here."

And then I burst into tears. Huge, racking sobs that rolled and shuddered through my body.

"Hey," Caspian said. "Hey, Astrid. It's okay. Don't . . ."

He moved closer, but he couldn't hold me. Couldn't put his arms around me, or move my hair back away from my face. Instead he just did the best thing he could. He let me cry.

"I can't believe she's really gone," I said through my tears. "It was my first day . . . alone . . . and her locker . . ." I cried harder. "I don't know what to do. I can't be me without her. I don't know who I am . . . or what I am. I'm empty. Just a shell."

Caspian leaned in close to my ear. His voice was low and soft. I had to slow my breathing to catch what he was saying. "You're *not* empty. You're strong and smart and talented, Abbey. Kristen will always be with you, but she's not *who* you are. You're Abbey. Just Abbey. Without Kristen, yes, but that's okay. That's what makes you unique."

I gripped the drawing and looked up at him. "Kiss me," I

said suddenly. Desperately. "Please. Please, somehow . . . just find a way to kiss me."

Sorrow filled his eyes. And heartbreak echoed in his voice. "I'm sorry, love. I can't."

Sighing, I leaned back against the bench. Defeat made me weary. Every bone in my body was tired. This was so hard. . . . "I know," I said softly.

We sat in silence for a while, in that close space with death surrounding us, until he said, "Tell me your best memory of her."

But I couldn't choose just one. So I talked until I couldn't remember any more.

The next day was better. And worse. Caspian took me to a movie to try to cheer me up. Of course there wasn't any popcorn sharing or make-out sessions during the boring parts, but for two hours I got to pretend to be *almost* normal.

It was all just a dream, though. A fantasy. Gone as soon as the credits rolled and the lights came on.

"I bet they don't even realize how lucky they are," I said under my breath, glancing back as we walked out of the theater and passed a particularly obnoxious girl who was swallowing her boyfriend's tongue. "They have no *idea* how much they take for granted."

We walked past another couple who looked like they were

two seconds away from public nudity. "Get a room," I growled.

The girl looked up at me and glared, which just made me madder. "Jealous?" she sneered.

Ignoring her, I kept walking. But I couldn't keep my mouth shut.

"It's not fair," I said angrily to Caspian, not even realizing that my tone was growing louder. "They have everything. Right in front of them. But do they appreciate it? *No*. They just keep acting like they have the right to do whatever they want, while *some* of us don't even have the chance to—"

Someone bumped into me.

"Sorry," a voice said. A voice that I recognized.

I turned around. "Cyn?"

"Hey, Abbey."

She had a funny look on her face. Like she'd just witnessed something horrible and didn't know what to do about it. "Are you . . . ," she started. And then that funny look came back.

"Am I what?"

Caspian moved next to me.

"Were you talking to someone?" She looked around, clearly trying to find the person that I'd come with, and for just a moment her eyes rested where Caspian was standing, before returning to mine.

"No. I wasn't talking to anyone. Maybe it was someone else?" I lied.

"Are you here alone?"

"Yeah." Lie number two. "You?"

"Same."

An awkward silence fell between us, and I didn't want to think too much about what level of crazy she might be grouping me into. I started to shift my position, to change my stance so that it was clear I was leaving.

She moved too. "My movie's gonna start. See you later."

I nodded, and we parted ways. When we were clear of the theater, Caspian asked, "Was that the girl from school who took Kristen's locker?"

"Yup. Just another person who probably thinks I'm crazy now. Wonderful."

He gave me a supportive smile. "She doesn't think that. And you're not crazy."

I smiled back at him, but I couldn't agree. Because deep down I still wasn't entirely sure.

It was later that night when I realized that the picture of Kristen that Caspian had drawn for me wasn't lying down on my desk like I'd left it, but instead was standing up on my dresser.

"Did you do that?" I asked, pointing to the drawing.

"Do what?"

"Put the picture there. I left it lying down, by my computer. Not on the dresser."

He glanced at it. "I didn't touch it. Did you move it so you could see it better?"

"No." I shook my head vehemently. "I left it lying down. By my monitor. Wait . . ." I remembered something different. "Maybe I left it on top of the printer."

I looked back and forth between the two. Did I move it? Or had someone else? *Someone like Vincent . . .*

"I could have sworn I left it lying down," I said. "I just can't remember if it was on the printer or by the monitor. But I know it was lying down. Not standing up. And *definitely* not standing up on my dresser."

I stared at it.

Am I going crazy? Did I leave the picture where it is now? Maybe Mom moved it . . .

Caspian interrupted me midthought. "Do you still want to read chapter five?"

"Yeah. Go ahead." I shook my head. "It's fine. It doesn't matter."

He looked doubtful but grabbed *Jane Eyre*. I settled into

bed and pulled the covers up. Lying down, or standing up, who cared where the picture was?

But I couldn't stop the sense of foreboding that was creeping over me.

In the dream, tree limbs held me down, and I thrashed from side to side to get free. Another one reached for my hair and whipped it out of my face, tangling it in wild snarls. I opened my mouth to scream. Felt my vocal chords stretch. And then break.

I tried harder. Arms straining, chest heaving, I screamed and screamed with everything inside of me. But there was nothing left.

Suddenly the world tilted. Or rather, I was tilting. Being lifted straight up.

My arms were still held down at my sides, yet I was floating in midair. My feet barely touched the ground. I was a strange minuet, with tree limbs as my strings.

"Watch," the forest whispered, all around me. "Learn."

The scene before me cleared, a path appeared. There was a figure dressed in black, flashing in and out of the trees as he ran. His hair changed from white-blond to black, and then back again.

Even without seeing his face, I knew who it was. Vincent.

As if my thoughts had called his name, he turned and grinned at me. His face was a horrible mask of features carved from stone.

 103

White and dried-out as bits of bleached rock. Only his eyes were alive—dark, burning coals of twin fire sunk deep into their sockets.

He kept running. Didn't break his stride, and I struggled to see who or what he was chasing. A gap in the trees revealed another figure, and shock came when I saw the black ball gown and dark, curly hair.

It was me.

He was chasing me.

My throat opened again, trying to force some sound out beyond the constricted airways, but the result was the same as before. Nothing.

Horror filled my veins, and I watched the other me slip back among the branches. Racing. Desperately racing for her life.

One last flash of color caught my eye before everything went dark.

A flame of red. Impossibly deep red hair.

"Abbey. Abbey, wake up."

Caspian called my name, and I opened my eyes, still seeing the color red in front of me. I thrashed my arms. They were trapped at my sides, tangled in the sheets.

"Easy," he said. "Easy. Are you okay? You were screaming in your sleep."

I freed myself and sat up. Trying desperately to remember where I was, my eyes locked with his, and then it all clicked into place. *A dream. Just a dream.*

"I'm fine," I said. "It was nothing."

"It didn't look like nothing. What happened?"

"I was being held down in a forest by some trees. And I think they were talking to me?" I shook my head. "I can't remember. But I saw something red . . ." I glanced over at the picture of Kristen. My heart started to pound again, and my hands grew shaky.

I knew without a doubt that Vincent had been here. He had moved it just to mess with my head.

"What can I do?" Caspian said.

I didn't know what he could do. I couldn't explain what was happening to me.

"Do you want some water?" he asked. "A blanket?"

"Just give me a minute." I tried to breathe deeply. Tried to make everything go back to normal. "Actually, I think I will take that water," I said.

Caspian moved to get up.

"Wait."

He stopped.

"I'll get it."

"Are you sure? I don't mind."

"I know. But I want to stretch my legs."

He nodded, and I got up slowly, limbs quivering like a fragile dandelion stem blowing in the wind. The bathroom felt like it was miles away, and my hand was still shaking as I turned on the light. Gripping the edges of the sink, I stared into the mirror, searching the eyes that looked back at me. There weren't any answers there, though. Only a cool blue reflection.

I turned on the water and cupped my hands together, bringing the cold, crisp taste to my lips. My cheeks were deathly pale, but the water I splashed turned them bright pink. When my legs felt more stable, and my hands were calm, I ventured out of the bathroom. Caspian was waiting by the door for me.

"Maybe you should switch rooms," he suggested.

"Why?"

"Because of what happened here. You never really dealt with it, Abbey. You just moved on."

I sat down on the bed. "Isn't that what people are supposed to do?"

He ran a hand through his hair. "All I know is that you came back to the place where you were attacked, and now you're having nightmares. It sounds like a problem with a simple solution to me."

"I know I'm sounding like a broken record here, but I'm fine. *Really*. Me having weird dreams is nothing new. It's no big deal."

He looked at me sternly. "I'm worried about you, Astrid. I only want what's best."

"I know you do. But if I give up my bedroom, then it's like he's won. I don't want to give him that power over me."

Caspian nodded. "I get it."

I glanced around the room, feeling antsy and restless. It was early, only 5:19 a.m., but I didn't want to go back to sleep. Spying my oversize sweatpants lying next to the bed, I got up and pulled them on right over the pajama bottoms I was wearing. My sneakers were there too, and I reached for them next.

"What are you doing?" Caspian asked.

"Going for a walk. Wanna come?"

"Of course. Call me crazy, but staying here as my girlfriend roams around outside in the dark while some crazed supernatural being stalks her isn't my idea of a good time. Where are we going?"

I walked over to the window and cracked it open. "To the cemetery. I want to see Nikolas."

~   ~   ~

The moon was almost full as we slipped through the side opening of the wrought iron cemetery gates, and it illuminated the grassy roads that covered the vast grounds in front of us. Once we got away from the main path, we headed for the woods that would lead us to Nikolas and Katy's house.

It was a bit creepy walking through the dark forest where the foliage started to grow denser, the tree branches thicker. Springy ferns and wild moss pressed in on us from every angle, and I tried not to think about the dream I'd just had about Vincent.

"I wonder what would have happened if I'd never heard of 'The Legend of Sleepy Hollow,'" I mused out loud to Caspian, trying to distract myself as we walked toward their house. "The town I grew up in, the school I went to, the places I visited? It's like all along, this was meant to be. My whole life was building up to this."

"To what?"

"You. Me. Nikolas. Katy. I mean, who could have guessed that the legend would be real and I'd meet the characters from Washington Irving's story?" I shook my head. "It's funny. Good funny. Not bad funny."

A small wooden bridge came into view, but I came to a stop before crossing it.

"What's wrong?" Caspian asked.

"Do you think it's too early? What if they're sleeping?"

"*Do* they sleep?"

"I . . . don't know."

But I started walking again. I had the strongest urge to see Nikolas, to ask him if he knew what was going on with Vincent or the Revenants, and to try to make some sense out of things.

We crossed the bridge, and when the familiar stone walls and thatched roof of their storybook cottage came into view, I wanted to break into a run. It was like coming home after a long trip.

Wisteria grew in a massive vine of trailing purple flowers and green leaves over the stone chimney on the left of the wooden front door, and it looked like Katy had been busy filling the front yard with new plants.

"I don't think you're going to have to worry about whether or not Nikolas is sleeping," Caspian said, and I turned back to face him.

"Why? How do you know?"

He pointed over my shoulder. "Because there he is."

I turned around. Nikolas was coming from the back of the house. He lifted his hand in a wave, and I returned the gesture, closing the gap between us.

"Nikolas! It's so good to see you!" I gave him a hug, thrilled that he was still here and still safe. I didn't know what was going on with Vincent, but just knowing that Nikolas was okay made me feel so much better.

His weathered face broke into a smile as he beamed down at me. "How are you feeling? Any ill effects from the incident with Vincent?"

"Oh, no, everything's fine. I had to wear a sling on my arm for a while, but now I'm as good as new."

"I am glad to hear it," Nikolas said. Then he nodded at Caspian. "I am also glad to see that things have improved for you since our last visit."

"Me too," Caspian said. "Hopefully we won't be seeing our nasty friend again."

Nikolas's face darkened. "I am sorry I could not be there, Abbey. It pains me that I am bound to this place."

"Your house?" I said absentmindedly. "I wouldn't mind being bound here."

"I am talking about the cemetery," he replied. "Katy and I cannot leave it."

I shifted my weight from foot to foot. "It's fine. Everything was, um, handled." I glanced down. Now that I was here, I didn't know what I really wanted to say. What was I looking for?

Caspian must have realized what I was feeling, because he said, "Is Katy inside?"

"She is," Nikolas replied.

"Then, I think I'm going to say hello," he said.

I shot him a grateful smile. "Thanks," I whispered.

He winked at me and then whispered back, "Just don't leave me in there *too* long, okay?"

I nodded, and he went inside the house.

Scuffing my toe in the grass, I tried to sort out my thoughts. "So . . . what are you doing up so late?" I asked Nikolas. "Or early. I guess you could be up early?"

He chuckled. "A little of both. What about you? This is an early time for a visit."

"Couldn't sleep. I've been having bad dreams so I thought maybe a walk here would help." I didn't want to talk about the dreams, though, so I said, "What's it like for you and Katy to sleep? *Do* you even sleep? Caspian said that it's a strange, almost dark place for him. Is it the same for you?"

He nodded. "We rest, but our bodies don't need sleep the same way they did when we were alive."

"Does time move fast for you guys too? How different is it for you and Katy compared to Caspian? What's a day for me can be a week, or even a month, for him if he falls into the dark place."

"It has been so long since I was a part of the living world that I have simply forgotten what normal time is," he said. "But yes, whole lifetimes can pass by in the blink of an eye."

"I wish school would pass by in the blink of an eye," I muttered.

Nikolas laughed. "Are you not happy at school?"

"*No* teenager is happy at school." I sighed heavily. "It's a painful experience."

He smiled.

"Speaking of . . ." I hesitated, then blurted out, "Does it hurt? When you die . . . what does it feel like?"

He didn't say anything, and I thought that this was it. I'd found the one thing that he would not answer. But then he surprised me.

"Dying was the easy part," he said evenly. "One moment I was there with my horse, preparing for battle, and the next, I was sitting on the ground. My horse was gone and so was everything else around me. Much time must have passed."

"It was that way for Caspian, too," I murmured.

"I did not understand what had happened to me at first," he said. "But eventually I learned. I thought I was trapped in purgatory as a specter, cursed to roam the land as punishment for my wicked deeds in life."

 112

"So the dying part didn't actually hurt?"

"For me, no. It did not."

I let out a sigh of relief. "That's good to know. What about the Revenants? When they helped you and Katy to be completed, did it hurt?"

Now he looked uncomfortable.

"Abbey . . ." He started and then stopped, pausing long enough to look back over my shoulder, into the woods. "I know that you are looking for answers, but I cannot tell you everything."

"Why not?" I asked. "You've been in my position before. You *know* what's going to happen."

"All I can say is that I do not know everything. It is different for each of us. And particularly now . . ."

"Now what?"

"Now that Vincent has interrupted the process, I am uncertain what will be done."

His words took a minute to register. "Uncertain . . . Wait, do you mean that there's a chance I *won't* get to be with Caspian?" Panic filled me at the thought, and I reached out a desperate hand. "That's not true, right?" I pleaded. "Tell me it's not true!"

"I cannot say," he replied. "It is not my place to make that decision."

"But I need to know! I need to—"

The sound of a door opening interrupted us, and Caspian came out of the house. "I think it's time to go," he said. "Your parents might freak out if they wake up and find you're not home."

"Good point," I said, then turned back to Nikolas. "I'm sorry if it sounded like I was getting upset with you. I'm just frustrated by . . . uncertainty."

"It is understandable," he said, patting my arm. "Come back to visit us again soon. We are always delighted to have your company."

Realizing that I wasn't going to be getting any more answers to my questions, I nodded. "I will. Bye, Nikolas."

I turned toward the woods, and Caspian followed behind me.

Once we were far enough away from the cottage, he asked, "How did it go?"

How did it go? I don't know. "Nikolas didn't have any answers for me," I said eventually.

"Answers about what?"

"Everything. Nothing. He wouldn't say. How did things go for *you*?" I asked.

"Fantastic. Katy and I talked about knitting patterns. I now know the difference between a purl stitch and a cross-stitch."

The expression on his face was so comical that I was glad to have something else to talk about on the way home. Now I was even more confused than when I'd first gotten here.

Chapter Eight

CRIMSON

❦

Ichabod became the object of whimsical persecution to Bones and his gang of rough riders.

—"The Legend of Sleepy Hollow"

There weren't any more false alarms or school-wide lockdowns when I went back to school on Monday, and I found Ben waiting for me by my locker after second period.

"Hey, Abbey," he said, fidgeting with the science book he was holding. "Can I walk you to your next class?"

"Yeah, sure. I'm going to civics."

He moved out of the way, and I opened up my locker door. "So," I said, exchanging my math book for a civics book, "have you been bombarded with girls asking you to the Hollow Ball yet? Or is it still too early for that?"

"It's not too early. I've been turning them down by the handful."

I raised an eyebrow at him.

"What?" he said. "It's true. I have to thin the herd a little bit."

"Thin the herd?" My eyebrow shot up even more. "Real nice." I turned in the direction that I needed to go, and he moved to my side. "You know who you *should* take?" I suggested sweetly. "Aubra."

He groaned. "You can't be serious."

"You totally deserve it with a comment like *that*. 'Thin the herd.' What are we, sheep? Elephants?"

His face turned serious, and he put up both hands. "I take it back, I take it back! There aren't enough Funyuns in the world to make me interested in someone that self-absorbed."

"She's not that bad, you know," I said. "She's not that great, either, but she's not *that* bad."

Ben shuddered. "Give me a thinker any day of the week. I like 'em brainy."

"Didn't think I'd hear that one from *you*." I rolled my eyes at him.

"What can I say? I'm an equal opportunity kind of guy."

A tall girl passed us, and I watched in astonishment as she tossed her hair and then smiled at Ben. "Man, you really *do* have to fight them off!" I said.

His face turned red, and he looked embarrassed. It was kind

of funny to see him acting all shy, but we were almost to class, and I still didn't know why he'd wanted to walk with me. Spotting a quiet corner by the water fountains, I steered him in that direction. "So, what did you want to talk about? Because I know it's not your girl problems."

He looked down at his feet. "I wanted to ask you something. But I don't know how to ask it."

"This isn't going to be another one of those awkward moments when you tell me how much you want me and I have to politely decline, is it?" I teased.

"No, no." Then he looked up. "Unless you want it to be."

"I'll pencil you in for next Thursday. You can declare your undying and eternal love for me then. Does that work for you?"

"Absolutely."

He shuffled his feet again, and I felt my patience wearing thin. I wanted to grab him by the arm and just tell him to spit it out already. "Seriously. What's up, Ben? What is it? You're making me nervous here."

He took a deep breath, like he was gathering up his courage, then said, "I've been dreaming about Kristen."

"You . . . have?" I hadn't been dreaming about her at all. Why was he?

"Yeah. And what's strange about it is—you know how when

118

you dream, there's always some part that's off? Like you can be going through your day at school, but everyone will have six eyeballs, or blue noses, or you'll be in your underwear?"

I nodded.

"It's not like that," he said. "These dreams are almost . . . real. Classes, and study halls, and stuff like that. We sit and talk about all kinds of things. For hours. It happens almost every night. Do you ever dream about her?"

I was almost tempted to say no. Some part of me didn't want him to know that *my* dreams about my best friend were upsetting. Instead I found myself saying, "I used to. But I never got to just spend time with her in my dreams. Something was always wrong, or weird."

"So you think . . . Do you think maybe she's watching out for me? Or haunting me?" He laughed self-consciously and tugged on a piece of his curly brown hair. "I don't even know if I believe in ghosts."

"I do," I said automatically.

"You do?"

I hadn't meant for that to slip out. "Yeah. I, um, I do."

Ben looked hopeful. "So do you think she *is* hanging around me?" He glanced around us, then lowered his voice. "It's not like I want people to know that I think I'm being haunted by a ghost, but . . ." A wistful smile appeared. "But I think it would be kind of cool if it did happen. With her."

Yeah, it's not so bad being haunted. Trust me on that one. "We were both connected to her. Me as her best friend, and you . . ." I smiled gently at him. "You as someone who wanted to be something more. There's a bond there. I don't think death can take that away."

"But it's not like she knew how I felt."

"I think you'd be surprised how much they know."

"They?" He looked skeptical.

"Ghosts. Spirits. The dearly departed." I waved my hand around. "You know."

He nodded in a vague sort of way that made me uncomfortable. *Dangerous territory, Abbey. Watch what you say.*

I put my fingers on his arm and made my tone very comforting and accepting. "What I mean is that you can believe whatever you want to believe. And I don't think there's anything wrong with believing that somehow Kristen knew how you felt about her."

His face cleared. "You're right. And I like the idea that she's happy. Wherever she is."

"Me too."

The bell rang, and I pulled away. "I have to go. I don't want to get a late slip."

"Thanks for talking to me about this, Abbey," he said. "But, uh, can we just keep it between us?"

I grinned at him, then turned to go to class. "Keep what between us?"

I skipped out of lunch early, and headed to my locker to beat the crowd. Cyn was at Kristen's locker—*No, Cyn's locker now. I'll have to get used to that*—and she was poking at something. Her freckled face turned to me as I approached.

"If you had to pick between a dead bug or a dead leaf, which would you choose?"

"Uhhhh, why am I choosing one of those things?" I asked.

"Just choose."

I reached out for my locker door and spun the combination. "I guess it depends on what type of bug. Is it like a butterfly, or a—"

"Ehhhhh." She made the sound of a buzzer. "Time's up. So you're going with bug?"

"I don't—"

She interrupted me again. "Your answer reveals a lot about you. I would have chosen leaf, but you chose bug. Why is that?"

"Technically, I didn't have time to choose anything. I just asked a question."

 121

She put a hand into her locker and pulled out a tiny terra-cotta pot. It was literally one of the smallest pots I'd ever seen. A lone plant stem bore three shriveled leaves, with the forth looking like it was barely hanging on.

"I like the almost dead ones," she said. "You think they're gone, but they're not." Her lips moved, and she whispered something that sounded like *"Ahtoo rah roorah ru shy el"* to the plant.

"What does that mean?" I asked.

"It's an ancient Gaelic blessing. A bespoke to the goddess of all living things. Plants like it." She moved to put the pot back, and I peeked over her shoulder. There were at least twelve other dead plants in there.

"Holy crap," I said. "That's a lot of plants."

I didn't mean for the words to slip out, but they sort of just did.

"Don't worry," she said conspiratorially. "I don't keep them all. I bury the ones that really don't make it. Most of them just need a little coaxing, though."

I didn't even know how to respond to that, so I just made some vague noise of agreement. *Who is this girl, and exactly how long am I going to have to have a locker next to her?*

With a bemused shake of my head, I opened my locker door . . .

. . . and froze when I saw what was there.

Cyn must have seen the expression on my face, because she leaned in. "What? What is it?" Her hand snaked out to reach for what was sitting there, before I could find my voice.

"Don't touch that!"

But I was too late. She had already picked up the blood-red bottle.

"It's perfume." She held it out to me, and I cringed. I didn't want to touch it. "Is something wrong with it?"

"It's not mine," I said. Was it a gift from Vincent?

She turned it over to read the name. "'Crimson.' I've never heard of that brand before." Opening the lid, she stuck it under her nose. "It smells heavy. And coppery. Like something . . ."

Bits of memory swam before my eyes.

Broken glass. Jagged edges. Sharp, cloying smells. And blood.

"It's blood," Cyn said swiftly. "*That's* what the smell reminds me of. Tangy and coppery at the same time. What the hell? A perfume that smells like blood? Who would want to wear that?"

Without even realizing what I was doing, I tore it out of her hands and practically ran to the closest garbage can. My fingers burned where I touched the bottle, and I flung the repulsive object into the mouth of the canister.

The overhead bell rang, signaling the end of lunch, and the halls flooded with people. They jostled my shoulders and crammed into my space. The hallways were tight with rushing bodies as everyone hurried to get to where they needed to be.

Suddenly a hand touched mine. Once, lightly, then grabbed hold. I looked down at the fingers wrapped around mine. They stroked my palm, and fingernails snagged painfully before letting go.

I looked up.

White-blond hair was all I could see, and Vincent smiled at me. "Hey, sweetheart."

Then he melted into the crowd. Like he'd never been there at all.

My knees locked. My chest tightened, and I wondered if I was going to faint in the middle of the hall. "It's not real," I chanted, trying not to pitch over. "It's not real. He's not here. You're just imagining it."

The halls cleared, and I was left standing there, still feeling his fingers on mine. Remembering the other time he'd pressed on my arm and had left his mark. A red welt driven deeply into my flesh . . .

Kristen came over, and I glanced at her. She was staring at me.

"Is everything okay? Why are you freaking out over perfume?"

Cyn. It was Cyn. Not Kristen. Kristen was dead. Not here. Not talking to me.

I came back to where I was. Back to the hallway, after lunch, and I wanted to scream. Wanted to cry. Wanted to make sure she'd seen what I'd just seen—Vincent. *Here.* Touching me.

But I stuffed all those feeling away. I shook my head, and found my voice. Smiling weakly, I said, "Secret admirer?"

She eyed me up and down. "I don't think so. That was some grade-A freak-out going on."

"It was a secret admirer I don't particularly want gifts from." *Do I tell her about what I saw? What if it wasn't real? . . .*

What if it was?

Then I remembered my dream about the forest and the red hair. I grabbed on to her arm. "You haven't seen a guy hanging around here lately, have you? A guy that creeps you out?"

She looked down and tried to shake me off. "Boundaries, much?"

I tightened my grip. "I'm serious, Cyn. If you see someone who tries to talk to you and is acting skeevy, stay away from him."

"Why?"

I *had* to tell her about it. No matter how crazy it made me sound. "I had this dream, and it might have been about you. Or maybe it was about Kristen. She had red hair too. But it was *dark* red hair, like yours, and a boy was chasing her . . . or me. He was chasing me. Or . . . I don't remember."

She pulled her arm away and gave me a strange look.

"Just . . . be careful, okay?" I said.

Because Vincent liked redheads. And Vincent obviously wanted to play.

As soon as I got home from school that afternoon, I told Caspian about the perfume bottle left in my locker.

"Any idea who put it there?" he asked.

I didn't answer. But the look on my face must have spoken for me.

"So you think it was him?"

"I think that I saw him there too. After lunch. He was in the hall and he grabbed my hand."

Caspian jumped up. "Do you still have the perfume? Where is it?"

"I threw it away."

He started pacing. "I can't believe this. He's stalking you! How am I supposed to protect you? We need some backup. I need to let Kame and Uri know about this."

"What are they going to do? Follow me around?" I groaned. "I don't want that."

Caspian stopped pacing and looked me in the eye. "From now on, I'm going everywhere with you. When your mom drops you off at school and picks you up, I'll be there. Hell, I might even start going to class with you."

I put my hand out, next to his. "You don't want to do that. You've already gone to high school once. Who wants to repeat *that* experience?"

"I just want to make sure you're safe," he replied.

"So come pick me up. Every day, if you want. Like glue?"

"Like glue."

Chapter Nine

NOW OR NEVER

... he summoned up, however, all his resolution ...

—"The Legend of Sleepy Hollow"

O n Wednesday I found a pile of broken glass surrounding
my locker. I wasn't sure if it was something left behind
by Vincent or just the remains of someone who'd been careless
with a Snapple bottle, so I told the janitor about it, and when I
came back after my next class, it was gone.

Everything changed on Friday, though. On Friday ... it got
weird.

I was trying to open up my civics book to page 352 in class,
when it fell across my desk with a heavy thump and opened to
a page on its own. It opened because there was something stuck
inside it.

I leaned in to get a better look.

There was a pile of small crescent-shaped crusty-looking things sitting there. Almost like dried-out pieces of hard candle wax. All of them were yellowed, except for one. It was bright red.

Picking up one of the yellow pieces, I examined it. *Is this earwax?*

That thought grossed me out, and immediately I put the yellow thing down. Using my pencil, I poked at the red one. It was shiny, and had a slightly rounded tip. *That* can't *be earwax. It almost looks like a . . .*

Fingernail.

It looked like a fingernail.

And then I saw the words scrawled across the pages:

they keep growing even after you're dead

I slammed the book shut and stood up so hastily that my chair hit the ground behind me, and everyone turned to look. I couldn't tell if they were looking because of the noise the chair had made, or because of the noise *I* had made. Something between a gasp and a scream.

Ms. Huffner stopped writing on the chalkboard. "Is everything all right, Miss Browning?"

"No . . . I . . . It's . . ." I just stood there, looking down at the pile of *fingernails* someone had put in my book. "I need to . . ."

It wouldn't come out. My words were stuck inside me and the room was spinning, and why was Vincent *doing* this to me?

"Do you need to go to the nurse's office?"

I guess I nodded or something, because she said, "Go on, then. You are wasting everyone else's valuable time."

Leaving the book behind, I fled the classroom. Out in the hallway the air was cooler, and the world stopped spinning. Sliding down against some lockers, I inhaled deeply and then leaned over to put my head between my legs.

With my eyes tightly closed, I tried to rationalize it all away.

Those weren't actually *fingernails. They were probably just petrified pencil shavings. Or old pieces of glue and eraser. Or bits of paper.* Nodding meant that I had to agree with those thoughts, so I did. It was easier that way.

Standing up slowly, I pushed myself away from the wall and detoured to the bathroom. I'd just go hide out in there until the bell rang.

At the end of the day, I went outside to hang out by the curb to wait for Caspian. Cyn was there, smoking a cigarette, and I sat down beside her.

"We're always running into each other," I said. "Have you noticed that?"

She exhaled and then shrugged. "That's what happens when you have nothing to do in a small town and a mother who makes you wait for a ride. You?"

"About the same."

She offered her cigarette to me, and I blanked. I'd never smoked before. Had never really felt the urge to, so it wasn't something I'd thought about.

She extended her wrist farther. "Are you going to take it, or just stare at it?"

"I've never . . . I don't smoke."

"First time for everything."

The cigarette butt ashed, and then the ash flaked away. It looked kind of gross, but she had a point. And it was now or never. It wasn't like I had my whole life ahead of me to change my mind.

I took it from her hand and placed it to my lips. It was thin and papery-tasting. Smoke wafted up into my eyes, and I inhaled deeply. I didn't know if I was supposed to count to ten or something, but finally Cyn said, "Whoa, whoa. Exhale."

I think I swallowed some of the exhale, because it felt like my lungs were going to explode. I coughed and choked, smoke wheezing out of me in little gasps.

Cyn laughed. But it wasn't a mean laugh, and as soon as I was able to, I was laughing too. It suddenly felt like I'd just done something monumental. Like climbing Mount Everest, or hiking the Great Wall of China.

She took the cigarette back and demonstrated. "Like this." After inhaling for a second, she pulled the butt away and tipped her head to the side, exhaling a stream of smoke.

"Let me try it again," I said, reaching for it. She handed it over, and I mimicked her actions.

The second time wasn't so bad, and I coughed only a little bit as the smoke leaked out of me. It was a strange feeling. One I wasn't entirely sure about.

"That one's almost out," Cyn said. "You want another?"

Little pieces of ash sprinkled down onto my jeans, and I glanced down, brushing them to the side. "No. I don't think so." I ran my tongue over my teeth. They felt funny. "My mouth tastes gross, like a combination of—"

A shadow fell over me, and I looked up.

"Smoking on school property is naughty," Vincent said, wagging his finger. "Are you being *naughty* schoolgirls?"

My first instinct was to scramble away from him as fast as

possible, but I tried to control myself. I didn't want to show him fear. Digging my palms into the asphalt beneath me, I felt the sharp sting of tiny rocks and hard cement.

"This isn't a spectator sport," Cyn said. "Get lost, asshole."

His hair was still blond, like Caspian's. And although it wasn't flat-ironed and lying across his face like it had been when he'd been on the bed in my bedroom, the streak of black was still there. It sent a shock wave through me. How closely he resembled Caspian.

Vincent sat down between us, and I was too scared to move.

"I like your hair," he said to Cyn. "Red is *definitely* your color. Mine, too."

"Don't care. Move the fuck on," she replied.

My senses were starting to flood with awareness, and I knew I couldn't sit there—*right next to him*—for much longer.

Cyn turned to stare at him, and I flattened my palms on the ground, readying myself. I had hit him once before. I could do it again if I had to.

"Did we invite you to sit here?" she said. "Who the hell are you?"

"Oooh, spicy! Abbey knows how much I like the spicy ones." He leaned into my ear and whispered, "*De*licious. Just like Kristen."

I pulled away, horrified.

Before I could stop him, Vincent reached over and laced his hand through mine. "As to who I am? I'm Abbey's boyfriend. Didn't she tell you? My name is . . . Caspian."

I jerked my hand out of his so hard and so fast that I fell forward off the curb and landed against the street. "No—no you're not," I managed to say.

Cyn gasped, and Vincent laughed. Then he stood up.

"Don't smoke too much, girls," he called, sauntering away. "Naughty, naughty, naughty!"

A minute later a black Mustang roared away from us, turning around a corner and racing past a stop sign. I rocked back and watched him go.

And then I leaned forward again, and puked.

Cyn helped me get cleaned up in the school locker room, and I kept apologizing to her. She kept telling me to stop, but I couldn't help it. I didn't know if I was apologizing for making such an idiot out of myself, or apologizing for feeling so helpless. Either way, it sucked.

"I can't *believe* that happened," I said, bent over the sink. "Talk about humiliating."

"It was probably just the cigarette," Cyn replied. "Or the fact that that guy was a *major* douche bag. I thought he looked like trouble."

I rinsed and spit. "Major douche bag" was only the half of it.

"Is he an ex?" she asked hesitantly.

"No."

I didn't say any more, and she didn't prod. I gargled and spit again, then turned off the water. We went back outside, and an old white Honda was sitting there.

"Come on," she said. "You're getting a ride."

"I can walk. It's not that far."

She pointed to the car, and her eyes went wide. "Get. In."

Her tone told me not to argue, so I followed orders. Cyn's mom didn't say anything as I got into the backseat, and Cyn was the one to ask for directions when she got into the front.

They dropped me off, and the house was silent when I walked in. That made me nervous.

"Caspian?" I called. "Are you here?"

There was no answer.

I headed to my bedroom as fast as I could, trying to quell the rising panic in my stomach. *Where is he? Why isn't he answering me? Did something happen?*

Pushing open the bedroom door, my heart sank straight to my feet when I saw someone lying on the bed.

 135

Vincent's here again.

I thought I was going to have a heart attack. My knees threatened to give out, and little black spots sprung up at the edges of my vision. *Breathe* . . . I was forgetting to breathe. I took a huge gasp of air and put one hand on the wall to steady myself so I wouldn't fall right over. And then the person on the bed sat up.

It almost felt like my heart was going to seize up again, only this time out of relief when I saw that it was Caspian.

"Abbey?" he said. "What are you . . . ? Are you okay?"

I clutched my chest. Caspian rubbed his eyes, and then he got up and came over to me. I put up a finger in response. "Just a minute. Just give me a minute. I think I'm having a heart attack. Twice."

He looked around. "What time is it? I was supposed to meet you at school. What happened?"

"I waited for you, but you never came. And then . . ." I glanced back at the bed, putting two and two together. "Were you *sleeping*?"

Caspian ran a hand through his hair, messing the back up a bit, and he glanced at the bed too. "I don't know. I don't remember what happened. One minute I was here and it was eleven o'clock. Then the next . . ." Realization dawned, and his look of confusion turned to anger. "I can't believe I fell asleep!"

 136

The sleeping thing concerned me, but I needed to wash off the remnants of seeing Vincent again before I could think about what it all meant. "It's not a big deal. Don't worry about it. I'm just going to go take a bath."

A strange look crossed his face as I passed by. "Is that smoke?" he asked. "And vomit?"

Embarrassment filled me. "Yeah. Cyn was waiting for her mom too, and she was smoking outside. I shared her cigarette and it didn't agree with me. Hence the hurling."

I limped into the bathroom and started pulling towels down from the cupboard.

"I didn't know you smoked," Caspian said.

"I don't. I mean, I never did before. This was just something new I wanted to try. Figured I wouldn't get another chance, so why not?" I turned on the faucet and adjusted the water temperature.

"Is this . . . going to be a permanent thing?" he asked slowly, a worried look on his face.

"God, no. Once and done. Now, can we please not talk about it anymore?"

He nodded, and I shut the door behind me. All I needed was a good soak in some hot water, and then I'd be ready to tell Caspian the important part.

About Vincent.

~ ~ ~

It wasn't until later that night that I was able to work up my courage to tell him about what else had happened. He'd just finished reading three chapters of *Jane Eyre*, and I didn't want to ruin the perfect moment. Time felt suspended when it was just me and him, together in our own little world, away from everything and everyone. Nothing mattered except the words on the page he was reading from, and the lilt of his voice as he spoke.

Closing my eyes, I took a breath and then said, "There's something I need to tell you, but I don't want you to get upset. So please don't, okay?"

Would he be even more upset with himself that he'd fallen asleep and missed the chance to make sure Vincent didn't do anything to me?

He closed the book and put it down on the bed. "On a scale of one to ten, how bad is it?"

"Probably a nine."

"Okay . . ."

"Just remember that I had a really bad day today, and I threw up in front of someone at school, and there was puke on my shoes," I said in a rush of words. "And Vincent Drake was there."

"At school?"

"Yes."

"You're sure?"

"Cyn saw him too. He came up to us outside and sat beside me."

"Did he hurt you?"

"Not exactly."

"What did he do?"

"Held my hand and told Cyn that he was you."

He was silent for a long time and then said, "Did you throw up before or after he was there?"

"Right after."

He leaned back and looked away. Finally I couldn't take it anymore, couldn't stand not knowing what he was thinking, so I asked him, "Are you upset? At me? At him? Tell me."

"I'm disappointed," he said. "It kind of feels like you kept this from me."

"But I didn't!" I justified. "I'm telling you now."

"Several hours after it happened."

"I . . . I just didn't know what to do."

"You could have let me in. You could have told me right away."

"But I'm telling you now. And you were asleep. And . . ."

"Well, I'm glad I know now," he said.

But he didn't sound glad. And I didn't feel glad. Instead I just felt worse.

Chapter Ten

WOLF IN SHEEP'S CLOTHING

Just then the shadowy object of alarm put itself in motion, and with a scramble and a bound stood at once in the middle of the road.

—"The Legend of Sleepy Hollow"

I knew right away that something was wrong when I woke up the next morning. Caspian was next to me, and he looked like he was taking a nap. But something was different. I could *feel* it.

"Caspian," I said. "Are you sleeping again? I thought you didn't need to sleep." I got up and walked over to the side of the bed where he was lying, and stood directly over him. "Wake up."

He didn't move.

"Come on, Casper. Wake up!" I said again, louder. My instinct was to shake him, even thought I knew I couldn't touch him. I called his name again and again, feeling a growing sense of unease. *Why is this happening? What does it mean?*

"Wake *up*. Why won't you *wake up*?" I said.

Finally I gave in. I reached down to touch him, and my hand went through his. But I didn't feel the buzz or tingle that should have been there.

I moved my arm back and forth—over his head, on his shoulder, up his arm. There was nothing. Not even a blip. It was like we were totally cut off.

I stumbled back, threw on a pair of jeans and a sweatshirt, and raced down to the kitchen. Sophie and Kame's number was there, on a business card they'd given to Mom, and I needed to talk to them *now*. I needed to know what was going on.

The doorbell rang as I was frantically digging through the junk drawer looking for the card that I knew Mom had stashed in there somewhere, and a second later there were voices coming from the foyer.

"Won't you come in?" I heard Mom say. "Let me go get Dennis, my husband. He'll be so pleased to meet you. It's wonderful of you to come introduce yourself to us."

Mom stuck her head in as she passed the kitchen, and said, "Abbey, would you please come meet Deacon Dwayne from Saint Paul's Pentecostal Church? He's new in town."

"Yeah, in a minute, Mom. I'm looking for something. Do

you know where Sophie and Kame's business card is? I thought it was in the junk drawer."

She crossed over to the fridge. "I moved it up here. Let's see . . ." She scanned rows of pizza coupons and Chinese take-out menus. "I don't see it. Must have fallen. Or maybe I put it in my purse."

Dad's voice echoed out to us as he greeted the deacon, and Mom got distracted. "Oh, good. Your father's in the living room. Come with me for just a minute, and then I'll find your card."

She grabbed my hand, and I reluctantly followed. I hoped that the deacon wasn't expecting fancy church clothes or anything, because I *wasn't* changing on his behalf. "Don't forget. I need that card!" I whispered. She nodded absently and kept pulling me behind her.

Dad was sitting on one end of the couch, with the deacon on the other end, and Mom hurried forward to fill the space in between. I ground to a halt, and my feet froze to the floor when I came face to face with him.

"I'm sorry to have kept you waiting, Deacon Dwayne," Mom gushed. "I'd like you to meet my daughter, Abbey." The deacon nodded benignly at me, his stiff black and white outfit barely allowing his head to move.

But he was no man of God. He was a wolf in sheep's clothing.

Deacon "Dwayne," indeed. *I see what you did there, Vincent Drake.* I narrowed my eyes at him and refused to sit.

"Don't be rude, Abbey," Mom prodded. "Come say hello."

"Do not be shy, my child," Vincent intoned in a gentle voice. "Come and sit with us."

A million thoughts ran through my head, but I couldn't pin any of them down. Caspian was here, but he couldn't help. I didn't have Sophie and Kame's card, and I didn't even know how to get a hold of Uri or Cacey.

"Come and sit," Vincent instructed again. "Fellowship with us."

"No, thanks," I said coolly. "I can fellowship from here."

"Have you not heard of the great scripture that says thou shalt honor thy father and mother?" he replied.

Mom nodded her head vigorously.

"Honor. Them." Vincent said, a hard edge in his voice. He moved one hand just a tad bit closer to Mom. Ever so slightly.

I don't think Mom or Dad even noticed it, but I did. It was a menacing move. There was definitely a threat there.

I walked over to the easy chair opposite Vincent and sat down. The seat seemed to rush up to catch me, and it surprised me.

"Now we are all one happy family," Vincent said, a pleasant smile on his face. "The Lord is pleased."

How long was he going to keep up this act? And why was he even bothering to put on such a charade?

"So, are you enjoying Saint Paul's?" Mom asked. "It's such a beautiful church."

"Oh, yes, it is. And they have wonderful youth services. I find myself very much drawn to ministries that help the children," Vincent replied, with an evil smile at me. "Young, wayward innocents are pressed upon my heart."

I gave him a dirty look.

"Yup, they have good kids' programs there," Dad offered. "Some of the best around."

"But it's not like they have them because they *need* them," Mom interjected. "Our kids are very well behaved here in Sleepy Hollow."

Vincent steepled his fingers and adopted a concerned expression. "Are they? I must say, I have heard . . . concerning things. About drug use, and teens becoming sexually active at such a young age."

Evil. He is pure evil.

Mom looked shocked, and Dad wouldn't meet my eyes. I guess the term "sexually active" was more than he wanted to think about.

"No," Mom said. "Our kids don't get involved in such things."

"Wonderful, wonderful." He looked concerned again. "What about other issues? Mental illness? Suicide?" Now Mom wouldn't look at me, and Dad cleared his throat loudly.

"Do you know anyone who has been personally affected by such a thing, Abbey?" Vincent directed the question to me.

What I wouldn't give to punch you in your lying smarmy face right now . . . "Nope. Like Mom said, we're all healthy, well-adjusted kids. Say, how are things going with the Catholics? They seem to be having problems right now, right? Maybe you could go help them out."

Mom gasped, and Dad finally looked at me long enough to frown. One side of Vincent's mouth pulled up in a smirk. And then it was gone.

"I must confess, I do not know how things are handled by the Catholic churches. I'm kept very busy looking after my own flock. I consider myself a shepherd in training, and I find that many of my sheep need . . . a certain kind of hands-on attention."

He cracked his knuckles, and the sound made my skin crawl.

Staring at him hard, I made a silent vow. *I am not going to let you get away with this.* "How long have you been with the church, Deacon Drake?" I said sweetly. "In general. I know Mom said that you were new in town."

"I fear that I have lost count how many years it has been. Or how many lives I've touched." His smile widened, and he licked the corner of his lips. "And it's Deacon *Dwayne*."

"Oh, did I get it wrong? I could have sworn that you said Drake."

Mom looked back and forth between the two of us with a slightly bewildered expression on her face. "Would you like some coffee? Tea?" she said to Vincent. "I'd be more than happy to make some."

"Actually, I have another appointment that I'm going to be late for if I don't leave now. So I will bid my farewells and say that I hope to meet again soon."

He stood up and shook Dad's hand, then turned to Mom. Being sure to angle himself so that I could get a full view, he leaned in to give her a hug with both arms. His hands lined up directly with her throat and he cast me another glance.

Mom! I wanted to scream. *Get away from him! He's the one who attacked me!* But I couldn't tell her. Who knows what he might have done then.

"It was very nice to meet you, Abigail," he said, pulling away from her. I noticed the use of my proper name. "You have lovely parents here. I would give thanks to God every day for such wonderful people in my life. Our time on this earth is so fleet-

146

ing. You never know when their time could be up. Even this day might be their last."

And with that subtle death threat, he walked out the front door.

I flew up to my room as soon as Mom found Sophie's card, and I dialed the number as fast as I could. Caspian was still asleep on the bed. I was starting to worry about him even more. All those times he'd described being pulled down into the dark place of sleep to make time pass faster didn't sound like a good thing.

What if he couldn't find his way back?

I paced beside him, silently willing Sophie or Kame to pick up their phone. It rang and rang and rang, and I was just about to leave an urgent voice mail, when Sophie picked up.

"*Sophie?*" I exploded. "It's Abbey. Vincent's here. Or was here. He dressed like a priest, and was threatening my parents, and Caspian won't wake up."

"Slow down. Slow down," she said. "What's going on? Vincent is *there?*"

"Yes. No. I mean, he was here, but he's not now. He just came by and stopped to talk to Mom and Dad." I told her what had happened. "I don't think they even realized what was going on. But I did."

Sophie swore. "We'll be right over."

"Something's wrong with Caspian too," I blurted out. "He won't wake up."

She was silent, and it didn't give me a good feeling.

"So-Sophie?" I asked. "Are you still there?"

"Yeah, sweetie. I'm here."

"What's happening to Caspian?"

"I think it would be better if we waited until we could talk in person."

"No! I think it would be better if you told me right now."

"I can't—" She exhaled loudly. "Just wait. We'll be right over."

The phone went dead, and I stared at it. It wasn't a good sign that she didn't want to tell me what was going on. Was this just normal we-cannot-say Revenant stuff? Or was there something more to it?

Ten minutes later Kame, Uri, and Cacey were in my room.

"Is everything okay?" Kame asked. "Are you hurt?"

I shook my head. "Everything's fine. Well, as far as me and Mom and Dad go. Caspian, I'm not sure about. Where's Sophie? And what are you going to tell Mom and Dad?"

"She's downstairs talking to them," Cacey said with a grin. "She's good at making things up."

Uri moved toward the bed. He pointed to himself, and I

nodded. Then he sat down next to Caspian. He laid one hand on Caspian's arm, and I *desperately* wanted to trade places with him. To be the one who could touch Caspian, and wake him up.

But I couldn't.

"This happened once before," I said. "He was supposed to pick me up from school and he never showed. When I got home, he couldn't even remember where he was."

Uri glanced over at Kame. Then shook his head.

"What's going on?" I cried, dangerously close to tears. "*Please*. Just tell me." I couldn't take it anymore. I couldn't take all their secrets and things they wouldn't say.

"You have to realize that there's not much we can do," Kame said. "This is an abnormal situation, and we're still all learning the best way to deal with it."

"Abnormal because of Vincent? Because he caused Kristen's death?"

He inclined his head.

"Or is this the abnormal part? Him hanging around me, stalking me, dressing up like a priest?"

"His . . . interference . . . is the abnormal part."

"So, then, what's going on with Caspian? Shades don't sleep, right?"

"It's not a normal sleep," he replied.

"What does that mean?"

"It means that we can't wake him up, Abbey," Cacey said.

She was standing next to the window, and I looked over at her, stunned. Then I looked at Uri. "She's making that up, right? Tell me that it's just her idea of a cruel joke."

"It's not a joke. We have no control over this," he confirmed.

I crossed my arms. "But I thought you guys were these mystical beings who were sent here to help Shades and their other halves. So help us."

Uri stood up and went to talk to Kame quietly. He kept glancing over at Cacey, and I got the feeling that she was being let in on the conversation too. Eventually Kame said, "Fine. I'm going to let you handle this. I'll be downstairs."

He shot them both a final look before he left.

"We think it would be best if we took Caspian with us," Uri said, turning to face me. "We want to take him someplace safe."

"That's fine. Where are we going?"

"*Him.* Not you," Cacey said. "You can't go."

"Oh, yes, I can."

"Oh, no, you can't."

"Why?"

"Because Vincent doesn't want the two of you to be completed. We haven't found out why yet, but it's what he wants. We need to be able to keep an eye on Caspian for as long as he's like this, and it will make it easier for all of us if you aren't there with him. Why draw Vincent to us?"

"But . . . but . . ." I couldn't think fast enough. Couldn't put together my words. They couldn't take Caspian away from me! "But what if Vincent finds you?"

"He won't," Uri said.

"What if Vincent finds *me*?"

"We've got that covered," Uri replied. "How do you feel about a short road trip?"

"A trip? While Caspian stays here? No."

Cacey moved closer and stuck her face right into mine. "Look, Uri is trying to say this a hell of a lot nicer than I am, but we're taking Caspian whether you like it or not. The way I see it, you don't have much of a choice." She looked down at her fingernails and picked at one of them. "Besides, if you come with us, you might even find something out."

She dangled that carrot of information in front of me on a well-practiced hook, and I couldn't say no. The chance to finally get some answers? I couldn't pass that up.

"Fine. I'll go with you. Just tell me one thing, where are we going?"

"Gray's Folly." Cacey looked gleeful as she practically rubbed her hands together. "An insane asylum."

Cacey told me that we'd only be staying overnight, so I packed a T-shirt, some jeans, and a couple of toiletry items in a small bag while she went downstairs with Uri. When she returned half an hour later, she said, "Okay. We're all set. You're officially spending the weekend at my house for a sleepover."

I glanced over at Caspian worriedly. "Kame, Sophie, and Uri are going to take care of him while we're gone?"

"Yup. Although it's going to be just Kame and Sophie. Uri's our driver."

"And why are we going to an insane asylum?"

"Looking for someone."

I didn't know if that meant we were going to be looking for a patient or for someone who worked there, but I decided to let it go for now. Reluctantly I shouldered my bag. Bending down near Caspian's ear, I whispered, "I love you. You're in good hands. I'll be back soon, and you'll be awake then." *I hope.*

I wasn't really sure about that, but with Caspian in this vulnerable state, I'd much rather have him be with the Revs who could take care of Vincent, instead of just me. "So tell me again why we can't stay here and just have you guys watch over us?" I asked.

"Too many questions." Cacey shook her head. "Our mind mojo is good and all, but after a while there would be too much to explain to your parents. Plus, do you really want Vincent coming back here again?"

"Right. Okay. Good point." I looked over my bedroom. "Then, I think I'm ready. Can you tell me where Kame and Sophie will be taking Caspian, at least?"

"Better if I don't. Trust me."

My face fell.

"Awwww, cheer up," she said, steering me down the stairs. "You'll forget all about it soon. I got us a road trip surprise. A twenty-four-pack of delicious Coke-a-Cola!"

Yay. That makes everything soooo *much better* . . . I smiled weakly at her and allowed myself to be directed downstairs.

I said a quick good-bye to Mom and Dad and then went outside to the Jetta. "How far away is it?" I asked, settling myself in and buckling my seat belt.

"About three hours. Upstate. Shouldn't take long," Uri replied.

Cacey was already opening a Coke and happily slurping away before we even pulled out of the driveway. She offered me one once we hit the highway, and I took it. I didn't want it, but God forbid I tell her that.

Time slipped away along with the scenery, and eventually I

saw a sign that read MENTAL HEALTH FACILITY 20 MILES AHEAD. Then another stating it was ten miles ahead, and another for five. At the one-mile mark I started to get a little bit nervous.

It was late afternoon when we arrived, and big rusted gates, one side emblazoned with an ornate *G*, the other with an *F*, blocked the way in front of us as the car came to a stop. Uri rolled down his window and said something to the guard that I couldn't hear. The guard nodded and checked his clipboard to confirm whatever Uri had told him. Then he waved us in.

A series of gray buildings came into view, like oversize blocks. Two small ones on the left, two small ones on the right, and a giant one in the middle. Barbed wire covered sections of the high walls at the top, and spotlights were installed in every corner.

"Looks like a prison," I muttered.

"It was," Cacey said. "Once. In 1825 it was built to hold all the prisoners that were waiting on death row. Then in 1943 someone thought it would be a good idea to turn it into a mental health facility for the criminally insane. Over the past twenty years or so they've expanded into accepting all sorts of people with mental illnesses and diseases."

"Lovely." *Exactly* the type of place where I wanted to spend my weekend. "And we're here to see someone?"

Uri pulled the car forward and found a parking spot. "Yup."

"A patient, or a facility worker?" I asked.

"Not sure yet."

Okay . . .

A nurse came to greet us as we got out of the car, and Uri went to speak to her. She shook her head, then ushered us into this weird little side building. It looked like a guesthouse or staff living quarters, because it was filled with half a dozen tidy little rooms.

"Looks like we're going to have to meet him tomorrow," Cacey leaned in to tell me as we walked down the hall. "Visiting hours are over."

I was shown to one end of the building and given a small, colorless room filled with only a bed, a wash table, and a picture of the crucifixion. A frozen dinner was brought to me on a dingy silver tray fifteen minutes later.

Cacey came in when I was almost done eating (or rather, when I was almost done tentatively pushing my spoon through the gloppy mess) and told me that we were in for the night and she'd be back in the morning. Sternly, she warned me not to leave the house, that there were strict rules about who was allowed to wander the property and I didn't want to be caught somewhere I shouldn't be.

I just shrugged and quickly agreed. Like I wanted to go wander around an insane asylum at night? No, thanks.

 155

~ ~ ~

The next morning, light filtered in through a small window cut high above my bed and woke me up. It was early, and I lay there for a while contemplating what it must have been like to live here all those years ago. When things like electroshock therapy and lobotomies were commonplace. Different rules, different medicines, different times.

What would they have done to someone like me? If someone had told them I thought I could see Caspian and Nikolas and Katy? Would I have been trapped here? Would I have ever gotten out?

The thought left me feeling grim, and my body was like lead as I got dressed. There was a small basin and a pitcher of water on a table nearby, and I washed my face and hands. A hot shower would have been nice, but all I really wanted was to just find whoever Cacey and Uri needed to see and get the hell out of there.

A knock came at my door, and I opened it to find Uri standing there. "Morning," he said.

"Morning."

"There's breakfast in the dining room."

"Okay." I grabbed my bag. I didn't want to come back here if I could help it. We walked silently down the hall, but I noticed that Cacey hadn't joined us yet. "Where's Cacey?"

"She snuck in the Coke cans last night and drank the rest

of that twenty-four-pack. She's not feeling too hot."

I laughed. Then I felt bad. "I hope she's okay."

"She'll be fine in a couple of hours. And then maybe she'll listen to me next time."

I shot him a look.

"Yeah, maybe not," he said wryly.

I was actually kind of relieved that she wasn't going to be with us. Without her around I might be able to get some answers. "So can I come with you, then?" I asked.

He hesitated. "I thought you might want to stay here with Cacey."

"Oh, no, that's okay. I'd much rather go with you." I didn't want my enthusiasm to show too much, so I added, "This place really gives me the creeps."

Uri laughed. "Where we're going isn't much better."

I gave him my best puppy-dog eyes. "Pleeeeeeeeeease?"

"All right. Fine." He sighed heavily.

"Do you mind if we skip breakfast?" I asked as we got closer to the dining room. The smells wafting out of there were revolting. "I'm not hungry."

"Fine by me. I hate hospital food."

He pushed open a nearby side door, and we went outside. There was a golf cart with a driver sitting there, waiting for us.

Uri sat down in the back and motioned for me to sit beside him.

We drove down a winding road and up a short hill before finally stopping in front of the middle building. The biggest one.

"Just stay with me, okay?" Uri said. "Nothing will happen, but better to be safe than sorry."

I nodded solemnly and followed him in.

We were buzzed into an entryway by a nurse who was simultaneously doling out pills into empty cups and entering something into a computer. She came around to get us, and we trailed behind her, walking past peeling walls and poorly lit patient rooms with their doors open. Her thick rubber-soled shoes made a squeaking sound that echoed eerily.

We rounded a corner and passed several more rooms. These all had closed doors.

"Treatment rooms."

The nurse caught me looking, and it was amazing how fast her head could spin around to say those words and then spin back again.

"Obviously you won't be seeing the insides of any of those. Strictly for the more severe cases. Although, I suppose a tour *could* be arranged," she said brightly.

Ah, no.

Uri must have agreed with me, because he politely declined

for the both of us. We passed an empty nurse's station and went around another corner, then came to a small room with a sitting area. "Here we are," the nurse said. "Go ahead and make yourselves comfortable." She gestured at two cracked brown leather chairs with a round table in between them.

Uri moved one of the chairs closer to me, and I sank down into it. He sat in the other one.

The nurse turned to leave, then stopped and whipped her head back around. "I'm sure both of you already know this, but liability requires us to give you an official warning. Don't go anywhere unattended, don't antagonize any of the patients that you may come into contact with, and don't believe anything they say. They are very sick individuals."

She didn't wait for a response, but only nodded her head and then marched back out the door.

I stared after her for a minute, kind of stunned. "What do they think we're going to do?" I asked Uri, speaking in a hushed tone. "Go around poking the patients with sticks?"

"You'd be surprised," he said.

I shook my head, and looked around again. "So, what do we do now?"

"Now we wait."

Chapter Eleven

NOT REAL

The whole neighborhood abounds with local tales, haunted spots, and twilight superstitions . . .

—"The Legend of Sleepy Hollow"

Settling back into my chair, I gazed around the tiny room. Gray walls, gray ceiling, gray floor. I saw where the facility got its name from. A large picture window, grimy with dust and old age, took up half the wall across from us. Metal bars covered it in square-inch increments. Overall, the aesthetic had all the same pleasing qualities that I'd imagined a police interrogation room might have.

A loud bang echoed from the hall and made me jump out of my seat. I could hear harsh sobbing from someone, but it was quickly silenced. My skin began to crawl.

"This hasn't been the greatest experience for you, has it?" Uri said.

"Not exactly."

"Sorry about that."

His words surprised me. The Revs didn't seem like the type to project the warm and fuzzy. Except for the whole mind mojo thing. That was definitely fuzzy. "Can I ask you something?" I said.

"Sure."

"Do you like being a Revenant?"

Uri stretched his legs out in front of him. "I don't have a choice. I am what I am."

"And what is that, exactly?"

His look told me that he "couldn't say" but I gave him an *Oh, come on*, look in return. Glancing over at the open door, Uri said, "It's hard to explain. Don't take this the wrong way, but most humans don't really get it." Then he said, "Do you like being a Shade's other half?"

I used his words and added a shrug. "I don't have a choice. I am what I am." Then I thought about it. "Or do I?"

"Abbey, I—"

"Come on, Uri. I'm not asking a whole lot here. Just talk to me. You don't have to tell me anything you don't want to, but . . . but I can guess, right? How about that? I'll just throw some stuff out there, and you can nod or shake your head. That way you're not *technically* telling me."

"I can't. Acacia will kill me."

"Acacia?" My ears perked up.

"Cacey." He clarified. "I mean Cacey." He scrubbed one hand over his face with the long-suffering look of someone who'd realized he'd just opened a can of worms.

"Acacia," I mused. "'Cacey' for short. Which means that 'Uri' could be short for something. We can start there."

He stayed silent.

"So if 'Cacey' is a nickname, and 'Uri' is a nickname, odds are 'Kame' and 'Sophie' are nicknames too."

"Not 'Kame,'" he finally admitted. "But 'Sophie' is short for 'Sophiel.' And I'm Uriel."

Now we're getting somewhere. I just have to keep him talking. "Why do you use nicknames instead of your full names?"

"We were given proper names at the ceremony when we became Revenants. But they aren't exactly traditional names. Modern people like easy, so it's what we do when we're here. It's easier to fit in that way."

He gave me a pointed look, and I held up two fingers. "I

won't tell anyone, I swear. Scouts' honor. Besides, I'm going to die soon. Who am I going to tell?"

He looked uncertain, but I pressed on. "How come no one will tell me when my exact death day will be?"

"That's the rule."

"Rule? There are rules?"

"Not 'rules' specifically. Guidelines. Humans don't know when they are going to die. That can't be altered."

"Yeah, but can't you make an exception here? I'm not the norm. I already know about you guys. I know about Vincent. I know about Shades."

Uri shook his head. "When the time comes, it will be revealed."

Well *that* was a frustratingly unhelpful thing to say. I couldn't let it distract me, though. "You keep saying 'humans.' Like we're something different. What exactly are *you*? I mean, beyond the helpers that come to make sure a Shade can be completed or move on?"

"We're not human," he said. "If you couldn't guess that already."

I nodded. "Vincent said he was a 'what' not a 'who.' I don't know if that means you're angels, or demons, or what."

"We're not any of those things. We're ..." He held out his hands like he was trying to contain something. "We're like ... energy."

"Okay."

"That's the best way to describe it."

"But where do you live? What about your car?"

"We have cars and houses only when we have an assignment here."

"Here? As in Sleepy Hollow here, or here as in Earth?"

"Earth."

Oh. "So . . . where are you when you're *not* here? On Earth, I mean."

"When we're not here, we're in this space that's sort of in between."

"Heaven?"

"No."

"Hell?"

He laughed. "Definitely not. Again, hard to explain. It's a place where there's nothing but energy and white light. No physical forms, no manifestations. Just pure energy."

"Okay, a little boring, but it's a Zen type place. I get it," I said.

"No. You don't. But that's okay."

"So one day you're just in this Zen lovey-dovey white energy space, and then the next you're zapped back to Earth to help a Shade or their other half be completed or pass over? How do you know what to do? Where to go? Do you get a Post-it note or something?"

"We work in teams, only two of us at a time. And when it's our turn, yes, we do sort of wake up here and then get our assignment."

"That's why Nikolas said it was a problem that there are five of you here," I replied. "There's only supposed to be two. He said that, too, but I don't think I really understood it."

Uri agreed. "Although we may occasionally have simultaneous assignments—which is rare, but it does happen—we are never in the same place at once. There is no need."

"So Vincent must have really screwed you all up, then, huh?"

"You could say that."

"How come everyone can see you and Sophie and Cacey and Kame, but they can't see Nikolas and Katy? Nikolas and Katy are different from me and Caspian because they've been completed, right?"

He nodded. "Humans can see us while we're here on Earth because, for all intents and purposes, we *are* human while we're here. Caspian is different because he's dead, and Nikolas and Katy are different because they've been completed."

I must have looked confused, because he said, "The easiest way to think about it is like blood types. Caspian is a certain type of ghost, say AB negative, while Nikolas and Katy are O positive. Both types are still blood, a.k.a. Shades, but if Caspian is completed, by you, he'll become O positive, like Nikolas and Katy."

"*If* he's completed? Why wouldn't I complete him?"

Uri glanced away. "Sometimes things . . . happen."

"Oh, you mean like with Washington Irving? Nikolas told me that he was a Shade, but he wasn't completed by his other half. She moved on."

Uri nodded.

"Why do Shades even need to be completed?" I asked. "No one's ever told me the reason why."

He wanted to hedge. It was written all over his face, so I tried a different tactic. "What about other Shades that need help crossing over?"

He took a moment to answer but finally said, "For now things are being handled. But this matter needs to be resolved soon. For everyone's sake."

"Okay, so you come down here, get your assignment, and then poof? You have a house and a car and clothes? What about ID? Credit scores?"

"We get what's given to us, in terms of houses and cars and clothes. Sometimes it's a Jetta, sometimes it's an apartment in a back alley, and sometimes it's Gucci. If we need an ID, that's available to us too. They can come in handy."

I remembered what he'd been wearing when I first saw him, in the cemetery after the bridge dedication. "You were given a mishmash of clothes this time, huh? You have this Goth meets prep meets skater boy vibe going on. Kind of weird. And the khakis? Not a good look."

"Most of the clothes are already there waiting for us, wherever we're staying. But Cacey loves to go shopping, and she drags me with her." Now he looked a bit embarrassed. "Sometimes it takes a while to figure out what century we're in."

"You guys need a built-in stylist-for-a-day when you get your assignments," I said. "That would solve everything. Oh, and a hairdresser, too."

Uri laughed again and touched his hair. It was longer than it had been in the cemetery. Instead of a fauxhawk he had mini dreads. "I think I'm a pretty good hairdresser."

I cocked my head. "Maybe for a boy." He smiled. "Do the other Revenants dye their hair?" I asked. "Sophie's always looks like it's not quite done right. Like she's a natural blonde and the red can't cover all of it up. And you all have eyes that are completely clear."

"Our coloring is the same because in the white space there's no pigmentation. That's why we all have pale eyes, pale hair, and pale skin. When we come to Earth, we can wear contacts, get a tan, and, yes, dye our hair. It's the only chance we have to live like mortals. Cacey likes to take full advantage. That's why she likes Coca-Cola so much."

"How long do you generally get to live like mortals? Before your assignment is up?"

"It varies."

"Like . . . ? Two days? Two years? Two months? What?"

"It just . . . varies." His mouth tightened around the edges.

That's all you're going to get from him on that, Abbey. Move on. "The superpowers must be kind of cool," I said instead.

"Superpowers?"

"Yeah, the mind-mojo thing."

"It's not really a power. More like the 'power of persuasion.'"

"So, you can persuade people to do things? Still cool."

"Not actually *things*—like barking like a dog, or pretending to be a chicken. We persuade them to go along with what we're saying. Or to forget that they saw us."

"I gotta say, that's pretty freaking sweet."

He smiled. "It definitely helps."

"When I first met you guys, I was really creeped-out," I said. "And then all of a sudden everything was fine. Was that the persuasion thingy?"

"That was it. It's like a calming agent."

"I totally need to get my hands on something like that. I have a couple of teachers at school who need to be 'persuaded' to forget about my homework." I grinned at him.

"Sometimes people experience a funny taste or smell when we use the persuasion on them," he said. "I'm not sure why."

"Yes! Burning leaves? Or burned toast?" He nodded. "Around you and Cacey I could smell it, but around Kame and Sophie I could taste it."

"I don't know what it is precisely, but I think it has to do with neurons misfiring. Like a short fuse."

"It doesn't really happen anymore," I mused. "Huh. I just realized that. And, you know, I don't get that creepy feeling either."

Uri looked away from me then, and stared at the window. He was probably getting tired of all my questions. But I needed a couple more answered. "Since I'm Caspian's other half, I'm the only person who can see him, right? I mean, living person? I always *thought* that but wasn't sure."

"Yes. Since you're the other half of him, there aren't any other pieces left for other people to see. He's the shadow that only you can see."

"I never thought about it that way. That's kind of weirdly lovely."

"I think so too."

"What about touch? Nikolas and Katy can touch Caspian, and so can you. How come I can't touch him?"

"Because you are the only one who is alive."

He said it kind of sadly.

"Oh."

"I really can't say any more, Abbey." He stood up from the chair and walked over to the window. "Will you stay here for a minute while I go check in with the nurse again?"

I wanted to tell him no. That I couldn't stay in this creepy place all alone, but I didn't want him to think I was scared. It was just a room. I could totally sit here by myself in a room. "Yeah. Sure. Take your time. I'll wait here."

He moved to the door.

"Just don't forget to come back and get me," I called out.

"I couldn't forget you," he said with a cheeky grin. "Cacey would have my head."

"That's true. She would!"

But he was already gone. I had no idea if he'd heard me.

I sat there for a while, trying not to think about people creeping around out in the hallways and waiting to poke their heads in at any minute and yell "Boo!" I kept myself busy by reciting president names and then humming Christmas carols until finally I couldn't take it any longer.

Hesitantly I got up from the chair and peeked outside the door.

No patients in sight. And no weird nurses, either. I walked quickly down the hall, trying to remember my way back to the front desk.

 170

I rounded the corner and then passed the empty nurses' station. *That means closed rooms are next, and then open rooms before I hit the front desk.*

Inhaling deeply, I tried to keep count of how many closed doors I passed. But the last door was open.

My feet automatically slowed, even though my brain was saying, *Hurry, hurry!*

I couldn't help it.

I looked in.

A flat bed on wheels was sitting in the middle of the room, completely empty. Heavy-duty straps were hanging down on all four sides, clearly meant to be used as physical restraints. Words were stamped on the straps, and I moved closer to see what they said. Half-faded ink read MENTAL HEALTH INSTITUTE FOR THE CRIMINALLY INSANE.

I took a step back. I needed to get out of this room. The air didn't feel right. It was stuffy. Where was the door? The walls were closing in. I couldn't breathe, and—

"Hi."

I spun around. The voice had come from behind me. It was high pitched and childish.

A girl was standing there, in a long nightgown that appeared to have once been frilly and white but was now stained and tattered. Shreds of lace wavered in little clumps around the edges of her wrists. A teddy bear with rubbed-away fur and only one eye hung from her hand.

I tried frantically to remember the "official warning," but all that kept coming to mind was, *Stick. Don't poke. Be nice.*

"Hi," I said eventually, moving slowly so that I was closer to the door. "How are you?"

She looked like she was my age, yet her voice was definitely that of a little girl. She took a sudden step toward me, and my heart sped up. "I lost my friend," she said sadly. "She died."

Oh. Wow. That was unexpected. I could feel my face softening. "You did? I did too."

She held up her teddy bear. "This is my friend now."

"Good. That's good." I didn't know if I should keep moving to the door or keep talking. Which one was the least likely to upset her?

"You're special," she said, moving toward me again and putting out one hand. "Pretty color."

She could see my color? Was she like Caspian? Or like me?

Suddenly the most horrific thought crossed my mind. *She's dead. I'm seeing someone else who's dead, and they're going to lock me away in here. Or maybe I'm already in here. Strapped to a bed. How can I tell what's real and what's not real? How can I ever . . .*

I could feel a little piece of my mind slowly start screaming, and I didn't know. Couldn't tell. Had no idea if this was an elaborate hoax set up by everyone just to get me here so that they'd never let me out, and how would I—

"There you are."

Both of us looked up.

A different nurse from the one Uri and I had followed was in front of us, arms folded. "Child, I've been looking everywhere for you."

Me? Is it me?

The girl in the nightgown turned and walked toward the bed. With the teddy bear still in one hand, she climbed up and then sat down. She put the bear on her lap and reached over for a strap. "I lost my mom," she said sadly. "She died."

I watched in mute horror as she slowly started to strap one wrist in.

"I lost my dad," she repeated. "He died."

"Poor girl," the nurse murmured, glancing back at me. "She had a mental breakdown. Has to be strapped in just to take her meds. Are you with the other visitor? The gentleman?"

All I could do was nod.

"Well, honey, let me go take you right to him. You must have gotten lost in this maze of a place. Just give me one second."

She went over to the bed, putting a hand on the girl's arm. "You don't need to do that. It's not time for your medication yet. Why don't you come with me? I'll take you to watch TV."

"Pretty color," the girl said, looking up at the nurse.

My heart whooshed with relief. *It's not me! I'm not crazy! She is.*

Gently the nurse undid the strap and helped the girl down from the bed. Scooping up her teddy bear, the nurse handed it to the girl and then led her to the door.

"You can follow us," the nurse said to me. "We're all going to the same place."

I wanted to laugh hysterically. I knew she meant that we were all going to the same front waiting area, but all I could think was, *You're right. Everyone goes to the same place.* I looked back at the bed as I left the room. *Some of us just get there faster than others.*

We shuffled slowly down the hall but eventually made it to the front desk. The nurse gave me a kind smile and pointed over to a corner, where I saw Uri talking to an older man with white hair. The man was wearing an old-fashioned white suit, and he looked like a college professor. A sad college professor. As I got closer, I could hear what they were saying.

"Don't you feel any sense of responsibility?" Uri asked.

"He's made his choice," the man replied. "It was not mine to make."

"But aren't you going to help us at all? You should be there."

"I can't. I'm sorry, but he won't listen to me."

Uri caught sight of me, and the conversation stopped abruptly. "Ready to go?" he asked me.

"Ready, like, an hour ago. You never came and got me."

"I was going to as soon as I was done here."

"How much longer were you going to be? You took a really long time. I had a slight run-in with one of the patients. But it's cool, I'm fine."

Something caught my attention, and from the corner of my eye I saw a male aide come to fetch the girl from the nurse. He was wearing leather pants underneath a scrub top uniform, and he looked like he could have been Johnny Depp's brother.

The male nurses wear leather pants here? This place is really *weird.*

"I guess we can leave, then," Uri said, drawing my attention back to him. "We've said all there is to say."

The man in the white suit didn't say good-bye to either of us but instead turned and walked down another hallway. I watched him go, wondering what exactly was going on.

"Did you find anything out?" I asked Uri.

He led me outside to the golf cart. The expression on his face was angry. "Yeah. I found out that we're on our own. The person I need isn't here."

Chapter Twelve

ADVICE

From his half-itinerant life, also, he was a kind of traveling gazette, carrying the whole budget of local gossip from house to house . . .

—"The Legend of Sleepy Hollow"

Cacey was waiting for us when we got back to the guesthouse. She looked like she still felt pretty awful, but after a short exchange with Uri in which he told her only that he was unsuccessful, we got in the car and drove away from the asylum without looking back.

All I could think about on the ride home was that girl. *What had her life been like before she'd gone in there? Does she have any friends that miss her? A best friend? That could have been me. . . .*

Uri's phone rang when we were almost to the house, and he answered it. He spoke briefly, then hung up. "Slight detour," he told Cacey. "We need to stop at the cemetery."

"Are we going to Nikolas and Katy's house?" I asked. I should have guessed that was where they'd take Caspian.

He nodded, and we drove through the open cemetery gates and headed for the far side. When we got to the trees, Nikolas and Katy were there, waiting for us. And so was Caspian.

I put my fingers on the door handle, ready to jump out and grab him.

"We'll go get him and bring him to you," Cacey said. "There are still people around."

"Yeah, okay. Just hurry." I would have agreed to just about anything as long as they went and got him right now.

Cacey and Uri got out, somehow managing to look effortlessly cool, like they were just taking a stroll, and wandered over to the trees. Uri pointed something out, making Cacey laugh, and then they came back with Caspian following them. Nikolas and Katy waved to me, and I smiled at them through the window.

When Cacey and Uri got back to the car, Cacey opened the rear door and leaned in to me, like she was saying something. "Get in," she told Caspian. He slid beside me, and I couldn't stop smiling.

"You're back!" I said. "What happened? You wouldn't wake up—"

"Are you okay? Did anything happen? Did Vincent hurt you?" he said at the same time.

He laughed and moved one hand closer, across the seat. I moved my hand closer to his, too, and felt the buzzing sensation.

"Were you with Cacey and Uri?" he asked.

"Yes. They took me with them to look for someone. But he wasn't there. Were you with Nikolas and Katy again?"

"Yeah."

"How long did it take for you to wake up?"

"I don't know." He glanced down.

Uri put the car into gear. "Okay," he said. "Let's get you guys back home." Then he grinned at me. "You didn't mind our little detour, did you, Abbey?"

"Nope. Not at all."

We shared a smile, and he actually looked a bit bashful.

"So, what do we do if this happens again?" I said as we drove. "Do I just call one of you?"

"We're going to be around more," Uri said. "All of us."

"That sounds more like a threat than a promise," Caspian whispered after they dropped us off at home and we walked up to the front door.

I laughed. "I think it's a little bit of both."

We went inside, and I called out, "Hi. I'm home."

I knew Mom was doing something in the kitchen because I heard her banging around. She caught up to me when I was almost all the way up the stairs. "How was your girls' weekend?" she asked.

"It was okay. Cacey got sick, so we didn't do much." Technically *almost* true.

"That's too bad. You'll have to plan another one soon." She turned away, then turned back. "Oh! Aunt Marjorie called while you were gone."

"She did? Why didn't you have her call my cell?"

"I didn't want to interrupt you guys. Just call her back when you get the chance."

"I will."

Crossing into my room, I tossed my overnight bag onto the floor. My bed looked super comfy, and it was calling my name. "Nap time?" I said suggestively to Caspian. "The bed I slept in last night was pretty crappy." He followed me over and I flopped down, rolling to one side. He lay down too, facing me.

We both lay there for a while, communicating silently. *I love you*, I wanted to say. *I missed you.* Eventually I settled for "Hi."

"Hi." He put out a finger and went to trace my arm. I felt the slow hum all the way down.

"That was pretty scary when you went to sleep like that," I said.

"I know. For me, too."

"What was it like this time? Was it different?"

"Not really. Just deeper."

"Like you couldn't wake up?"

"Yeah. Like I wouldn't ever wake up."

"What are we going to do?" I asked, looking deeply into his eyes. "About this. About us . . ." I put one hand up and made a frustrated gesture.

"I don't know. Wait? See what happens?"

"How long can we wait? How long can we go on like this?" I closed my eyes. "I'm scared of something changing. I'm scared of what it means when you fall into this sleep that feels like you'll never wake up from."

"Are you scared of me?"

"No!" My eyes flew open. "Why would I be scared of you?"

"Because of me." He moved his hand, and it went through mine. "Who I am. What I am."

"You can't help that. You are what you are." I propped my hand under my head. "It's funny, though. Uri and I were talking about the same thing today. We went to this insane asylum that used to be a prison."

"They took you to an *insane asylum*?" He looked shocked.

"Well, more of a mental health institute now. But, yeah. It wasn't really all that bad."

"I can't believe they took you there. Especially after . . ."

"After what happened when I went to go stay with Aunt Marjorie? And seeing Dr. Pendleton?" I said.

"It seems a bit insensitive," Caspian replied.

"I don't think they meant it that way. They didn't seem to think anything of it. It's hard for them. They're here only part of the time." I told him what Uri had said about the white energy space, and what happened when they got their assignments.

"So there are more of us?" he said. "More Shades?"

"I didn't get an exact count, but it didn't sound like many. And they come at different times. It just happens when it happens."

He looked at me intently. "I'm glad they made us in twos, then."

My cheeks felt warm, and I looked down. "I thought I saw another Shade today," I said. "At the asylum. There was a girl there, and she mentioned having a friend die. Then she said she could see my color. It was kind of spooky. Turns out she was a patient. Had a mental breakdown."

"And you thought it could have been you," he guessed. "That you could have been that girl."

Sadness filled me. "Yeah. I did. She just looked so lost and alone. I wanted to help her, but I couldn't. It was . . . tough to see."

"She'll get the help she needs if she's in there. It's the right place for her."

"How do we know what the right place is? For any of us? She didn't ask to be put in an insane asylum. She didn't ask to have a mental breakdown. It just seems so unfair. So random. None of us *really* have a choice in life."

"Are we still talking about her?" he asked gently. "Or you?"

"Her. Me. Don't you get it? We're both the same."

He leaned in closer. He was almost right on top of me. "No. You're not the same. For one thing, she doesn't have me."

A little laugh bubbled out of me. "Ego much?" But I smiled so he knew I was teasing.

"No, I don't mean it like that. I mean that she doesn't have me to love her. You do."

Love. Love. Love. The word spun around in my brain and made me feel all fizzy in there. Closing my eyes, I nestled closer to him. Not touching, but close. Oh, so close. "November first, November first, November first," I chanted. "Please come fast."

~ ~ ~

I called Aunt Marjorie back after dinner that night. Caspian was up in my room, and I sat down on the porch to make the call.

"Hi, Aunt Marjorie. It's Abbey," I said. "How are you?"

"Well, bust my britches! I'm great! How are you, sweetie?"

I had to cover up the receiver so I could laugh. "I'm good, Aunt Marjorie."

"School start yet?"

"Oh, yeah. They finally reassigned Kristen's locker this year and gave it to someone new."

She made a disapproving sound. "That must be hard to see."

"It was, at first. But now it's a little easier. The girl, Cyn, is really nice. That makes it better."

"How did your summer schoolwork go?"

"Good. I passed my science test." That was the unexciting part of the end of summer. I couldn't tell her the other part, about Vincent. "Are you taking your plane out anymore? Or is it too cold?"

"She's still going up. Not as often, though. I have to keep an eye on the engine and make sure the block heater doesn't get too cold. It's a bitch to unfreeze midflight."

 183

I laughed. "Aunt Marj, you are the coolest aunt ever."

"I try," she said. "So how are the other things? Fitting into your hole again?"

"My hole?"

"Round peg, square hole? It's a metaphor for life. If you're the square peg in a square hole, you fit back in."

That makes sense in a strange sort of way. Aunt Marjorie logic. "Actually," I said, "yeah. I am finding my place."

"See? I knew you would. And you were worried about going back."

"You were right. And I can honestly say, I wouldn't be the same person if I hadn't come back."

"Then, everything was meant to be."

"Hey, Aunt Marjorie," I said, "if I don't ever get the chance again, I just wanted to tell you how much I really appreciate everything you did for me. Especially the advice about love and being sure and all that. My head is a lot clearer now, and I can make decisions easier. So, thanks."

"Decisions?" she said. "Planning something?"

"More so, just now I know what I need to do. And I'm at peace with that."

"Are we talking about being at peace with ourselves because we are strong, individual, confident women who don't need men, or are we talking about being at peace with a decision that involves something drastic?" She sounded alarmed.

"I don't know what you mean by drastic, but it's the right choice for me."

"Abbey, you've discussed this with other people, right? Talked to someone else about it?"

"Well, yeah, actually, but it didn't work. They don't understand me. I tried to talk to Mom and Dad, but they just got upset."

"You can talk to me. *Please* talk to me. You have other options. This is a serious decision! I know it might seem like the world is ending now, but there's more in store for you. Just hold on. Some boy isn't worth it!"

"Worth what?"

Now she sounded flustered. "Are—aren't you talking about hurting yourself? Because a boy dumped you?"

I know I shouldn't have laughed, but I did. "Um, no. That's not what I'm talking about."

"It's not?"

"*No*, Aunt Marjorie. I'm talking about having a clearer idea of where my life is headed. For the future."

"Oh." Relief flooded her voice. "Oh, that's good. Very, very good."

I shook my head at the phone. Hurting myself because a

boy dumped me? I don't know where she'd gotten *that* from. "Okay, then. So are we good? All clear?"

"All clear."

"I'll call you again soon."

"Okay, sweetie. Talk later."

I tucked my phone away and looked up. It was a beautiful night out, with clear skies and a big silvery moon. But there weren't any stars.

Getting up, I dusted off my jeans and headed back inside. Luckily, I had my own set of stars. And someone to look at them with.

The letter from Aunt Marjorie came two days after our phone call, and I realized she must have written it pretty much *right* after I'd called her. I found it in the mailbox when I got home from school, and sat down on the front steps to read it.

Dear Abbey,

I feel that this letter has been a long time coming, mostly because I feel that you should know something very important about me. The irony that it seems like recent boy troubles have been on your mind is not lost on me, especially in light of this news.

I am not one to judge, so please do not feel that this is me judging you, or passing my opinions or thoughts on to you. You are my great-niece, whom I adore and cherish with all of my heart. Whatever choices you have made in life, and will continue to make in life, I fully support. Wherever that may lead you.

In the long run, however, I feel that you deserve to know this because I fear I may have given you the wrong idea of how smoothly life went for your uncle and me. Even though we haven't discussed your uncle in great detail, please know that I loved that man with everything I had. With everything I was. In fact, I still do. He was kind and patient and wonderful. There will never be another person on this earth who is the kindred soul to me that Gerald was.

Our love was strong. And fierce. As I've told you before, when it hit me, I _knew_. I knew beyond anything else that he was the one for me. There were happy times, and sad times, because such is the way of life, but above all, there were _good_ times. Always, always good times.

I could fill these pages with memories of all the good times, Abbey. Pages and pages of good times. But what I think is most important for you to know, what something deep in my soul tells me you need to know, is about the bad times.

Gerald and I were married right after he joined the Navy. He was a scientist. A fixer and builder of things. After he'd returned home from his tour of duty, he told me a story once. About how his platoon had been sent on a top secret mission to spy on a new project that the enemy was developing. On the night they were supposed to go in, someone tipped off the other side, and Gerald and his platoon walked straight into a trap. He was so scared that he started to recite elements of the periodic table. The "scientist's prayer," he always called it.

One of the guards recognized what he was saying and put him and the platoon members into a different cell. A safer cell. Every day, until they were rescued three weeks later, the guard came in to talk to Gerald, and even snuck him in extra food. It was because of those extra rations that the platoon managed to stay alive.

The guard who snuck in the extra food used a woman to do it. A woman who got to know Gerald. Who fell in love with Gerald, and he with her.

I tell you this, Abbey, not to besmirch the man I loved. He admitted what he had done, which was the unforgivable. He'd had an affair. But in the end, though it took me some time, I forgave him.

The reason why I'm telling you this is because of what he did. He betrayed my trust. Yet in the end, I was the one made stronger by it. I was the one to overcome adversity, as you have so recently done.

The day that your uncle Gerald told me of his affair was the day I started taking classes for my pilot's license. In some ways his admission freed me to follow that part of my soul that longed for something more, and I will always be grateful to him for that. And yet . . . And yet I regret that I waited so long. That I waited for _him_ to free that piece of me. I wish I had done it for myself.

You've been through a lot, Abbey, and it breaks my heart to know that you have gone through such trying times alone. Losing your best friend, and in a sense part of yourself (for who are we, really, when our dearest friendships suddenly end?), is something that I wish you would have never had to experience. Although I know that it has made you a stronger person, I'm still your auntie, and I don't want you to have pain. Ever.

All I want for you, Abbey, is to live. Live and love like nothing has ever broken your heart before. And choose.

Choose wisely. Choose freely. Choose for you.

All my love,
Aunt Marjorie

I sat there for a long time, rereading the letter and thinking about what she was saying. Even though she didn't know what was truly going on, in the end her advice to me was that it was really all about *my* choice to be with Caspian.

Choose wisely. Choose freely.

I knew what choice I would make.

Chapter Thirteen

An Opportunity

He came clattering up to the school door with an invitation to Ichabod to attend a merry-making or "quilting frolic . . ."

—"The Legend of Sleepy Hollow"

The first week of October came and went before I even knew it, while I was on a strange buddy system with the Revenants. One of them was pretty much always nearby. When Caspian dropped me off at school in the morning, I'd see Cacey there, talking to the other seniors. Sometimes it would be Sophie, stopping in to discuss real estate with the school secretary in the afternoons.

It wasn't so bad at first. And it seemed to be working. There wasn't a peep out of Vincent. But after the second full week of being trailed by bodyguards, I was starting to feel caged in.

"We need to tell them to relax," I whispered to Caspian. We had scooted in the side door to school early one morning before classes started, and we were hanging out by my locker. Kame was walking the halls. "Can you say something to them?"

"I don't know if that's a good idea."

The bell rang, and the outside doors opened up.

"Please?" I pulled out the big guns; I pouted a little.

"What if Vincent is waiting for them to stop hanging around before he does something again?" he replied. "I don't want to take that chance."

The hallways filled with students coming in from outside, and lockers started opening. I kept my voice low. "Okay, fine. They don't have to stop their protective-detail thing. But can it be toned *down*? Like, can you and I actually go somewhere just to hang out without feeling like they're watching our every move?"

Even in my bedroom it didn't really feel like we were alone anymore, knowing that one of the Revs was always downstairs, or outside watching the house.

"I'll talk to Uri about it," he said. "But no promises, okay?"

My pout turned into a grin. "Okay!"

Caspian groaned. "I mean it. I'm not promising anything. If

they think it's best to keep doing what they're doing, then it's going to stay that way."

"But you *will* talk to them?"

"Yes. I *will* talk to them."

"That's all I ask." I stuffed my book bag into the bottom of my locker and pulled out the first set of books I'd need. "Okay. Gotta run. See you after."

"Have fun," he said. He grinned at me, and I blew him a quick kiss before he turned to leave. I was just about to shut my locker door when I realized I forgot to grab a pencil.

"Shoot."

"What's up?" Cyn's voice drifted over the top of her locker, startling me.

How long has she been there? "I, uh, just forgot to grab something." After reaching for a pencil, I slammed the locker door shut. "Got it now. Catch ya on the flip side."

I gave her a quick wave, but she just stood there and watched me go, wearing an odd expression on her face.

Ben caught up with me at lunch and slid his orange plastic cafeteria tray next to mine. Beth joined us a moment later. She'd been eating lunch with me since the first day of school.

"Meatloaf surprise," Ben said, staring down at the quivering blob of gray mush in front of him. "Surprise! No meat."

Beth laughed. "And yet, you're still going to eat it. Aren't you?" She had a small tub of wilted lettuce in front of her and was steadfastly picking out all of the brown bits.

I pushed my spork around in my meatloaf. "It's not too bad if you cover it with gravy. Then you can't tell what it is."

"I'll stick to my salad, thanks." Beth picked up a tiny forkful of lettuce and chewed. "Did you guys see the new posters the cheerleaders put up for the Hollow Ball this year? It's supposed to be some art-deco thing, but it looks like crap."

Ben snorted some of his meatloaf surprise.

"It's true!" she said. "It looks like someone took twelve buckets of paint and just splashed it all around. And I think that someone was blind."

"Hey," I said. "Blind people can create amazing art. I saw this exhibit in the city once that was just incredible."

"Let me rephrase." Beth tilted her head to one side and thought about it, lettuce dangling limply from her fork. "A blind someone who isn't a professional artist and doesn't have an ounce of creativity in their body. Better?"

Not really, but okay. "I can't believe that it's October already." I changed the subject. "Where did the last two weeks go? I never even saw them putting the posters up."

"You *didn't*?" Beth looked shocked. "They've been putting them up, like, every two feet around the whole school. And the bathroom walls are plastered with 'em."

I shrugged. I'd been too busy thinking about the Revs and Caspian to pay any attention. "Who are you taking to the ball?" I asked her. "Lewis? Or someone new?"

"Depends on what day of the week it is. If you ask me on a Monday, I'm going with Lewis. But if you ask me on Thursday? I'm thinking Grant, a cute junior I have computer class with."

"Does it matter what day of the week the Hollow Ball falls on?" Ben asked.

I nudged him with my knee. "Ooooh, good question."

"I don't get it," Beth said.

"Well, if you tell Grant on a Thursday that you'll go with him, but the Ho' Ball falls on a Saturday, does that change things?"

Beth stuck her middle finger up at him, and Ben just laughed.

"I'm sure whoever you go with, you'll have a great time together," I said.

"Thanks, Abbey," Beth said sweetly. "I think so too."

I moved my sludge-masquerading-as-food around a bit more. No amount of gravy was going to help it. "Ugh, I'm so done."

"Me too." Beth pushed away her salad and then downed a

carton of milk. "I have to—" Her phone buzzed, interrupting her. She looked down at it. "Aaaand, it's Monday."

She punched a couple of buttons, then looked up and glared at the table two rows away from us. "He's sitting *right* over *there*. But does *he* come to *me*? No. *I* have to go to *him*. Gah!" Gathering her tray, she shot us an aggravated look. "Bye, guys. Time to go make Monday happy. Thursday's looking better and better."

I gave her a pitying smile. "See ya. Good luck."

Ben just shoveled in another mouthful of meatloaf and grunted.

"Well, that was fun," I said, watching her go.

"Hey, how well do you know the new girl?" Ben said suddenly. "Cyn."

"Okay, random much?"

"Yeah. Sorry." Ben gave me a cheesy grin. "But still, how well do you know her?"

"Why? Are you hoping I'll play matchmaker? Do you want to ask her to the Hollow Ball?"

He looked uncomfortable. "I thought about it, but now I'm not sure."

"Why? What is it?"

"Don't take this the wrong way, okay? But she was asking me about you."

"Asking what?"

"Like if you talk to yourself, or talked to Kristen, or anything like that."

She must have heard me talking to Caspian this morning.

"What did you tell her?" I demanded.

He put up both hands in surrender. "Nothing. I just wanted to let you know. She said that it was cool, no big if you do," he said quickly.

"She probably just heard me singing along with my iPod," I muttered.

Ben nodded and looked like he wasn't even giving it a second thought. "Anyway, I just wanted to know if you guys had, like, a history or something."

"Nope. She's cool, I think."

But I wasn't very sure about that.

"So, then, you *don't* mind if I ask her out?"

His grin was obscenely flirtatious, and I flicked a piece of leftover salad at him. "Hornball."

On Friday, Ben met me at my locker again and danced his way down the hall to see me.

"Cute," I said. "Trying to impress all the single ladies?"

"Nope. Just you."

"Color me impressed."

He reached into his back pocket and pulled something out, using one hand to shield it like a magician drawing cards. "*This is what should impress you.*"

He held out two tickets.

Silently I groaned as soon as I saw what they were. "That's supposed to impress me? Paper?"

"Not just any paper but two magical tickets to a fantasy land called the Hollow Ball." He dangled them in front of me. "There are only two weeks left. These babies are a hot commodity."

"So why are you showing them to me?"

"Because I'm asking you if you want to go."

"*Ben . . .*"

"*Abbey . . .*"

"I don't know." I groaned out loud this time.

He brandished the tickets again. "Come on. May I *please* have the honor of your company at the Hollow Ball? Or something like that. I showed you all of my best dance moves."

"Why me?"

"Because when I heard Beth talking about who *she* was taking at lunch the other day, and didn't hear you talking about who *you* were taking, I knew who I wanted to spend the evening with."

"A *friendly* evening?" I said.

"I can't promise that once you see me in my studmuffin tux you won't want to rip the clothes right off my body. But if that happens, I'm sure we can find a nice, quiet place."

"I'm sure I'll have a hard time controlling myself," I said dryly.

His face perked up. "Is that a yes? What time should I pick you up?"

"That's an I-don't-know. Let me think about it."

He opened up the front page of the Spanish book I was holding and stuck the tickets inside. "Here. Now you can make your choice. And if you choose not to go with me, you can take someone else. I'll understand."

My mouth dropped open and I shook my head at him. "Ben. Why are you such a nice guy?"

He turned to dance back down the hall. "It's just my nature."

"I think you should reconsider," Caspian said again as we walked home from school that afternoon. I'd told him about the tickets Ben had given me, and Caspian had made the same argument the entire way home.

"No. I don't want to go."

"This is the only chance you'll get to have a senior prom. Do you really want to miss out on that?"

"It's just a stupid dance. Besides, I can't go with the person I *really* want to go with, so why go at all?"

"Lots of people take dates who are just friends to dances. It doesn't mean anything, and at least you won't miss the opportunity."

I raised an eyebrow at him. "So you're saying that you want me to go on a date with Ben?"

"Not a date-date. And he better keep his hands to himself."

"Or you'll what?" I teased.

"I can throw things, you know." His smile disappeared. "This is important, Abbey. It's a rite of passage that I don't want you to look back on and regret missing."

"Do you really think I'll regret missing a rubbery chicken dinner in bad mood lighting?" I laughed. "That won't happen."

"Please, Astrid?" he said quietly. "Please go? For me."

Caspian knew how to pull out the big guns too. Sexy eyes, and lips, and hair that he kept brushing away . . . "I'll think about it," I said. "That's what I told Ben, so that's what I'll tell you, too. Okay?"

"Okay."

"I can't *believe* my boyfriend is trying to talk me into going to the prom with another boy," I grumbled. "On what planet does that even make any sense?"

"I'm doing this for your own good, you know," he replied.

I snorted. "So if I go, do you think that means the Revs will go too? That would be kind of funny, seeing them try to blend in. I can just imagine their outdated formal wear." Then I cocked my head. "Speaking of, I haven't seen them around as much. Were you able to convince them to give us some space?"

"Yeah, I talked to Uri. He agreed to tone it down. They're still hanging around, but I think now they definitely take longer lunch breaks." He shot me a grin. "Trust me, though. One day you'll thank me for pushing you to go to your senior prom. Dances are a lot of fun."

"Oh, yeah?" I said, raising an eyebrow. "And how do you know that?"

He looked sheepish. "I've been to my fair share."

"Mmm-hmm. Really."

He ran a hand through his hair and looked embarrassed. "What can I say? I was the mysterious, quiet guy. Girls wanted to get to know me."

I moved closer to him, feeling a surprising stab of jealousy spike through me. "And how many girls did *you* want to get to know?"

"There *were* quite a few dances . . ." A mischievous smile tugged at his lips.

"And?"

"And . . . I don't kiss and tell."

"Ooooooohhh." I narrowed my eyes.

Caspian laughed. "I love when you get all grumpy, Astrid. It's quite adorable." He held a finger next to my cheek. "This number right here is the number of girls I've danced with that I wanted to get to know. *One.*"

My heart melted a little. "Me?" I said hopefully.

He nodded. "You."

I thought about what Caspian had said about the prom all weekend but was still undecided, and I found Beth and Ben standing next to the flagpole before school Monday morning, having a heated discussion about the best way to rig the pulley if you wanted to send something heavy up. Like a body.

"You guys have the *weirdest* ideas," I said, joining in. "Like, seriously weird."

"Do you think it could be done?" Beth asked.

"It's totally possible," Ben replied. He launched into some long explanation that involved physics and weight and mass versus matter, as my eyes glazed over.

"Yes, but *why* would you do it?" I just shook my head at him.

Cyn walked over, smoking a cigarette and wrapped up in a long black coat. "How's it hanging, peeps?"

I didn't know how to act around her. I wasn't exactly mad at her, but I wasn't entirely comfortable, either. "We're analyzing the merits of hanging a body on the flagpole," Ben said.

"Vertical or horizontal?" she asked.

"Vertical. Unless we're talking a stiff stiff."

"What would happen if the body didn't have a head?" said Beth. "Ooh! That would be the coolest thing ever!"

"Doable," Ben said.

They all looked at each other and grinned.

I laughed loudly, and it echoed around us. *My friends are really strange.* The bell rang, and the group turned to go. I stood there for a moment, gazing after them as they walked. That thought sinking into my brain. *My friends . . .*

"Yo, you coming?" Beth yelled.

"Yeah." I smiled down at the ground. "I'm coming."

"All right, superstar." Ben grinned at me as I walked out of English. "What color bow tie should I wear? I know you probably don't have a dress yet because girls have to wait until the last minute for everything, right? I know the 'girl rules.' But just let me know when you know, so I can get the right one."

"The right color bow tie?" I gave him a confused look. "Um, what?"

"For the Hollow Ball? I got your note. In my locker."

A suspicious feeling filled the pit of my stomach. "Can I see the note?"

He dug into his pocket and pulled out a folded slip of paper. I recognized Caspian's handwriting right away. He'd even taken the time to draw little hearts.

One word was all there was: YES.

Clearly all signs were pointing to yes.

Why fight it? I sighed. "Yup. It was about the Hollow Ball."

"I knew you couldn't resist me." He grinned, then said, "Beth's going with Lewis, so do you want to rent a limo with them? We could take Candy Christine, but the limo is classier."

Ugh. This means dress shopping... "Um, yeah, sure. That's fine with me."

"Okay. I'm on it. Oh, and what about the wrist flower thing?"

"Corsage?"

"Yeah."

"Don't worry about it."

He looked relieved. "Okay. Great. Let me know about the bow tie, though. Gotta go."

"Will do," I called as he walked away. *I'll get on that just as soon as I'm done chewing my boyfriend out.*

~ ~ ~

When Caspian came to pick me up at the end of the day, I was waiting for him. Arms crossed. He read my face. "You found out about my note, didn't you?"

I glanced over at Cyn, who was rearranging her dead plant menagerie to make room for another one. "Not here," I said quietly.

"All I wanted to do was—"

"Something that I didn't want you to do," I interrupted. "I told you I wanted to make my own decision. Why didn't you respect that?"

Cyn paused and glanced over her shoulder at me.

I moved away from her, away from Caspian, and started walking down the hall. We needed to finish this discussion somewhere private. Where no one could hear me. I didn't let loose again until we were home, in the safety of my room.

"How could you *do* that?" I stormed, stalking around the bed. All of my words were pent up inside me and ready to burst out. "I just can't believe it."

"I thought it would help."

"Help? How is making the decision for me helping me? In what way, shape, or form is that 'help'?"

"I'm sorry," he said. "I shouldn't have—"

But I was too mad to listen. "Now I'm going to *have* to go. I told Ben yes, and I can't back out. How is that fair to me?"

"You're right. I'm sorry. It was a stupid thing to do."

I paced back and forth. "This *also* means that I'm going to have to go dress shopping. Most likely with my *mother*. Which is never fun, by the way." I blew out an angry breath. "And now—"

"Astrid." He stood up, and came to face me. "Give me the note."

"What? Why?"

"Because I'm going to write a new one. I got you into this. I'll get you out. Consider it already done."

I fished the note out of my pocket. It was crumpled around the edges from where Ben had been holding it. As I stared blindly down at it, all I could see was the expression on Ben's face as he talked about his bow tie and the limo. Then I saw him giving me the tickets in case I said no.

Caspian reached for it.

"Wait." I sighed, holding it back. "You can't. I'll feel bad."

"He'll get over it."

"Yeah, but *I* won't get over it."

He paused, hand outstretched. "I don't want to make you do anything you'll regret."

"Other than the dress shopping with my mother, the only regret I have is that I won't get to go with you." I exhaled again and sat down. "Actually, I think that's what I'm really mad about. Going with Ben is no big deal. It's the fact that if I want to go at all, it has to be with someone other than you." I glanced up at him and said softly, "I want to be there with *you* as my date."

"I know. I want that too. Believe me, I actually thought about . . ." He shook his head. "It's selfish, but I actually thought about telling you not to go. To stay here with me."

As he said that, I realized how much it must have hurt him to push me to go with Ben. All so I wouldn't miss out on my senior prom. "I'm not letting you off the hook for pretending to be me and writing that note," I said. "But I understand why you did it."

He went over to my desk and opened up a drawer. "I, uh, have something for you. Something that I hope will act as a peace offering." Reaching down into the drawer, his hand disappeared.

"Damn it," he said a minute later. "Damn. I can't . . ."

"What?" I got up and went over to him.

"I can't pick it up." He glanced at me, eyes wide with panic. "I can't touch it."

Panic flared inside me too. "Try again. You can do it."

He reached his hand down again. With the same result.

"One more time," I pleaded, refusing to believe what was

happening. Or almost happening. Refusing to believe that the loss of control over his sleeping, and now this, might mean he was fading away from me. "Try again. *Please*."

He did, and this time the results were different.

With a look of relief, he pulled out a small square item draped in a piece of blue cloth. He placed it down on the desk.

"It worked that time, see?" I said, trying to keep the edge of desperation out of my voice.

"Yeah." He was doing the same thing too. Affecting a falsely happy tone. Nudging the item toward me, he said, "Open it."

I picked the object up and slowly peeled away the fabric. A small piece of wood was revealed. On closer inspection I could see that it was actually resting on top of a second piece of wood. The edges were smooth and round, sanded down to perfection. And the wood had been stained a light cherry color. Tiny crank handles were at each corner.

It was surprisingly lightweight, and fit comfortably in my hands.

"What is it?" I asked.

"It's a flower press. You place a flower in between the two pieces of wood, like a sandwich. Then you turn the handles to tighten it, and it flattens the flower. It takes five to seven days for the flower to dry completely."

"How did you . . . ? Where did you . . . ?"

"I went to go see Nikolas today, and he made it."

I turned it around and around to look at it. "This is one of the most amazing things I've ever seen. Now I just need to get some flowers." I smiled up at him. "Thank you, Caspian. I love it."

He stuck a hand into his front pocket. "It wasn't a bribe or anything. I don't want you to think that. But I *did* think it would be in my best interest if I had a present to give you today."

"Today, of all days, when you just so happened to promise Ben that I'd go to the dance with him?" I raised my eyebrow.

"Totally and completely had nothing to do with that."

Laughing, I cradled my gift closer. "Let's just say, then, that you're a very good present picker. And an even smarter boy-friend."

Chapter Fourteen

EARLY GRADUATION GIFT

It was, as I have said, a fine autumnal day; the sky was clear and serene, and nature wore that rich and golden livery which we always associate with the idea of abundance.

—"The Legend of Sleepy Hollow"

Mom was in the kitchen when Caspian and I got home from school the next day. "Do you have any plans right now?" she asked me. "I mean, when are you going dress shopping with Beth?"

Mentally I prepared my argument. Beth and I had made plans last night. "We're not going until Wednesday. But I have homework to do. Why?"

"A lot of homework? Or can it wait?"

I cast a side glance at Caspian. "That depends. Can you just tell me what's up?"

Excitement was written all over her face. She could barely contain her grin. "I want to take you somewhere. But it's a surprise."

"I'm not sure if I can—"

"Just go with her, Astrid," Caspian said to me. "She's excited."

I shook my head slightly at him. I had no clue what Mom's surprise was, and didn't know if I was in the mood to find out.

"Go," he said sternly. "Come *on*. Look how happy she is."

I sighed. I knew when I was beat. "Okay, yeah, I'll go," I said to Mom. "Homework can wait."

"Oh, good!" she squealed.

"Just let me take my stuff upstairs and get changed, okay?"

She nodded, and I trudged toward the stairs. Caspian followed behind me. "You are in *so* much trouble," I said to him quietly.

He just grinned.

When we got upstairs, I threw my book bag onto the bed and went to change my jeans. "If she 'surprises' me with a bad prom dress again, you're going to have to make it up to me in a major way," I called out from my closet. "I am totally serious."

"Just humor her," he replied. "I'm sure it won't be like that."

"Are we talking about my mother here? Because I thought we were."

"I know, I know. But if she does, then you have my permission to take it back."

I laughed loudly. "Your permission? Oh, I'm so glad." I switched shirts and came stalking out. He was still grinning in a maddening way. Like he knew something I didn't. "*Major* sucking up," I reiterated. "I don't know how yet, but I'll think of something."

He came over to me. "You are being a very good daughter," he said softly. "Think about how happy your mom will be. This is a good memory for her. For when . . ."

For when I'm gone.

I sighed and looked up at him. "You're right. But I'm totally doing this for you, you know." He nodded, and I grabbed my phone. "All right, all right. I'm off, then. Wish me luck."

"You won't need it," he said. "How bad can it be?"

Mom was waiting for me downstairs, and we both hurried out to the car. "Where are we going?" I asked, getting in.

"Still a surprise," she said. "Are you hungry? Do you want to grab a snack somewhere first?"

"What did you have in mind?"

"Gelato?" she suggested. "We can stop at the new place downtown."

"Yeah, sounds good."

We both buckled, and Mom pulled out of the driveway.

Halloween decorations were up at each house that we passed, straw-stuffed scarecrows and pumpkins at every corner. White trash-bag ghosts hung from the lampposts that lined the town streets, and ghoulish, grinning orange papier-mâché masks filled shop windows.

"You know tourism is up by thirty-three percent this season," Mom said casually. "It looks like it's going to be a great holiday."

"Good for business."

"It *is* good. You can't overestimate the importance of customer traffic. It's all about location, location, location. That's an important thing to think about when you're a business owner."

We came to a little Italian ice stand with a red, green, and white striped awning, wedged in between a shoe repair store and a bank. It advertised Momma Mia's Icy Treats.

"They have gelato here?" I questioned. "Are you sure it's not just Italian ice?"

"How can they have one and not the other?" she said.

"True. But I'm really in the mood for gelato now, so if they don't have it, I might not get anything."

Mom laughed. "If they don't have it, then I'll take you somewhere else. Okay?"

"Okay."

We moved to get in line, and I squinted to read the tiny, almost illegible hand-printed menu sign. "Frozen ice, frozen slushies, frozen fruit bars . . . ," I read out loud.

"Aha! Gelato!" Mom said.

I read lower. "Yeah, but they only have four flavors."

"Still, gelato is gelato."

Mom put in her order for a scoop of vanilla bean, and I got one scoop of lemon custard. "At least they have *good* flavors," I said as they handed us our bowls. "This looks delicious."

"Mmm-hmm," Mom agreed, dipping her spoon in. "Let's walk," she said a minute later.

We wandered down the sidewalk, passing several stores along the way. Each window was decorated for Halloween.

"What's your favorite season?" Mom asked. "Halloween or Christmas?"

"Hmmm, tough one." I sucked on the edge of my spoon as I thought about it. "With Christmas you have trees and lights and cookies. But with Halloween you have candy, pumpkins, and apple cider."

"Oooh, good point. I love apple cider."

"I guess they're both good for business here in Sleepy Hollow," I said.

Mom nodded eagerly. "You are so right." She got that

excited look on her face again, and finished up the last of her gelato. Throwing the empty cup and spoon away, she glanced around us with a secret smile.

"Do you know where we are?" she finally asked.

I scraped the bottom of my bowl and then threw it away too. "Uh, yeah. Downtown."

"No, I mean *where* downtown."

"Next to the . . ." I looked around and immediately recognized the bay window. "My shop! We're at my shop."

Mom's smile grew even bigger. "Go look at the window."

I glanced over. There was a piece of cardboard hanging there, but the FOR RENT sign was gone. My heart sank.

Someone else got it. Someone else is renting it, and now I'll never have the chance to open Abbey's Hollow.

"It's gone?" I said sadly. "Did someone rent it?"

"Just go look at it," Mom said again.

I ventured closer. The cardboard sign said FUTURE HOME OF ABBEY'S HOLLOW. I stared at it, then turned back to Mom. "What does that mean?"

She pulled a key out of her pocket and dangled it in front of me. "It means, do you want to go inside?"

"Yeah, of course. But I don't get it. What's going on?"

"Just come with me. Let's go inside."

She walked over to the entrance and put the key into the lock. Pushing the door open, she gestured for me to follow behind her. I stepped inside the shop and couldn't believe what I saw. It was clean. *Clean*, clean. No cobwebs, no dirty windows. No blown-out lightbulbs or dust-streaked surfaces. Everything had been freshly painted with a coat of white paint. Some new bookshelves lined one corner, and the floors were actually shiny.

"What do you think?" Mom asked, standing in the middle of the room, arms spread wide. "I know white isn't the most glamorous color, but it's just a base coat. I wanted there to be something other than that old tan shade that was here before."

"It's gorgeous, Mom. I can't believe everything is so *clean*. I've never seen it look this way before. But I still don't get—"

She held out the key. "Happy early graduation, Abbey."

"What? I . . . ? You . . . ? *What?*"

"I called Mr. Melchom. The rent is paid up for a year. Since it was on the market for so long, I convinced him to cover all the utilities for the first six months too. So your expenses should be minimal at first."

I still couldn't believe it.

"Take the key." Mom laughed, shaking it at me.

I held out my hand, and she dropped it into my open palm. *Is this really happening? Did I really just get handed the keys to my shop, with no strings attached?* I glanced down at it. "Mom, I . . . I don't know what to say."

She wrapped her arms around me and squeezed. "Do you like it? I wasn't sure what to get you, and then I thought this would be the perfect gift."

"It *is* perfect. Thank you. Thank you so much! I love it!"

Walking around the room, I took it all in. It was like looking through someone else's eyes. Everything was fresh and new. Suddenly I could see so much more. I could see myself *here*.

"Mom," I said, trying to find the words to express what I was feeling, "I . . ." But I couldn't find them. I didn't know how to tell her I was sorry for every mean thing I'd ever said, or how I wished we would get to have more time to spend together. Mere words couldn't tell her that she was the best mom ever and I was glad she was mine.

She must have known somehow what I wanted to say, though, because she nodded. I just smiled.

We stayed for a while after that, talking about options for paint colors and window treatments, and what artwork would look best hanging on the walls. I told Mom my idea about making it a fall-themed shop revolving around "The Legend of Sleepy Hollow," with pumpkins and old books, and she loved it.

~   ~   ~

When I got home, I was practically bursting with excitement as I hurried up to my bedroom. I couldn't wait to tell Caspian about the shop.

But when I opened the door, I saw him on the bed. Asleep.

I grabbed my phone and dialed Kame and Sophie's office number. Uri picked up.

"Hey, it's Abbey."

"Hi. Everything okay?"

"Caspian is asleep again." I tried to keep the panic out of my voice.

Silence met me on the other end of the line. Then he said, "Why don't you just give it some time?"

"Like, how much time?" I asked. "An hour? A day?"

"However much time it takes."

I told myself to count to ten, trying not to scream in frustration at his answer. "Why does this keep happening, Uri?" I said. "Does it mean he's slipping away from me?"

Silence again.

"I'll take that as a yes. One of you is around here somewhere, right?" I asked quietly.

"Kame. He's in the neighborhood. Do you want him to stop by?"

"Can he do anything?"

"No."

"Then I'll just wait. As long as Vincent's not around, I'm fine."

He said good-bye, and I hung up the phone, feeling angry and frustrated. All my feelings of happiness were completely gone. Settling myself in next to Caspian, I propped my chin in my hand, wondering how long it would take for him to wake up this time.

I had a hard time sleeping that night, feeling like Caspian was so far away from me, and I kept waking up. Around two a.m., I decided to grab something from the fridge. A snack might keep me distracted, at least for a little while.

A light was still on in the living room when I passed by, and I peeked in. The TV was turned down low, an old Western movie playing, and Dad was snoring away in the recliner. I shook my head and crept back out to the kitchen.

I found a turkey and cheese hoagie in the fridge and pulled it out, checking the expiration date. It was still fresh. I cut it in half and then wrapped up the remainder to put back. After stacking a couple of pickles onto the plate next to it, I carried my prize into the living room.

I found the remote by Dad's hand and flipped though the channels, pausing every now and then to take a bite of my sandwich. *Halloween III* was on, so I left it and settled in. Dad's snoring grew louder and louder, until finally I reached over and shook him.

"Dad. Dad, wake up."

He rolled over. "I'm awake." And then he sat up. "I'm awake. What time is it?"

"Almost two thirty."

"What are you still doing up?"

"Couldn't sleep. Got a snack." I held up the plate.

He glanced over. "Is that a pickle?"

I held one out to him, and he took it. We both sat there for a couple of minutes, crunching loudly on the cold vegetables. When I was done, I placed my plate on the coffee table and stretched out on the couch. The room was bathed in the blue glow of the flickering television screen.

"I heard that you and Mom went downtown," Dad said. "To see the shop?"

I hit the remote and turned down the volume a bit more. "Yeah, she took me right after school. It was great."

"So, what do you think about it?" he asked.

"What do I think? I love it. The chance to have my own shop? It's my dream."

Dad looked pleased. "I knew you'd like it."

"Are you still planning to help me out with the business plan?" I cast him a sideways glance. I'd taken much longer than intended to actually finish the damn thing.

"Are you done with the first draft yet?"

"Yup."

"Show it to me, then, and I'll take a look at it. We can probably work something out."

I grinned at him. "Talk about a great graduation gift."

He reached over and put a hand on my arm. "Your mother and I are very proud of you, Abbey. It takes a lot of effort to have your future mapped out at such a young age, and we want to do everything we can to support that. We believe in you, and we know you'll do great things."

His words hit something inside of me that triggered a bittersweet ache. I *wanted* them to be proud of me. "I can't promise that everything will work out," I said. "But I can promise that I'll do my best. And I'll work my hardest. It means a lot to me that you guys are so supportive of this. Especially since I know you wanted me to do something different."

Now Dad looked a little teary. "I can't tell you the thoughts that ran through my mind when we found out that someone had broken into the house and . . ." He trailed off and cleared his throat gruffly. "Well, I just never want to see that again. It really brought home a lot of things and made me start thinking about the future. Your future."

Now his words triggered something different inside of me. Regret.

All this talk of the future and the excitement of seeing the shop today as such a real, tangible thing had made me totally forget about my actual future.

The one I didn't have.

Chapter Fifteen

MORE THAN FEAR

The common people regarded it with a mixture of respect and superstition . . .
                                    —"The Legend of Sleepy Hollow"

Caspian still hadn't woken up by the time I had to go to school the next morning, and I hated leaving him behind. I made a quick call to Sophie, and she assured me that she'd stop over to chat with Mom and keep an eye on things. I felt a little bit of relief knowing that at least she'd be there if he woke up.

I spent most of the day thinking about Abbey's Hollow, and the fact that I'd been handed my dreams on a silver platter, yet I wasn't going to live long enough to see them come true. It wasn't until Mrs. Marks called on me in English class to read part of a poem that I was jerked out of my contemplative mood.

I stood up, clearing my throat. As my eyes filtered over the page in front of me, bits and pieces started to assemble themselves into images inside my brain, and I noticed the beautiful flow and rhythm the poem had. Then I really began to notice the words.

We are the hidden people
lost and in between.
So much of none
yet still, begun.
Shadows draped upon our walls.

We are the hidden people,
and when you think the end has come
you'll turn and see.
There are none.

We are the hidden.
People.
All one.
For hidden you will become.
Something more than fear,
it resides here.

As Mrs. Marks asked the class questions about who the poet might have been talking about, all I could hear were the words "We are the hidden people," and I thought about what that meant. Thought about it in a whole new way.

The poem was about me. About what I was going to become.

Shades were the hidden people. The other half. Living in the shadows. Part of this world and the next. Here, but not here. And I understood that, in a way no one else could.

As the bell rang, I couldn't get it out of my head. *Something more than fear, it resides here.*

Was I afraid? Yes. And no. But I was special. Unique. My gift was to be one of the hidden people.

It was who I was meant to be.

Beth caught up with me after class and pulled me back into the present. "You ready to do this thing?" she called, coming down the hallway from the opposite direction. "I have my mom's car."

"What thing?"

"Shopping? For the Hollow Ball? Today's Wednesday."

"Um, yeah." I wasn't crazy about the idea of not going home to be with Caspian, but Sophie still hadn't called my cell. Which meant that he hadn't woken up yet. "Sure. Just let me dump my books off at my locker. I don't have any homework that can't wait until tomorrow."

She came over and waited beside me.

"Any ideas where we should go?" I asked.

"There's this specialty dress store in Jersey," she said, giving me an arched look. "I know. Jersey, right? But I have a friend who swears by it. Says they have the best designer stuff for half the price. They probably get it after it falls off a truck, but, hey. I'm not going to complain."

"We'll probably be gone all afternoon, right?"

"Uh, yeah. Why? Do you have an afternoon curfew?" Beth laughed.

I smiled weakly at her. "No, no. Just want to make sure my mom doesn't call and bug me about it, like, a million times. No big."

"Okay. Let's go, then." She clapped her hands together.

I crammed my books into my locker and then followed her outside. A dusty blue Chevy was sitting by the curb, and we got in. Beth turned up the heat as we drove away from the school, and she started talking about Lewis right away.

We headed away from Sleepy Hollow and across the Tappan Zee Bridge. I stretched my legs out in front of me and shifted in my seat. Already I was wondering if Caspian was okay. What if he was asleep for too long? What if this time he didn't wake up?

"...and then he said that I should just go with Grant if that made me happy. Ugh. Boys."

Beth glanced over at me, waiting for me to say something.

But I'd zoned out completely.

"Are you daydreaming, Abbey?" she said with a little smile. "You know, there's a cure for that. . . . A hot boy. I mean, a hot guy. Forget boys. Who needs 'em?"

I smiled back.

"Do we need to go cruising for some hotties?" she asked. "We can still crash the beach house for a weekend. Granted, it's the off-season, but you never know when a cute lifeguard in training might show up or something."

I laughed. "No. We don't need to go pick up a lifeguard hottie. Although, I appreciate your willingness to help me out on that one."

"It's the thought that counts."

I remembered those words coming from someone else. Caspian had said them to me once. I glanced away, out the window. A pickup truck passed us on the right, with two guys in the front seat. They were keeping pace with us, and Beth noticed.

"That driver is kind of cute," she said. Leaning over, she

smiled flirtatiously at them. The driver honked his horn, and his passenger did some sort of hand motion that either meant *Call me* or *Give me more*. I couldn't tell which.

"Keep us on the road, Beth," I said with a grin when she kept looking at them.

"You never know. Those could be our Hollow Ball dates."

The truck edged forward, the driver holding up a sheet of paper next to his window with a phone number scribbled on it. *Hey, hotie, textt me*, it said.

I burst out laughing as Beth made a face. "At least we know they can spell," I said to her. She stepped on the gas, blowing past them with a smile, and her laughter filled the car.

"Oh, well. Guess neither one of them was Prince Charming after all."

We came to a ramp and slowed down, pulling off at exit twenty-four. The road went through a little town with a speed limit of thirty-five, which Beth had a hard time staying at, and we bumped along the way. The town was one giant pothole.

"We're looking for Denim Street," Beth said, keeping an eye on street signs. "How fitting."

It came up on our left, and she made the turn. A bright orange cement building with a pink and green striped awning sat surrounded by vacant storefronts. The parking lot was filled to capacity. "Guess the secret's out," I mused. "Looks like everyone else knows about this place too."

"Great," Beth said. "I hope there's still some good stuff left."

We parked two blocks away and walked down to the store. Two girls were struggling with a giant puffy garment bag that was snagged on the exit door, with another girl pushing behind them, trying to make her way out.

"I hope we don't get trampled or anything," I whispered as we ducked under the garment bag and slipped in.

"Stampede!" Beth said, mimicking a cowboy.

We walked into the main showroom, and immediately I saw why it was so busy. Rack upon rack filled the massive place, all sorted by designer, color, or occasion. It was a free-for-all. Girls everywhere were pulling out handfuls of dresses at a time.

"How are we supposed to find what we want?" I asked, taking it all in.

"Start at one end and pull what you want. Pull what you're unsure of too, in case I want it, and I'll do the same. But be careful. I heard about this brawl that started over in the Betsey Johnson section, and it took the cops to pull everyone apart. Assault and battery charges were filed."

"Jeez, Beth." I looked at her. "What did you bring us into?"

"Don't worry," she said. "Just stick with me. All my years of running track will come in handy when I book it from one end of the room to the other to beat out the girl who is grabbing the perfect gown."

"Oh, I'm definitely sticking with you. No doubt about it."

We headed into the fray, and divvied up sections. I found myself on one end of a metal rack, thumbing through dresses and shouting back to her when I found something.

"There's a pink dress with one shoulder strap and some sequins on the hem here," I called out. "You want it?"

"Light pink or hot pink?" she asked.

"Hot pink."

"If it's in my size, pull it."

I yanked the dress off the hanger and draped it over my shoulder, then continued flipping through the plastic dress coverings. I wasn't sure what I wanted yet. Purple? Blue? Or maybe something pink? To match Beth.

A little voice in the back of my head started whispering, *What color would Caspian like? Something green to match his eyes? Or black? To match the stripe in his hair?*

I tried to push those thoughts away. I tried *not* to think about the pang that hurt my heart.

"Yo, Abbey!" Beth suddenly called. "What about this?"

She held up a deep red sleeveless satin dress that looked

like something a flamenco dancer would wear to do the tango in. It had a plunging neckline, a thigh-high slit, and black roses embroidered along the bottom.

I walked over and gave her the pink dress. Then I took the red one. It was daring. Something I'd never pictured myself wearing, but it fit Ben's crazy personality to a T. "I kind of like it," I said. "I'm gonna try it on."

Draping it over my arm, I went to go find a fitting room. There was a line a mile long, but eventually a room opened up, and I went in. I had to wiggle my way into the dress, and it fit me like a glove. I stood back and took in my reflection.

The slit was high, the top low, but it looked damn good. I piled my hair on top of my head and held it up with one hand. A few wispy curls straggled down around my ears, and I turned to check out the back. It was a sexy dress, and for a moment I wondered if it was *too* sexy to wear for a friend date with Ben. But the longer I looked at it, the more I had to have it.

It was perfect.

A knock came on the door, and I opened it a crack, sticking my head out to see who it was. Beth stood there, shifting a huge pile of dresses from one arm to the other. "I thought I saw you grab this dressing room," she said. "Can I come in? This line is atrocious."

"Yeah, sure. But I'm going to go with this dress, so I'm done."

She nudged the door open wider, and her eyes grew large. "Yup. That's the one. Ben is totally going to want to do you."

I could feel my face get warm. "That's *not* the look I'm going for. Maybe I should get a different—"

"If you don't get *this* one, Browning, I will kill you. *Slowly.*"

"Are you sure?"

"Yes!" She shuffled into the small space, and piled the heap of dresses onto the changing bench nearby. "That's the one. *Get it.*"

"Okay, okay," I said. "I'll get it."

Beth turned away and bent over to pick out a dress. Loosening the plastic, she pulled one out and hung it up on the hook by the mirror. As I changed back into my regular clothes, all I could hear was the whooshing of voluminous fabric as she struggled to find the arm and neck holes.

"Do you need help?" I asked.

"Nope." Her head popped through. "I got it." She glanced at herself in the mirror and made a face. The bottom of the white dress she was trying on stood out from her body in a huge ball of bunched-up fabric.

"It's . . . poofy," I said.

"'Poofy' isn't quite the word I'd use. More like 'fugly.' Next."

She bumped into me as she pulled her arms free, and I tried to move out of her way, but there wasn't enough room. We did a little dance back and forth, but I was trapped up against the wall. "I think I'm going to just leave," I said. "That okay with you?"

"Yeah."

I cracked the door again, and then stood waiting outside. "Are you having any luck?" I called after a while.

There was a muffled curse, and then she said, "Nope. Just tried on the third one. I have about twelve more to go."

Twelve? Good Lord. "Since you still have so many, do you mind if I go take a walk? I'm bored out of my skull."

"Go ahead."

I started to walk away, then came back. "Oh, hey. I left my dress in there. Do you want me to get it?"

"Nah. It's fine where it is."

"Okay. Call me when you find the one."

I quickly left the dressing room behind, and went outside. The cool air was a blast of relief on my skin, and I didn't even realize how hot it must have been in there.

Most of the nearby storefronts were empty, but I walked up to each one anyway, peering into dirty windows to see what had been left behind. One store still had a bunch of racks and display shelves with what looked like old pharmacy bottles stacked high against the wall. I could only imagine what the old labels would say.

Tearing myself away from the window, I walked farther up the street and found the antiques store we had passed on the way in. It was small, and looked like it was crammed with junk, but with the way Beth was going, it looked like I was going to have plenty of time to kill. Why not give it a shot?

So I went in.

Chapter Sixteen

THE PERFECT DRESS

❧🜚❧

The gallant Ichabod now spent at least an extra half hour at his toilet, brushing and furbishing up his best, and indeed only suit of rusty black . . .

—"The Legend of Sleepy Hollow"

Old toys and busted-up junk filled the shelves of Clutter and Cobwebs Antiques, a cross between a really bad estate sale and a going-out-of-business dollar store. As I looked closer, I could see remnants of yard sale stickers here and there. "Nice," I muttered.

It seemed like a waste of space, and I was just about to leave when a steamer trunk caught my eye. It was pushed out of the way, half buried under a pile of moth-eaten fur coats in the back of the clothing section. But there was something about it that drew my attention. . . .

The trunk looked old. A lot older than any of the other stuff surrounding it, and it was covered in faded stickers. Shoving the coats out of my way, I knelt in front of it. The stickers were from everywhere—Madrid, Ireland, France, Turkey, Indonesia, Brazil.

A white piece of fabric hung out of the corner, trailing forlornly down the side. It looked really fragile.

I had the briefest notion that it was a wedding dress. That I'd just found someone's long-forgotten wedding dress, but as I lifted the lid and removed an old wooden tray filled with handkerchiefs and gloves, I saw that I was wrong. It was a gown. A ball gown.

Digging deeper, gently pushing my way past petticoats and nightgowns, I pulled at the edge of the silvery-white fabric. It felt like gossamer in my hands.

Slowly, ever so slowly, it came free, and I lifted it up from the trunk. It was the most beautiful dress I had ever seen.

A full, flowing skirt fell away from the front in a graceful V shape, the color of a fresh pearl. Little silvery capped sleeves looked dainty and ethereal, while a black lace overlay ran from the corseted bodice down to the floor. It almost looked like someone had taken two dresses and put one on top of the other, then taken scissors and cut away the front so that the bottom dress could peek through. It was stunning.

I pulled it close, and a faint wave of rose scent drifted up to me. Closing my eyes, I was suddenly lost in a flood of hazy images.

Waving good-bye as your beloved goes to sea . . . Waiting for him, handkerchief in hand, stained with fresh tears . . . Red roses, given at a Christmas dance, now dried and pressed for all eternity . . . A watchful bride, walking the shore as she prays for her sailor to find the bottle she's tossed into the waves . . . A stolen kiss . . .

Pulling the dress away from me, I stared down at it.

That all felt so . . . real.

Which was crazy. I had no idea where this dress had come from or who it had belonged too. And yet something . . . something was calling to me. Even now, as I pushed it away, my fingers kept creeping back into the soft fabric.

It felt like mine. It felt like home.

Hardly daring to breathe, I looked at the tag. It was marked with pencil, and had an odd size on it. I didn't know how it compared to my size, but I couldn't let the dress stay there. I had to try it on. A sign by the front register said that dressing rooms were in the back, so I headed there.

Once inside the small room, I barricaded the door and hung the dress on the metal hook on the back of the door. Soft folds of fabric fell gracefully to the floor, whispering for me to try the gown on.

I took my clothes off swiftly. Carefully unlacing the front of the bodice, I tried not to pull too hard in case the strings were fragile. It opened easily, and I stepped inside, pulling the dress up over me. I held my breath until every last fold was in place and the front strings had been tightened once again, before daring to look in the mirror.

It wasn't me. And yet . . . it was.

I looked closer, staring hard into the reflective surface. Somehow the dress had given my waist definition and had magically created an impressive amount of cleavage that *certainly* hadn't been there before. Tiny capped sleeves graced my arms, while the black lace netting gave it a decidedly wicked look. The full fabric of the skirt rustled delicately as I turned from side to side to admire every angle. It was Gothic. It was Victorian. It was Gothic and Victorian all rolled into one, and I was in love.

But what would I wear it for?

It wasn't right for Ben and the Hollow Ball. The red flamenco dancer dress suited him better. But this one? This dress was pure romance and lost love. Pure . . . *Caspian.*

As soon as that thought entered my mind, I knew. I knew

what the dress was for. This is what I would wear somehow, or someway, for *him*. For when we could be together on November first.

His death day.

I reached for the front laces slowly, and began to carefully undo them. I wiggled my arm out of the right sleeve first, and then the left. As I pulled the dress over my head, the bottom rustled past me and I caught an odd sound as it went past my ear. Almost like a crinkling.

Did something just rip? I turned it over to look at it.

The hem looked fine. It wasn't ripped. And there weren't any leaves or dirt that could have caused the sound. Flipping it up, I examined the other side. There was a small slit. But it didn't look like a tear or hole. It was a perfectly clean slit. Like someone had cut it.

Pulling it closer, I peered at it. Then I held it up to my ear and moved the fabric around. The rustling noise came from within.

I stuck my finger into the hole and felt something wedged inside there. It was hard to get it loose, but eventually I turned it the right way, and a slip of paper drifted out. It was tiny, old, and yellowed, with spidery cursive writing. I knelt to pick it up.

Holding the paper up to the light, I read the words:

When he shall die,

Take him and cut him out in little stars,

And he will make the face of heaven so fine

That all the world will be in love with night

And pay no worship to the garish sun.

—William Shakespeare

"Wow," I whispered. Those words were beautiful. And someone had thought so much of them that they'd tucked them into their clothes to carry around with them? I folded the paper back up and put it inside my pocket. I would keep it close to me, too.

Grabbing the dress, I draped it carefully over my arm and went to go find out what it cost. It didn't matter what the price was. Somehow I'd find a way to pay.

The store clerk was a mousey-looking old man, who peered up at me from behind the counter with thick-lensed glasses, and a hearing aid in each ear. "Do you want that?" he asked me as I approached.

"I didn't see a price on it anywhere," I said. "I was wondering—"

"It's just an old dress, right?"

"Yeah, but—"

"Clothes are ten dollars. You got ten dollars?"

Ten dollars? Of course I had ten dollars. "Are you sure? That's all this is?"

He chuckled roughly. "If you want to give me more, missy, you can."

"Ah, no, that's okay." I didn't want to rip him off, but if that was the price, then that was the price. I fished out a ten-dollar bill from my wallet and passed it over.

"Do you want a bag?" he asked, taking my money. He held up a white plastic grocery bag, and I knew there was no way in hell I was stuffing my dress into that tiny thing.

"That's okay," I said. "I'll just carry it."

Suddenly he stood up. Peering closer.

"Did you get that from the trunk?" he asked, eyes turning sharp.

"Which trunk?" I said defensively. I didn't know if he was going to try to get more money out of me.

"Steamer." He waved a hand. "In the corner. With the tags on it."

I couldn't help myself. I glanced over at it. "Yes," I said reluctantly. "Why?"

"Came from a lady." His eyes narrowed. It looked like he was trying to remember. "A widow. She lost . . . She lost her . . ." His eyes grew cloudy again. "She lost her husband. At sea, I think."

A chill ran down my spine. *Lost her husband . . . waiting, by the sea . . .*

Just like I'd pictured it. And even if he was wrong, even if the trunk hadn't been hers, just the idea that he thought it might have been was eerie.

"Okay," he said suddenly, back to the present again. "You enjoy it. Bye-bye now."

I nodded and slowly walked to the door, dress clutched tightly in hand, and that little slip of paper tucked safely in my pocket.

When I found Beth back at the dress store, she was standing in line, trying to juggle my red dress and a black dress, while simultaneously pulling out her phone. "Hey," she said, looking up at me. "I was just going to call you. You're definitely going with the red one, right?"

I nodded.

"Here you go." She handed it off, and then caught sight of what was in my hands. "What's *that?*"

"Um . . . Halloween costume?" I replied.

"Okay." She looked at me like I was a bit crazy, then shrugged and turned back toward the line. I peeked over her shoulder. "What did you pick?"

"Since you're going with the sexy red dancer dress, I went

with one of those too. We're going to bring a little Latin flare to the Hollow Ball." She held her dress up so I could see it. It was super short, matte black, with ruffles that zigzagged along the hem and up one side.

"Niiiiiice," I said.

She stepped up to the counter to pay, and I moved behind her. I couldn't see who was at the register, but I recognized the tone. "Will this be all for you today?" a bored female voice asked.

My head whipped up. "Aubra?" I moved out of line so I could see her.

She gave me the barest hint of a smile. "Hey." Then she turned back to Beth. "Cash or charge?"

"Charge." Beth sat her purse up on the counter to dig through it, but it fell over. A tube of lip gloss and the perfume sample I'd made her went rolling. "Sorry," she said, but Aubra was already reaching for the perfume.

"What's this?" She opened it and sniffed.

Beth pointed back to me. "Abbey makes perfumes. That's an exclusive one she made for me." She said it with such an air of superiority that I had to hold back a grin.

Aubra smelled it again. "Smells good. Vanilla." She capped the tiny bottle and reluctantly gave it back to Beth, who was standing there with her hand out.

"Can you make one of those for me, too?" Aubra asked, looking past Beth and directing her question to me.

"For a price," Beth replied before I even had a chance to open my mouth. "Of course, it won't be this blend exactly, since it's an exclusive. But we can work something out."

I cast an amused glance between the two of them.

Aubra nodded at Beth, then rang up her purchase. She motioned for me to move forward next, and I placed the red dress on the counter, being careful to hold on to my white dress. She tallied up my total, and I slid some cash across to her.

"So when can you make a perfume for me?" she asked, putting my dress into a plastic garment bag.

"Uh, I guess whenever," I said.

"There will have to be a deposit," Beth broke in. "Half of the formulation fee up front, and the other half on delivery."

"How much will that be?"

"We'll get back to you," Beth said as she smoothly reached across the counter and picked up my dress. "Come on, Abbey. We have to go."

I shrugged at Aubra, and followed Beth outside.

"That was awesome!" she exclaimed, turning to grin at me as we walked to the car. "Can you believe it? She is *so* totally sold on that perfume."

 245

"I need to hire you as my salesperson," I joked.

"You've got that right." Beth agreed. "I never liked Aubra. She's such a bitch. We'll have to jack up the formulation fee to include an I-hate-you charge."

I laughed at her. "We can't do that. Besides, I'm not even sure I *can* make her a perfume."

"Why not?"

"Because it's hard to make perfumes for other people. Especially when I don't know them that well."

"But you don't really know me. I mean, not super well. And you made me one."

"That was different."

"How?"

"I don't know." I struggled for words. "It just . . . was."

"You can totally do this, Abbey. I'll pimp you out to a bunch of other people I know too. They'll eat it up."

"I'm going to need that shop space sooner than I thought," I mused absentmindedly.

"What shop?" she asked.

"My shop. My mom paid the rent for a year on a storefront downtown as an early graduation gift. So I can start Abbey's Hollow."

Beth turned to stare at me. "She did? That's *sweet!*"

"Yeah. I just didn't think I'd ever get the chance to actually follow through."

"Why not?"

"It's complicated."

"Well, complicated or not, I just scored you your first client, sister, so I'm thinking I need to become your partner."

I stayed silent on that one, but it was an interesting thought. I'd never pictured anyone other than Kristen helping me out at Abbey's Hollow. To imagine Beth there was strange.

Chapter Seventeen

THE SÉANCE

... and haunted fields, and haunted brooks, and haunted bridges, and haunted houses, and particularly of the headless horseman, or Galloping Hessian of the Hollow . . .

—"The Legend of Sleepy Hollow"

Caspian was finally awake when I got home, and I was thrilled to get the chance to tell him about everything that had happened.

I hid the white dress behind the red one in the back of my closet, and spent most of the night talking about Mom and Dad's graduation gift and my shopping trip. I left out the part about what I'd found at the antiques store, but it was so good to just be able to lie in bed and talk with him again.

The only thing that didn't come up was how long his sleep had lasted this time. And there was a moment of uncertainty when I rearranged a pillow to get more comfortable and it fell off the bed. He reached for it, but he couldn't pick it up. Couldn't grab on to it.

I quickly told him that it was fine where it was, and I moved on to a funny song that I'd heard on the radio at the store today, but his eyes were worried even as he agreed.

Since I stayed up half the night talking to Caspian, I woke up the next morning feeling like a zombie. Cyn must have noticed me dragging through the day at school, because she kept asking if I was okay. After lunch she waited by my locker, resting the back of her head against it.

"So, I'm thinking about having a séance," she said abruptly. "You want in?"

I turned to her. "Are you serious?"

"Yeah. Haven't you ever been to one before?"

"Yeah, right. Sure." I snorted with laughter. "Séances are common occurrences around here."

"They're not? This *is* Sleepy Hollow, right?" She looked surprised. "I would have thought in a town like this it would be a weekly occurrence."

"Nope." Then what she'd said dawned on me. "What do you mean, 'a town like this'?"

She made a gesture with her hands. "You know. Historical. Haunted. The mascot of the whole damn town is a headless ghost on a horse. Don't tell me you can't feel it. There's an undercurrent of . . . something here." Her eyes glazed over and she stared off for a minute. Then she blinked. "So, do you want to come?"

"Where and when?"

"We need someplace spooky. Know any spooky places around here?"

There was the cemetery. But that wasn't really spooky. At least not to me it wasn't. And it didn't feel right to think about holding a séance there. It felt sacrilegious. "Not really," I said.

"We'll have it at my house, then. It has an attic. I'm at 24 Main."

"Are you sure that's . . . ?" I didn't know how to word it, so I just looked at her, hoping that she got my meaning.

"What? Spooky enough?"

I nodded.

"Oh, yeah." She laughed derisively. "It's spooky enough. Trust me. The deaths of a thousand dreams reside there. I can feel it. Hell, *I* die a little each time I have to go back there."

She looked so unhappy that it actually made me uncomfortable to see her that way. "So, yeah, okay," I said hastily. "When do you want to have it?"

"Tonight."

"*Tonight?* That's . . . soon."

"It feels right. I generally go with what feels right and don't question it." Cyn shifted away from the locker and turned to head down the hall. "Be there at nine o'clock."

She was almost out of earshot before I realized what I wanted to ask her.

"Hey, why exactly are we *having* a séance?" I yelled.

"To summon up the dark spirits and confer with them, of course," she yelled back. "Mwahahaha!"

I told Caspian about the séance when he came to pick me up, and we talked about it on the way home from school. I thought he'd be against it, but he surprised me by saying that it sounded like fun.

"You're going to come?" I asked, astonished.

"All séances need a ghost," he said with a smile. "Isn't that the point?"

It was nice to see this playful side of him. I thought that the incident last night with the pillow had really shaken him up. I smiled back. "Will you put on a good show?"

"I aim to please. You know that."

There was something more behind his words, and the look

in his eyes had my heart beating faster. Suddenly all I could think about was the white dress in my closet and the fact that his death day was almost here.

When we got home, Sophie was there with Mom and they were both bent over the kitchen table. A bunch of papers were spread out between them.

"Hey, sweetie," Mom said as I walked in.

Sophie said hi too, and tipped her head at Caspian when Mom wasn't looking. I slid my book bag next to the chair and went to grab a bottle of water. "What are you guys doing?"

Mom looked up, all excited. "I'm studying for my real estate license. Sophie is walking me through the process."

"She is?" I paused with the water bottle halfway to my mouth. "Why?" I directed my question to Sophie.

She smiled at me. "Since I've been spending *so much time* here lately, I thought it would be something fun for us to do together."

So much time. Right. Hanging around in case Vincent stops by again. I nodded at her and chugged the rest of my water. "Have fun." Turning my back, I walked up to my bedroom with Caspian. And found Cacey there.

Waiting for us.

She was messing around with the perfume supplies on my

desk and didn't even bother to act guilty that I'd found her paw-ing my stuff.

"Seriously, what is *up* with everyone wanting my perfume?" I said.

She glanced up. "Oh, hey, Abbey."

"Cacey." I lifted an eyebrow at her.

No *Sorry I was looking through your personal belongings when you weren't here*, or *Whoops, you caught me!*

She just smiled sweetly at Caspian. "How are you, dead boy?"

"I'd be a lot better if you weren't pissing off Abbey right now." He crossed his arms and scowled at her, but Cacey just threw her head back and laughed.

"Trained him right up," she said with a wink at me. "Isn't he just the cutest little guard dog *ever*?"

Her voice had a syrupy-sweet quality to it that grated on my nerves, and I almost found myself wishing for the burning smell and creepy crawly spider sensation that she used to bring. "Did you need something, Acacia?" I asked. "Even *you* have to be bored of hanging around this place for so long. Anything new?"

"Ooooh, *someone's* been talking to Uri. He spilled the beans about my name, huh?" She shook her head and then sat down at the desk chair and swung her foot.

"He spilled the beans about a lot," I said.

"Oh, Uri," she sighed. "Between the two of us, he's the nicer one. If you haven't gotten that yet," she said in an exaggerated whisper.

I rolled my eyes at her.

"As far as what we have on Vincent? Nothing. That is why I'm here. And you are *so* right, by the way. I'm ready to move on."

"Do you guys have any idea where he is?" I prodded. "Or what he's doing?"

"Nada. Zip. Zilch. We've got nothing."

I let out a frustrated breath and paced over to the bed. "So, what's next? Can I please have some idea? What are we waiting for?" I didn't want to say it, but I was almost ready for them to just take me and get it done with already.

I glanced over at Caspian. *Well, maybe not ready yet . . .*

"Can't you guys just use your mind mojo to find him?" I asked. "You can communicate telepathically with each other, right?"

"Only with our partners," she replied. "Which means that I can only communicate with Uri, Sophie can only communicate with Kame . . . You get the picture."

"But what about the mind-bendy thing? The feel-good mojo? That affects others. Can't you tap into that?"

Cacey shook her head. "It only works with humans. Sure,

there's the persuasion bit. A very little bit, but it's mostly just memory *reading*."

"Is that like mind reading?"

"No. Memory reading. Just what I said." She looked annoyed.

"Explain it to me."

"We can tap into memories. Whatever happened to someone at an earlier time."

"So, wait, you can read *all* of my memories?"

I fought hard to keep myself from blushing, but I could feel the heat creeping up as thoughts of Caspian and the hotel room instantly flooded into my brain.

"Recent ones, mostly. Uri's better than I am at going back farther. And Sophie and Kame are really good. That's how we knew so much about you and Kristen. For now, I can . . ." She broke off and squinted a little. "Okay, there's one." She shut her eyes.

I tried to turn away. Tried desperately to think of something—*anything* other than Caspian and the hotel room . . . the towel . . . no shirt. . . . And then there was the lotion.

"Oh, gross!" she yelled. "Do *not* want. I did NOT need to see that! Cool it, Abbey. Put a shirt on, dead boy."

Caspian just looked confused. "What's—"

"Never mind," I blurted out, forcing myself to think about the puppy I saw in a store window at the mall during Christmas when I was twelve. He'd been so cute and fluffy, and I got to pet him—

"Thank you," Cacey said immediately. "Thank you, thank you, thank you. That was a *much* better one."

I stared down at the floor. My face was never going to feel normal again. I was always going to have a scarlet ring of shame around my ears.

"Aaaaaaanyway," Cacey said a moment later. "I'm just here to let you know that we're still keeping an eye on things, so keep playing it cool. If you see Vincent, let us know. Don't accept rides from strangers. Don't eat Halloween candy that doesn't come from your neighbors, yadda, yadda, yadda. You know the whole safety drill. Understand?"

I glanced up at her. "Yeah, we got it."

"Good." She stood up. "Then, I'm off." She waved to Caspian, then turned to me. "Oh, and I heard about this big prom thing coming up? Just FYI: Don't be surprised if you see me and Uri there." She started to move toward the door, but stopped. "Do they still serve Coca-Cola at those things? Or do I need to bring my own?"

I just laughed. I couldn't help it.

"I'm taking it that's a no?" she said. "I don't need to bring my own?"

"No," I said eventually. "You don't need to bring your own soda. They'll have drinks."

"Cool. Then, have fun. Drink smart. And use protection." She slipped her hand into her back pocket and withdrew something before tossing it to me. "And by that, I mean this."

I glanced down at it. "A phone? I already have one of those."

"Yeah, but he doesn't." She nodded at Caspian.

"You got a phone for *me*?" he said in clear surprise. Then suspicion crossed his face. "Why?"

"So in case you need to reach us right away and you can't get to her phone, you have your own."

Caspian and I shared a look. It made a lot of sense, and I couldn't help but wonder why we hadn't thought of it sooner.

"Oh, and don't worry about the bill," Cacey called, continuing out the door. "You're covered by the Revenant calling plan. The long-term contract, however, is a bitch."

She laughed again as she went out the door, and a minute later I heard her downstairs talking with Mom and Sophie.

I flopped back onto the bed, feeling like I'd just been run over by a truck.

Talking to Cacey was exhausting.

~ ~ ~

Later that night Caspian and I left for Cyn's house right before nine. Main Street wasn't that far away, so it would only take us about two minutes to get there. I was actually a little bit surprised at how close she'd been this whole time.

On the way there we passed Mr. and Mrs. Maxwell's house, and I noticed two things right away. The first was that even though it was dark outside, their house looked *really* dark. And . . . empty. The second was the reason why it looked that way: the FOR SALE sign in the yard. I came to a complete stop in the middle of the road and just stared at it.

"What's going on?" Caspian asked, coming to a stop beside me.

"That's the . . . For . . . It's . . ."

I couldn't even speak. All I could do was point.

"Isn't that—"

"The Maxwells' house," I blurted out. "*Kristen's* house. For sale." I stood there, just looking back and forth at the sign and their empty house. I couldn't believe it. They'd just upped and moved? What about Kristen? What about her room?

"This doesn't mean they don't love her anymore," Caspian said, reading my mind. "You know that, right?"

"Yeah, but how can they . . . ? Why would they . . . ? I didn't even know they were thinking about leaving," I said softly.

Caspian stood there with me in silence, until I realized that we were going to be late for Cyn's séance. "We should go," I said, reluctant to pull myself away.

Caspian looked at me questioningly. "Are you sure? We can skip tonight."

"And miss all the fun?" I shook my head firmly. "No. Let's go."

Because it didn't matter how long I stood there and wished for things to change. The Maxwells had made their decision. Now it was time to make mine.

When we got to Cyn's, the porch light was out and we had to bump our way up the dark walkway. The doorbell stuck when we pushed on it, and it kept buzzing and buzzing and buzzing. I was just about to cram my hands over my ears and tell Caspian we were leaving, when the front door finally swung open and Cyn peeked out.

Her wild red and green hair had been tamed back, pulled into a smooth mane that flared out from beneath a witch's hat. Dark eyeliner rimmed both of her eyes, making them look large and exotic. As she moved forward to greet me, I saw that the little black dress she was wearing was sheer, and almost see-through. Jealousy reared its ugly head and I almost wished that we had gone home. I didn't want Caspian to get a glimpse of any part of her beneath that dress.

"Hey, Cyn," I said, moving to block his view.

She threw both arms around me in a giant hug. "So glad you could make it, dahhhhling. Do you like the hat?"

"Love it."

She gestured for me to come in, and I stepped through the door. Caspian followed quickly behind, but when he passed Cyn, I could have *sworn* that her eyes focused on him for a moment. I held my breath to see what she would say.

A crash came from above us, and then loud laughter. Cyn's eyes flitted away from where Caspian was standing, and drifted up. "Ben's here," she said by way of explanation.

"Ahhhh, I see. Then the party's already started."

"Yup. Follow me."

I tried not to pay attention to the living room as we crossed through it. It wasn't that it was dirty, or even cluttered. Far from it. It just had a vague, unlived-in look about it. None of the furniture matched. No pictures hung on the walls, or sat above the tiny TV. And there wasn't a single personal possession in sight.

Cyn led me to the stairs, but she didn't say anything. I

couldn't tell if she was embarrassed by the way her house looked or just didn't care. We climbed up two flights, and then came to a door. The door was attached to more stairs that led the rest of the way.

"The attic," Cyn said slowly as we walked up. "Watch out for bats."

Automatically I ducked my head, and she laughed.

"I'm teasing. There haven't been any bats up here for a couple of weeks. Well, live ones, anyway. I found a skeleton in one corner, but I left it. Maybe we'll be able to contact its former owner tonight. Do you speak batanese?"

I wished that I could have reached back for Caspian's hand and held on to it. I didn't want to see *any* bats, living or dead. Then I felt that buzzing sensation on the back of my leg, and I glanced at him. He smiled at me and whispered, "I'm here. I won't let the bats get you."

I smiled back. *November first, November first, November first.*

I took one final step up from the last stair, and the room opened into a wide space. A few chairs had been set in a semi-circle, but almost everybody was sitting on the floor, spread out along a Persian rug with a black cast-iron pot in the middle of it.

Ben, of course, already had his shoes off.

"Hey, girl," Beth called. She was sitting next to a boy I didn't recognize, but he looked a little bit younger than us. *Grant?*

"Hey, Beth. Ben." I waved to both of them.

Cyn pointed to a girl I didn't know, sitting beside Ben. "That's Sara—from my art class—and Mark." Her hand went to a boy slumped in a giant leather chair. He put up one finger, then let it drift back down again.

"And Grant," Beth chimed in. "From computer class." She gave me a look, and I smiled knowingly.

"Hey, Grant," I said. He was kind of cute in a geeky tech-boy kind of way.

"Hey, Abbey," he replied.

Suddenly Ben did something that resembled a magic trick and made a candle "disappear," and the girl he was next to, *Sara*, encouraged his every move. He went to make it come back again and knocked over the lid of the black pot sitting in the middle of the rug. It fell heavily to the floor, and everyone laughed.

"Where do you want me to sit?" I asked Cyn, hoping that Caspian would be able to find a spot close by me.

"Wherever."

I realized that they were already sitting in an almost closed circle, with an opening on the other side of Sara. I gave her a small smile as I went to sit down beside her. My back was to a supporting post, but there was enough room for Caspian to sit behind me, which he did.

"What should I do?" he asked softly as soon as we were settled in. "Make stuff move? Levitate?"

I gave him a brief shrug. I didn't know what else he could do. And I *really* didn't know what Cyn had already planned.

"Maybe I'll just make the curtains move or something."

I glanced over at the diaphanous white curtains hanging from a nearby window. Then I gave him an almost imperceptible nod. That was a good trick. I didn't want anybody freaking out *too* much.

Be honest. You don't know what he can or can't do, and you don't want to find out here in front of everyone. What if he tries to move something and can't touch it? Do you really want to see that and not be able to react?

Ruthlessly I squashed that thought down and pasted a smile on my face. I didn't want to think about that right now. "Are we ready to get started?" I asked loudly, with a note of forced cheer. "Let's get this séance going!"

Ben hooted and drummed his hands against the floor. "Yeah!" he said. "Let's see some ghosts!"

Cyn went over to a small cupboard and took out some candles and matches. Then she came back to us and held them up.

"We're using red, green, and black candles tonight," she said. "Red for love, because we want the spirits to know that we come with love in our hearts. Black for the veil, because they will have to pass through it to reach us. And green for protection. We don't want anyone here who isn't welcome."

The candles were passed from one hand to another, and I ended up with a red one. Cyn lit the first one and then got up to turn out the lights. Flames wavered and wax dripped as we lit our candles off of one another.

When Cyn returned, she sat at the opposite side of the circle and drew her feet up in front of her. They were bare. At her side was a potted plant.

She stuck a hand into the pot and withdrew some of the dirt, muttering something to herself and rubbing the dirt between her fingers. She closed her eyes for a moment, and when she opened them, she tossed the dirt into the black pot on the rug. "Everyone ready?" she said.

I nodded.

It was then she noticed that I had a red candle.

"Abbey . . ." She trailed off and frowned, looking like she was concentrating hard. "Black," she said suddenly. "You need a black candle."

Okay. I shared a look with the Sara. Her face was eager.

"You." Cyn pointed at her. "Switch candles."

Sara obediently handed me her black candle, and I handed her my red one.

"That's better." Cyn nodded. "Okay, Ben, will you light the candles in the pot?"

He leaned over and lit them.

"We have one of each candle in the sacred vessel," Cyn intoned. "Black for the veil, red for love, green for protection. There is also a ring of earth." She stopped and whispered, "A.k.a. dirt," and a low giggle escaped from Sara. Cyn continued, "To bind the candles together and act as a grounding force. We came from earth, and thus we shall return to it."

I could feel the slight tilt of my lips as I watched her. *I bet Cyn doesn't even believe any of what she's saying. She probably got this from* The Vampire Diaries *or something*. But I had to hand it to her. She definitely fit the role of an ancient pagan priestess.

"Now, everyone just close their eyes and concentrate," she said. "Think of someone you'd like to speak to and repeat their name over and over in your mind. I shall begin the incantation *now*."

My eyes flew to Ben as soon as she said that, and his eyes met mine. *Don't think Kristen, don't think Kristen, don't think Kristen,* I mentally pleaded with him. As much as I desperately

265

wanted to see her, or hear from her, I didn't want it like this.

Not like this.

His gaze skittered away, and I couldn't decipher what he was thinking.

It's just pretend, I told myself. *She won't really come through. This is just a stupid thing that stupid teenagers do. Relax, Abbey. Just relax.*

I almost had myself convinced when Cyn started talking again.

"Lift the veil, come forth," she said urgently. "Lift the veil, come forth. Lift the veil, come forth. I beg of you. Lift the veil, come forth. Lift the veil, come forth. *Lift the veil, come forth!*"

The last time she said it, her voice turned to a scream and my back went ramrod straight. I sat up and inhaled sharply. Every hair on my arms lifted, and a cold sensation slithered down my spine.

Chapter Eighteen

A Message

꧁❦꧂

But all these were nothing to the tales of ghosts and apparitions that succeeded.

—"The Legend of Sleepy Hollow"

"Is anyone coming through?" Ben asked Cyn, leaning over to her. "Helllooooo. Are you with us?"

"Who's here?" Sara asked. "Is there anyone with us?"

Someone snickered. I think it was Beth.

"Can you ask my grandmother to come through?" Sara said, loudly and eagerly. "Rose White. From Boston, Massachusetts. Can you bring her through? Is she here?"

"Chill, girl," Beth muttered. Then Grant whispered something low to her, and she turned to him, giggling.

"I am channeling . . . Michael Jackson," Ben said suddenly. "Whoo! I'm feeling the urge . . . the urge . . . to dance!" He stood up and did something that resembled a moonwalk, singing

"Billie Jean" the whole time. Beth clapped her hands for him just as he was about to grab his—

"You *guys*," Sara interrupted. "This is *serious*."

"Silence!"

We all looked at Cyn. Her eyes were closed, but she had a look of determination on her face. "Someone is at the door. Trying to come through."

She lifted her head but kept her eyes closed. When she spoke again, there was something different about the texture of her voice, and she couldn't seem to get out a complete thought. ". . . have to warn . . . ," she said. "Trouble. Coming. Trouble."

We all watched, mesmerized, as her body started jerking. Then her head fell forward.

"Oh, shit," Beth said, finally breaking our shocked silence. "Is she, like, having a seizure or something?"

I couldn't tell if this was all part of the show, or if something really was wrong. Either way, though, it was too much. It had gone on for too long.

"Cyn?" I managed to get out. "Cyn, are you okay?" I went to put my candle down, and the instant it left my hands, Cyn's head lifted up. Her eyes opened, and she screamed. A hoarse, terrible scream.

We all gasped.

Cyn started weeping. She covered her face with her hands, and then all of a sudden, she pointed at me. "You're next! You're next, and he's coming, and you better be careful. He wants you and he means to have you. You're next! You're next! You're next!"

I was frozen. She was talking about him. *Vincent.* Was it Kristen trying to warn me away from her killer? Or was it Cyn just playing me?

"Whoa, okay," said Ben. "I think this is enough, Cyn. You scared us all pretty good." He tried to put a hand on her arm, but she shook him off.

"If you think what happened before was bad, just wait," she said. "A little blood is *nothing*." She sobbed again. "He will tear you to pieces! He will rip out your heart and soul just as surely as he did mine. Nothing will stand in his way!"

Cyn reached out to me, bumping the pot so that it was dangerously close to tipping over. Someone dropped their candle, and it rolled across the floor, away from the group. Several heads turned to watch it.

"Let's go, Abbey," Caspian said behind me, standing up. "I don't know what's going on, but she's fucking crazy."

I scuttled back a bit. Closer to him, yet helpless to move away any farther. I was desperate not to hear what she was saying, and at the same time I was desperate to hear more.

 269

Cyn lunged. And then grabbed my face.

"Abbey, Abbey, can you hear me?" she asked.

"Kristen?" I whispered. Low enough so that no one else could hear me. "Kris, is it you?"

She put one hand up against my cheek, and up close I saw her eyes. I would have recognized those eyes anywhere. They weren't Cyn's eyes. They were Kristen's. "I'm sorry," she said urgently. "Sorry this happened to you. Sorry . . . because of me . . ." Her words faded.

"It's okay, Kristen. It's okay. Just stay. *Please*. Stay—" My voice broke.

She smiled again. "You were my best—"

"There's so much I have to tell you," I replied. "So much you don't know. So much to talk about—" I found myself gripping her hands fiercely.

Her eyes widened. "Be careful, Abbey! Be careful!"

And then, as if on cue, all the candles went out.

Someone screamed, and a flare of sudden panic grabbed hold of the room. "Who just touched my ass?" Beth shrieked.

"Make it stop, make it stop," Sara was saying in a small voice. Mark yelled for someone to find the damn light switch, and I held very still.

Cyn's hands were cold, and she was completely quiet.

"I got it," Ben said. The overhead lights flickered on a moment later. "Is everyone okay?"

I glanced at Cyn. She looked confused. But more importantly, she looked . . . like her. Her eyes were green again. Not brown.

"Why am I over here?" she asked. Then she saw our hands. "Did something happen?"

"What do you remember?" I asked her swiftly. Quietly. "Anything? Do you remember starting the séance?"

"No. Was it fun?"

I didn't know how much to tell her. What had just happened here? So I settled for "Yup. It was fun."

The rest of the room was buzzing with quiet conversation. No one was paying any attention to us, but I couldn't stay. Couldn't sit there and pretend that nothing had happened, when it felt like my insides were being turned upside down.

"I need to go," I said. "I'm helping . . . helping my mom out tonight. With a project."

"Are you okay?" Caspian asked me. "Love, are you okay?"

Getting to my feet, I quickly jerked my head at him. "So, yeah. I guess I'll see you at school, then," I said to Cyn. "Thanks for inviting me."

I headed to the stairs before she could say anything else, calling a quick good-bye to Beth and Ben and leaving them behind as fast as I could. It felt like all of my nerve endings were jangling together and crashing under my skin—like I'd touched a live wire and couldn't shake the sensation.

Caspian followed me through the house. When we made it out the front door, he finally spoke. "What the hell was *that* all about?"

"I don't know. I think . . ." I gestured inarticulately. "I think it was Kristen."

"Abbey." He stopped walking. "It wasn't her."

"Why not?"

"Because she's not here. She's dead."

I crossed my arms. "*You're* dead. And I can still see you."

"That's different." He ran a hand through his hair. "You *know* that's different."

"But it was her, Caspian. I know it! Cyn's eyes changed and everything. She was channeling Kristen or something, and Kristen was trying to warn me. About Vincent. Why don't you believe me?"

He sighed. "I just don't think it was her. Can we agree to disagree? All I'm worried about is whether or not you're really okay." He moved closer and put out a hand near my cheek. The faint hum where his hand would have touched my skin was a welcome distraction.

"I'm okay," I said softly. "I am. I'm okay."

He looked down at me, green eyes intent. "Then let's go home?"

I nodded. I didn't know if that meant this conversation was over, or if it meant we'd discuss it more once we got there, but I didn't care. All I wanted was the safety of my own bed. "Yeah. Let's go home."

As soon as I stepped through the front door, Mom pounced. "Where *were* you?" she asked.

"At a friend's house," I said wearily. "Why?"

"Because I didn't know where you were, and I was worried about you."

"I was fine, Mom." I crossed to the fridge to grab an apple.

"You can't just—"

"Just what? Just go hang out with a friend? I didn't break curfew, so what's the big deal?"

Suddenly she came over and wrapped her arms around me. Taken by surprise, I just stood there. "You're right," she whispered as she held on tight. "I'm just a mom who worries too much. And I worry because I have something important to ask you."

 273

Trying not to let my impatience show, I said, "What is it?"

"Do you think—" She stopped, and paused. Then started again. "Do you think that it would be possible for you to stay at a friend's house for Halloween weekend? Maybe Beth's? Or Cacey's?"

"Why?" I said suspiciously.

"Your father and I would like to go away for a mini vacation. There's this romantic little B and B in Connecticut that I've been dying to stay at for years, and now is the off-season. We're getting a great rate, plus an automatic upgrade."

She looked hopeful, and I felt some of that hope transferring to me. Mom and Dad were going to be out of the house for Halloween weekend? That meant I could have the *entire day* of November first to be alone with Caspian.

A touchable Caspian.

I'm going to get the chance to be with Caspian. Here. Alone! That thought was happy enough to make me forget about what had just happened at Cyn's.

"Yeah, Mom," I said with a slow smile, catching Caspian's eye. He was smiling too. "I can stay at Beth's."

"Really? That's great! I'm so glad that works for you, Abbey. I didn't want to push you too hard with things being so . . . unsettled."

"Unsettled" must be code for the break-in.

"You and Dad totally deserve a weekend away. I hope you have fun. And enjoy yourselves." *Okay, so that's a bit much. . . . But, whatever it takes to get you guys out of the house.*

She beamed at me until eventually I stepped out of the hug. "Okay. I'm going up to bed now. School tomorrow."

"Okay, sweetie. Sleep tight. See you in the morning."

"Night!" I called, trying to hide the huge grin covering my face. I wasn't going to "sleep tight" tonight at *all*. This turn of events was too exciting.

Turned out, I was right about the not-sleeping part. But it wasn't because of excitement. It was because of bad dreams.

My bed was soft and squishy—unnaturally so—and I squirmed around, trying to find a spot that felt better. I tried to throw a hand above my head to readjust my pillow, but my hand stayed put. It wouldn't move.

Frowning, I looked down at it. The room was too dark for me to see anything. Shifting my weight, I went to turn over and switch sides. But I bumped into something hard. And cold.

Fear rode up on me, and I wiggled my shoulders, forcing my hand to move an inch. It jerked to the left, and hit something cold and hard there, too.

 275

Frowning again, I tried to sit up. Tried to focus.

I couldn't move.

"Help!" *I opened my mouth to form the word but no sound came out. My throat flexed and constricted, but there was no voice.* "Help!"

I tried again. Gasped. But still, nothing.

"No one can hear you, silly," a voice said in my ear. "It's just you, me, and the maggots."

I clamped my lips shut as revulsion turned my stomach. It's not her. It's not Kristen!

"I've been waiting for you," she said in a singsong voice. "Now we can lie here for an eternity together and keep all our secrets. All of our secrets, forever and ever."

I squeezed my eyelids shut, holding them as tightly closed as I could. This is a dream. You're dreaming. It's not real. Just open your eyes and you'll see. This is a dream. It's all a dream.

Suddenly there was light behind my closed eyes, and when I opened them, I could see a wooden plank being lifted above my head. A clod of dirt hit my face, landing dangerously close to my mouth, and I could taste the earth.

Instantly a spray of dirt showered down upon me, and I was hopeless. Surrounded by cold, hard wood. Above my head. Below my feet. At my sides. . . . I was in a coffin.

I couldn't hold back the scream of fear and anguish then. And this time sound came out.

My hands unclenched, and gripped the edges of my clothes. My beautiful Victorian white dress that I'd been saving for Caspian's death day. "No!" I screamed, glancing down at it. "No! This isn't real!"

A shadow fell over me, and I looked up. Vincent stood there, his dark head blocking out the sunlight.

"How do you like it?" he asked, his teeth growing monstrously larger with every word. "It's your new home. I built it special."

"Let me out of here!" My voice was working now, and so were my fists. I banged them on the sides of the wood as hard as I could. "Let. Me. Out!"

"And leave your best friend down there to rot away all by herself?" Vincent laughed. "I couldn't do that. That would just be . . . cruel."

His laughter filled my head. His voice was so loud that I shoved both fingers into my ears to try to drown him out as a red rose was tossed down upon me.

"Ashes to ashes," he said, then tossed another one. "Dust to dust."

"Noooooooooo," I screamed again. "Nooooo!"

"This is what happens. After." Kristen's voice was back again.

"This is what happens after you fall in love," she said. "Just take it from me."

A bony hand wrapped around my wrist. With every fiber of my being, I wanted to shake it off. Wanted desperately to climb out of that hole and leave everything behind. But instead I did something worse.

I turned to look at her.

She was nothing but a skeleton head, with no skin and only globs of hair. Her jawbone worked with a creaky back and forth hinge motion, and the teeth looked like they were ready to fall free from their sockets.

My stomach revolted. I was going to be sick.

"You should have known," the head cackled. "Look at me. Just look at me!"

Chapter Nineteen

TELEPHONE

... it is a favorite story often told about the neighborhood round the winter evening fire.

—"The Legend of Sleepy Hollow"

I told Caspian about my dream the next morning, and he was just as unsettled about it as I was. He thought maybe it had something to do with what had happened at the séance, but I wasn't so sure. Deep down I was worried that it was a whole subconscious metaphor for me being afraid of death and all that.

I was thinking about it at school on my way to fourth period, when I ran into Cyn. She was coming down the opposite hall, and I turned to go the other way.

Cyn hurried to catch up as soon as she caught sight of me.

"Abbey, wait!" she called.

I was tempted to ignore her. I couldn't stop thinking about that dream, and it felt like dark clouds were hanging over me with every step I took. I really wasn't in the mood to talk about what had happened with her and Kristen. But I stopped anyway.

"What is it, Cyn?" I said slowly.

She looked around us and pulled me over to a section of empty lockers. "I wanted to talk to you about last night. Are you pissed at me?"

I shifted my books. "No. It's not you. I'm just in a bad mood."

"Is it because you heard?"

"Heard what?"

"It's stupid."

"What is it?" I demanded. "What's stupid?"

She glanced down at the floor. "God, I could use a cigarette." Then she glanced up at me. "Trying to quit."

She was wearing some type of bangle bracelets, and they all clanked back and forth as she fidgeted. It was an explosion of sound that felt like nails on a chalkboard.

I wanted to shake her as she stalled. "Just *tell* me, Cyn," I finally said.

"It's douche bag Mark. He told a couple of people about what happened at the séance."

What do they know? What did they hear? "Told people what?"

"About the lights going out. He said that you got scared and bailed. I told him he was an asshole, and then I keyed the side of his car to make sure he got the point."

"Thanks?"

I tried to look serious, but I couldn't help but laugh. He was spreading rumors about me being afraid of the dark, and Cyn thought *that* would upset me? It was like that game we used to play in elementary school, telephone. God only knew what the rumor had morphed into now. Talk about funny.

"Why are you laughing?" she asked.

I choked back another giggle. "Because," I said. "That's pretty much the stupidest thing I've ever heard. Compared to the things they were saying about me when Kristen died . . ." I shook my head. "It would take a lot more than that to upset me."

"Yeah, okay. Glad you find it funny," Cyn said.

"I do find it funny. But thanks for sticking up for me. I really appreciate that."

She gazed at me with a mix of humor and disbelief on her face. Then her expression turned serious. "Abbey, did I say anything to you at the séance? About being careful?"

Now it was my turn to fidget. I ground the heel of my shoe into the wooden floors and stubbed my toe against the bottom of the locker doors. "I don't remember. Maybe. Why?"

 281

"It's just this feeling I have. Sometimes I get these . . . I don't know how to word it. They're just . . . feelings. But this one's telling me you should be careful. I know you warned me to watch out, but I'm thinking maybe you should too. Okay?"

The second bell rang. Now I was technically late for class.

"Yeah, I will," I said nonchalantly, turning away from her.

"We cool?" she asked.

"Absolutely. Catch you later."

I peeked back at her only once as I walked away. She was still standing by the lockers, frowning, playing absentmindedly with the bracelets on her arm. I didn't know what was going on with her, or what it meant, but somehow, or some way, Cyn had channeled Kristen.

Now I just wondered how long it would take for her to realize it.

I didn't wait for Caspian to come pick me up after school, but started home right away.

When I got there, I found a note from Mom saying that she would be out for the evening taking real estate classes with Sophie.

"Not a problem," I said out loud to the note. I just wanted to see Caspian.

282

As soon as I thought his name, I paused. *Where* is *Caspian?* *Is he still up in my room?*

I took the stairs two at a time, knowing, just knowing, what I was going to find. *Please, don't let him be asleep. Just let him be busy. Drawing.*

My book bag fell out of my grasp and landed on the floor with a thud when I saw him. He was asleep again, but he wasn't on the bed this time. Instead, he was slumped over in my desk chair. His pad and pencils lay on the desk in front of him.

It didn't look comfortable, and his face . . . His face was the worst part. It was contorted in agony, in a grimace that must have happened right before he fell asleep, fell into that dark place. It looked like his dreams were haunting him.

I rushed over and knelt beside him, putting out a hand.

It went right though without the familiar tingle. I couldn't do anything. Couldn't move him, or smooth back his hair. Couldn't wake him up and tell him it was all going to get better.

My fingers fumbled in my pocket, and I found my phone. I dialed Sophie and Kame's number, but it went straight to voice mail. I hung up and tried again, but it happened again. Finally I decided to call the only other Revenant number that was listed on my phone.

Cacey's.

She didn't even have her voice mail set up, just an automated voice that repeated the number I had dialed and told me to leave my message. Growling in frustration, I waited for the beep, then said, "Guys! I've been trying to call you. These little things called cell phones don't work if you don't pick up on the other end, you know. Caspian is asleep again. And ... he doesn't look good. Can one of you come over and help me move him? Call me, okay? Bye."

Stepping over to the bed, I sat down on the edge, determined to keep a vigil until someone called me back.

But the call never came. Two hours and six more tries later, I threw the phone across the room and began to pace. *This has to mean something. The séance, the warning from Kristen, the look of pain on Caspian's face. Something is happening.*

My head was pounding, probably because I needed to eat dinner, but I wasn't hungry. After a long look at Caspian behind me, I wandered downstairs and settled on some tea and crackers. It was bland, but it made my head stop aching, at least.

Getting up to throw away the empty cracker box, I stopped when I saw the nearby container of recyclables. There were two empty tin cans sitting on top (sliced cranberries), and a strange thought crossed my mind. Of a game we used to play in elementary school. Telephone . . .

What the hell. I needed something to keep me occupied.

I grabbed the cans and rinsed them out, patting them thoroughly dry with a paper towel. Then I peeled off the labels and threw them away. I found the string in the junk drawer and pulled a sharp knife off the counter. Positioning the knife on top of the tin, I hammered down with my fist, and the blade poked a jagged hole through. I repeated the motion with the other can. Then I pulled out a long piece of string, threaded one end through the hole, and tied it into a large knot. I left plenty of slack and tied the other end into a knot in the hole of the other can.

Tucking the tins under my arm, I went back upstairs. I felt a little silly when I got there, glancing down at my homemade tin can telephones, and it took a couple of minutes to actually work up the courage to use them.

Wedging one of the tin cans in between two books to hold it still, I propped the books up by Caspian's ear. Then I pulled the string until it was taut, and carried the other tin can into my closet. I was able to close the door and thread the string out under the bottom, so I could sit inside. Somehow it made me feel less silly if I didn't have to face him as I spoke into an empty cranberry can.

I leaned my head back against the wall. "Testing, testing," I whispered. "One, two, three."

There was no reply, but I hadn't been expecting one. I guess mostly what I'd been expecting was the chance for someone to listen.

"I don't know if this is going to work," I said, putting the open end of the tin can up to my mouth. "This is a game that I played once in third grade. The strings are pulled tight so you can hear sound and words across it. Like a telephone wire."

The stuffed bear sitting next to me stared up with one glassy eye. I pulled him into my lap and stroked his dark, smooth fur.

"I'm really scared," I whispered, hoping that somehow Caspian could hear me, wherever he was. "What if I can't do it? What if I'm not strong enough? What if I tell the Revenants that I . . . I don't want to die? What if I beg for a second chance?"

Tears burned behind my lashes, but I refused to let them fall. "Oh, Caspian. That's what I'm afraid of most of all. What if I'm not strong enough to be with you?" I shook my head. "I don't know if I can become nothing. If I can become just a shadow of life. And what if you think I don't love you enough to want to be with you?"

I hugged the bear tightly against my chest.

"I have all of these thoughts always going around and around in my head. I *want* to be with you. I want that more than anything. So how can there still be a part of me that doesn't? How can there still be a part of me that wants to cling on? That wants things ... other things. Like my shop."

I closed my eyes and fell silent for a minute. It felt like I was betraying him somehow. By confessing all of this, I was exposing all of my inner secrets and fear. It was embarrassing. And overwhelming.

"I still want *you*, though," I said. "But why do I have to choose? Everything I want, it comes with a price. I *should* be happy that I get to be with you. And yet I want ..."

I put the tin can down. Pulled it away from my lips. I couldn't tell him what I really wanted; him *alive*, and Kristen alive, and Vincent Drake out of the picture and no more Revenants hanging around.

Lifting the can back up for my farewell, I whispered, "All I want is for you to know that I love you. And I hope I'm strong enough for you." *And I wish you could hear these words ...*

Caspian finally woke up two days later, on Friday, the day of the Hollow Ball, and I was sick with worry about him the whole time he was asleep. Cacey had eventually called me back, but I hadn't answered the phone, and she didn't leave a message. He couldn't remember how much time he'd lost, and that scared me. We didn't really talk about it, though. What else was there to say?

On the way to school that morning, I took a quick side detour through the cemetery, and Caspian went with me. Kristen's grave was only a foot away, but I felt apprehension fill me as I drew closer. Tonight was a big night. Slowly I stepped up to the tombstone.

"Hey, Kris." I brushed away some dead leaves scattered on top. "Tonight's the Hollow Ball." It was chilly outside and I stuffed my hands into my pockets. "I'm going with Ben. I hope that . . . I hope that's okay."

A weird, prickly feeling ran down the back of my scalp, and I glanced over. Standing across from me, on the far side of the cemetery, was an older man in a white suit, staring at me.

I squinted, and stared back, positive that I'd seen him somewhere before. He looked so familiar.

But the memory wouldn't come to me.

"I have to get to school," I whispered to Kristen. "I just wanted to let you know that I'll be thinking about you. I miss you. And I love you."

I laid my hand on the top of the stone, but when I looked up again, the man was gone.

Chapter Twenty

THE HOLLOW BALL

❦

It was toward evening that Ichabod arrived at the castle of Heer Van Tassel, which he found thronged with the pride and flower of the adjacent country.

—"The Legend of Sleepy Hollow"

I made last-minute plans with Beth and Ben for the Hollow Ball right after the bell rang for last period. "Are we doing the limo at seven or seven thirty tonight?" Ben asked. "I have to let the driver know."

"Seven thirty," I answered. Beth nodded her agreement.

"Your dress is red, right?" Ben said.

"How did you—"

"I told him," Beth said. "Yeah, it's red," she confirmed.

"I'll stick with a red bow tie, then, and I'll be there around seven thirty to pick you up. I'll be wearing my sexay suit." Ben wiggled his eyebrows at us before turning to walk away.

Beth laughed, and I rolled my eyes at him. But I couldn't help a small smile either.

"Are you going to the salon with me?" Beth asked as soon as he was gone. "My aunt works there and she does hair and makeup. I can totally get her to squeeze you in."

"Yeah, sure, I guess." Hair, makeup, the dress . . . it all seemed like such a process to go through.

Beth squealed. "Awesome! Drop your books off, then, and let's go, girl! Time is wasting, and we have to get beautiful."

Caspian was nowhere to be found as I made my way to my locker, so I sent him a quick *Gng 2 do hair w/ Beth* text.

A few seconds later his text came through. *Ok, have a great time.*

I turned to Beth with a forced smile. *This is fun*, I told myself as we headed outdoors. *Just go and have fun with your friend.*

I tried to keep my thoughts, and my expression, happy as we drove to the salon. But even with nonstop laughter from all the other senior girls around us getting ready too, I couldn't stop myself from thinking that this was it. This was the last chance I was going to have to spend time with Beth and Ben. The Revs wouldn't have been sticking around all this time if it wasn't going to be soon. If the day I was supposed to die wasn't almost here.

As false eyelashes were applied to my eyelids, and my nails

were buffed, trimmed, and painted, it became harder and harder to keep the smile on my face.

"Hair up, or down?" Beth's aunt, Lucinda, asked.

I didn't answer quickly enough, and Beth poked my arm.

"What do *you* think?" I asked her.

"If you want sexy, I'd suggest up." Her smile turned mischievous. "And if the date goes *really* well, you can always let it down later."

"What about half up, half down?" I said. I didn't really want sexy for Ben. That just felt . . . weird. "Could we pull the one side back and maybe put a flower in?"

"Oooh, a red rose. Yes, that's it," Lucinda said. "With your coloring it will be beautiful."

Beth was in the next chair over, getting her dark hair piled high and talking to Lucinda's right-hand man about Grant. "Nice," she said, pausing to eye me up as Lucinda got to work. "Good choice."

"Thanks." I smiled back at her.

When we were finally finished, Beth dropped me off at home. Caspian was upstairs, sitting in my desk chair. He was reading a book, so I entered my room quietly so I wouldn't disturb him.

"Hey, Astrid," he said.

My special name made my heart trip, and I went over to him. Even after all this time, my first instinct when I saw him was to try to put my arms around him. "Hi," I said back shyly.

He gazed up at me. "You look beautiful."

"Thanks." My cheeks were on fire.

"Tonight's the big night, huh?"

"Yeah."

"Will you be careful?"

"I will. Cacey said she and Uri will be there, so don't worry about Vincent. Besides, I don't think he'd try anything. Too public. He seems to prefer alone time when he's terrorizing me."

He stood up and moved close. "Be careful about Ben, too." His tone was half joking, but the serious half was still there. "I know I was the one who pushed you into this, but you're still my girl."

I stood there for a while, just looking up at him, trying to convey what I was feeling without words. Eventually he cleared his throat and took a step away. "I don't want to interrupt you. You should probably be getting ready."

"Okay," I said, mourning the loss of his closeness.

"Do you mind if I stay up here?" he asked softly, not meeting my eyes. "I don't think I can see you. All . . . dressed up and stuff. For him."

"No, no, that's fine. I don't want it to be awkward. In fact, I'm going to get dressed downstairs. More . . . room down there. Are you sure you're okay with this?"

He nodded. "Of course. I like Ben. He's a nice guy."

I went over to the closet and put the white Victorian dress behind the red dress in its garment bag. I wanted to surprise Caspian with it, and this way I could put it on downstairs when I got home. A tight ball of nerves sprung up in my stomach. *Tonight, at midnight, will officially be November first. Caspian's death day.*

I was ready, and yet so *not* ready. What if he didn't like the white dress? What if he thought it was too old fashioned, or hated the way it looked on me? What if . . .

No more what-ifs. One thing at a time. Hollow Ball now. Caspian tonight. Just get through the Hollow Ball with Ben first.

Hanging the dress over my arm, I nudged the closet door open and grabbed some black strappy shoes. "I guess I'll see you when I get back, then?" I said to Caspian as I made my way out.

He nodded.

"Mom and Dad are leaving for the weekend tonight. They'll be gone until Monday afternoon, so . . ." My throat felt tight, and I didn't want to start crying and ruin all of Lucinda's hard work. "I wish I was going with you," I said softly. "I'll miss you."

Caspian nodded again, and with a final glance behind me, I walked out the door. Leaving my dead boyfriend behind so that I could go to the dance with someone else. All because he wanted me to.

Mom was beside herself with excitement when I went downstairs to get dressed, and kept checking on me every five seconds. After the fourth interruption I told her, "Just stop. Chill. If I need anything, I'll call for you."

But she had the camera ready when I finally came out of the bathroom, and immediately started snapping pictures.

"Mom, I'm not even completely dressed yet," I said. "I need to put my shoes on."

"I know, but—*snap*—this is such an exciting moment and I—*snap*—want to make sure I have pictures of everything." *Snap*.

Ignoring her, I went to the couch and sat down to put my shoes on. But my dress was too tight to bend in, and I kept contorting myself at awkward angles. "Hey, Mom, I think I need some help now."

She came right over. "I'm here. I'll take care of it."

I slid my foot into the shoe, using the edge of the couch for balance, and Mom buckled it. Then she did the other one.

Dad came into the living room as soon as she was done, and whistled. "You look beautiful, sweetheart." Mom grabbed him and pulled him beside me to take some pictures as I glanced at the clock.

I still had fifteen more minutes of this until Ben would be here.

"All right, Mom," I said through gritted teeth. "Let's take some pictures."

She posed me and Dad by the fireplace, by the window, in front of the fridge. Then she wanted some pictures of herself with me. We stood in front of the bathroom mirror, by a vase of flowers, in front of the steps . . .

I was never so happy to hear a car beep outside. Ben was early. By a whole minute.

"Oooh, good. He's here! Now I can get some pictures of the two of you!" Mom squealed.

I glanced at Dad. "Don't worry," he whispered. "We're leaving by seven fifty, so there won't be too much more of this."

"Yeah, thanks, Dad," I said. "It's *already* been too much of this."

Mom ran to open the door when Ben knocked on it, and he stood there with a bashful look on his face. A dozen white roses were in his hands.

"Come in!" Mom said. "Don't you look handsome?"

Ben was in a charcoal gray suit with a red tie, and I had to admit, he *did* look pretty good. It was definitely a "sexay" suit.

He stepped into the house. "Since you said no corsage, Abbey, I got you these."

He held the flowers out to me, and I took them.

"If I may?" he asked, pulling one of the roses free. I nodded, and he turned and handed it to Mom. "This is for you."

"Oh, well . . . I just . . . I . . ." Mom was ten shades of red, but she looked ecstatic.

"Awww, aren't you just adorable?" I said to Ben.

He grinned.

"Let me get some pictures!" Mom said, taking the roses from me. "I'll just put these in the kitchen." Before I could hustle Ben out the door, she was back. "Okay. Let's get some over here."

She directed us to stand in front of the fireplace, and the stairs. Ben had no problem just smiling through all of it. We took pictures outside, in front of the house, by the limo, walking up the steps . . . until finally I told Mom that we needed to go pick up Beth and her date.

Mom started to get all teary, and that was when the hugging began. "Have fun," she said. "Be good. Be safe and all that."

She clung to me, and I patted her back. "Yeah, okay, Mom."

"Your father and I are leaving tonight and we'll be back Monday," she said. "I've left some extra money on the dining room table. Don't forget to take it with you. Are you staying with Beth or Cacey?"

"I'm staying at Beth's."

I made a mental note to tell Beth about our "sleepover" this weekend so that if Mom called she'd know what to say.

"Everything will be fine, Mom. You guys have fun too, okay? I love you," I whispered to her.

Ben offered me his arm. "Bye, Mr. and Mrs. Browning," he said. "I'll take good care of her."

"I bet you will," I said, and snorted. But he just grinned at me again.

Stepping carefully, I walked down the front path to the waiting Hummer limo as Mom and Dad waved good-bye. Just as the car door was closing, I looked up. We were directly in line with my room, and I could see Caspian looking out the window.

Something wet ran down my cheek, and I brushed it away. Looking down at my fingertip, I saw it was a tear.

Hastily dabbing at the corners of my eyes, I told myself to stop. I'd be back in a couple of hours and everything would be fine. I'd get to see Caspian then.

But my heart still hurt when we drove away.

~ ~ ~

When we pulled up to Beth's, she was outside, laughing and posing for pictures with Grant. "I guess she went with computer class guy?" Ben said, glancing out the tinted windows.

"Looks like it."

"Hey, Abbey," he said suddenly. "You know that séance at Cyn's the other night?" His voice was low. "I thought that maybe you'd want to talk to Kristen. If you had the chance. But I'm glad you didn't say anything. It didn't feel right with everyone else there, you know?"

I was kind of surprised he was talking about that. And surprised that he'd felt the same way. "I thought the same thing about you, too," I replied. "That you might want to talk to her. I was really glad that . . . didn't come up."

"I think she would have liked the fact that we're here together," he said.

"Me too," I said slowly. "Me too."

"I still dream about her," he said softly, a faraway look in his eyes. "I don't know what that means, but I think it's a good thing." Then he shook his head. "Hey, enough of this. Let's go grab the final two members of our party and have some fun. What do you say?"

"Let's do it!" I gave him a big smile, trying to push Kristen out of my mind. Trying to push away the fact that Ben was dreaming about her, while I, her best friend, only had nightmares.

We arrived at the Hollow Ball by eight fifteen, and the reception hall was beautiful, done in pale blue, off-white, and silver decorations. You never could have guessed that it was normally a convention center.

Beth looked *amazing* in her black dress, and Grant was adorable and funny. Between him and Ben, none of us could go longer than five minutes without laughing.

I caught a glimpse of Uri once, holding a can of Coke in one hand, and he gave me a brief nod. I smiled back at him, before catching up with Beth and Grant again. The only thing missing was Cyn, and I realized that I really *was* missing her.

"Hey," I said to Beth in between songs. "Do you know where Cyn is? Did she come?"

Beth swayed to one side, with her arms up above her head as a pounding beat started. "Haven't seen her."

"Oh." I cast another glance around. "I'm going to check outside. See if she's smoking."

Beth nodded, barely noticing when I left. She seemed to be having a ton of fun with Grant. It looked like she'd made the right choice.

The cool night air bit into all of the more exposed parts left behind by the skimpy material of my dress when I stepped outside, and I shivered. It didn't look like anyone was out here.

I thought about calling Caspian. To see what he was doing, and see if he was missing me as much as I was missing him. It was almost like I was split in two. One part of me was having a great time being here with Ben and seeing Beth so happy, getting this chance to have this time with my friends was more than I could have ever hoped for.

But the other part of me longed to be home with Caspian. To be waiting as the clock turned to midnight . . .

A loud voice from the alley beside me caught my attention, and I saw a girl in a pink dress trying to practically climb on top of a boy standing next to her. The boy moved, distancing himself, and I saw a flash of gray.

Ben?

"Ginger, don't. I'm here with someone else."

His words confirmed that it was him, and I tried to shrink back into the shadows. If I could see them, they could probably see me. And I didn't want that.

"But don't you want to?" her drunken voice slurred. "I've been waiting all night for you. Come 'ere. Just give me a li'l kiss . . ."

"Ginger. I'm serious. I said—"

I moved out of the shadows then. "Ben?" I called. "Ben, I was looking for you. You promised me the next dance." I walked over to him, and the girl, Ginger, was practically falling out of her dress. Her hair and makeup looked awful. I had a brief twinge of compassion for her.

"He's mine, bish," she said, moving clumsily toward me and trying to stand up straight. "Go fine your own man somewhere else, ho."

Compassion? Gone.

Ben gently moved her to the side. "She's right, Ginger. Are you going to be okay out here?"

"You're *leaving* me? Leaving all of *this*?" She looked out-raged, but still managed to flounce her hair. "Fine. Whatevs. *Bye*."

Turning to totter clumsily back to the front door, she left Ben and me standing there. I managed to wait a whole thirty seconds before bursting out into laughter.

"You know how to pick 'em, Ben." I said. "Another ex?"

"Regretfully," he replied. "Ready for another dance?"

"If you can handle all of *this*," I said with a snort of laughter.

We went back inside, where the DJ was announcing that the next song was "for the ladies." I turned to Ben. "You ready for another dance, sexay man?" He brushed imaginary dust off the collar of his suit, and did a silly move with his hands.

"I was born ready."

I took his outstretched hand and followed him to a clearing on the dance floor. Ben put his arms around my waist, and I hugged his neck. A slow intro had already begun to play, and the space around us quickly filled in with the crush of eager bodies.

I laid my head against his shoulder and closed my eyes. Ben was a good guy, a *really* good guy, but he wasn't the one for me. And we both knew it.

I lifted my head after a couple seconds of moving back and forth, and stared up at him. "You know, you really are a great person, Ben," I said. "I don't know if I've ever told you that, but you are."

He looked down. "Thanks, Abbey. You're pretty great too."

"I'm really glad I had the chance to get to know you better," I said. "And for the record, I think that you and Kristen would have made a great couple. I wish you could have had that."

"Me too," he said softly, and I laid my head back down on his shoulder.

We were almost to the end of the song when a sudden melancholy filled me. Sorrow, clear and striking, came over me, and it wasn't just the slow music or the soft lyrics.

Somehow I knew that this was the last time I'd see Ben.

I slowed my movements, and came to a halt, moving my hands from his neck to his arms. "Ben," I said urgently, "I want you to have the best of everything. Everything that life has to offer. The best school, the best job, the best house, the best wife, the best kids, the best family . . . Make yourself happy, okay?"

He glanced down. I was gripping the sleeves of his suit. "Okay, Abbey. But isn't it a bit early for this? I mean, graduation isn't for another six months."

"I know. But I just want . . . Just be happy. I just want you to be happy."

He gave me a strange look. "Let's save the well wishes for—"

A teary-eyed Beth suddenly pushed her way through the crowd and interrupted us. Immediately I came to a halt and reached out a hand for her. "What's wrong?" I asked over the noise. "What happened? Are you okay?"

"It's Grant. I never should have brought him!"

I pulled her over to the side of the dance floor, and Ben followed us.

"What happened?" he asked.

"Something with Grant," I yelled over the music. Thinking it would be a bit quieter away from the main stage, I left Ben behind and dragged Beth over to a table. I put my arms around her as she tried to stop crying. Her shoulders shook pitifully.

"What happened, sweetie?" I said. "Can you tell me?"

"He's an asshole," she said. "He was making out with this drunk girl outside. I went to go find you, and found *him* instead." She burst into sobs again. "I never should have picked him over Lewis!"

Ben came over just in time to hear the last part. "I'll go find him," he said, his tone menacing.

"I'm fine, I'm fine," Beth said suddenly. Pushing herself away from me, she stood up straight and fixed her hair. "I don't need him. I'm going to call Lewis."

Before I had a chance to stop her, she was pulling out her phone from her bag. She turned away from me, and I could hear her talking. A minute later she turned back and snapped her phone shut. "Great. Lewis can't come. He's home with his sick little brother and can't leave him."

She looked so miserable that I wanted to do whatever I could to make it all better. I glanced over at Ben. "Can you call the limo company?"

"Yeah, sure." He pulled out his phone. "On it."

After ten minutes of waiting, Ben finally talked to someone and made arrangements for the limo driver to come back early.

"We'll all head out now," I said. Then I looked at Ben. "Unless you want to stay?"

"I can't let you guys leave your senior prom early because of me," Beth protested. "I'll be fine. I can just get a ride back on my own."

I shared a glance with Ben. "I'll go with her," he said automatically.

Beth started to protest again, but I wouldn't let her.

"At least *you* stay, then, Abbey," she said, "so Ben can come back and you guys can have fun."

"No. I—"

"Please?" She looked heartbroken, and I couldn't help but give in.

"Okay. Fine. Whatever."

"Okay, good." She wiped the tears off her face.

Ben's phone vibrated, and he looked down at it. "That's the limo company. They're here."

"Are you sure you're okay?" I asked Beth again.

"I'm a little embarrassed, but I'm fine," she said. "You stay here. Have a good time." She gave me a hard look, then suddenly hugged me. "Take care of yourself, Abbey," she said quietly. "Okay?"

"Yeah, okay." I pulled back from her. It was a strange thing for her to say, but she was already turning toward Ben. "Ready?"

He held out his arm, and she took it.

"Try not to take advantage of her tonight, okay, Ben?" I said with a smile, watching them go. "Don't do anything I wouldn't do."

"I'll be an absolute gentleman," Ben called back, with a roguish wink. "See you in an hour."

Beth waved at me, and they disappeared through the doors.

I was still on the dance floor when the next song came on. Within seconds My Chemical Romance's "The Ghost of You" was playing.

I stood there, the bass growing louder, the beat growing harder. The lyrics were haunting, and they echoed in my ears as my eyes closed. The song took over, and I found myself swaying in time to the music as I sang along. "At the end of the world, or the last thing I see . . . You are, never coming home, never coming home . . . Never coming home, never coming home."

It was then that I realized I was crying. Swiping both hands across my cheeks, I rubbed away the tears, and bits of my makeup, before going back to the table where my purse was waiting. I wanted to go home. Caspian was there while I was here, and it was almost . . . I glanced down at my phone. *Almost midnight.*

I shot a quick look around me, but I didn't see Cacey or Uri to ask if they could give me a ride, and I wasn't about to hang around waiting. I didn't know how long Beth and Ben would be. *Maybe I can walk.*

Putting my phone back into my purse, I was pulling my hand away from it when all of a sudden it buzzed. I didn't recognize the number.

"Hello?"

"Abbey? Hey, it's Cyn. I know this is kind of weird, but . . . were you just going to call me?"

A creepy feeling settled at the back of my neck. I laughed weakly. "Are you stalking me, Cyn? I was just trying to see who I could call. I need a ride home from the dance."

"I'll explain everything when I get there," she said. "Wait outside."

While I waited for Cyn, I texted Ben that I was getting a different ride home, and she pulled up in a silver Audi about five minutes later.

"New car?" I asked, one eyebrow raised. "Holy crap, Cyn. You were holding out on me."

She unlocked the passenger side. "It's not mine. I . . . borrowed it. For the evening."

I climbed in. The interior was all sleek black leather and

chrome gadgets. She gunned the motor, laughing as I frantically scrabbled to grab hold of the seat belt. "You really do have a thing for cars, huh?" I said.

"You don't know the half of it. It's sort of a hobby of mine."

I slid a hand over the smooth dashboard in front of me in awe. "Seriously, Cyn. Where did you get this? Is it rented?"

"No. It's not rented. I told you, I *borrowed* it."

The way she said "borrowed" made me feel unsettled. "We're not going to get pulled over because we're riding in a boosted car, are we?" I said seriously. "I really don't need that right now."

"There won't be any cops."

I shot her a look.

"Trust me," she said. "I do this sort of thing all the time."

"You steal cars all the time?" I knew my jaw was hanging open.

"Not steal. Okay, *technically*, steal. But I see it more like borrowing. I always return it in the morning. And they never know."

"They never know? You wouldn't happen to be friends with Kame, would you? Or Sophie? What about Cacey and Uri?"

"Who?" She frowned, and I tried to read her face. Tried to see if she was bullshitting me. "I don't know any of those people."

I looked at her closely.

"Honest. I really, truly don't," she said.

"Then, what do you mean, 'they never know'?"

She shrugged. "It's sort of a gift that I have. I tell someone that I want to borrow their car, and they give it to me. Then I tell them that I'll return it in the morning, and they don't remember a thing. It just kind of . . . works."

My life was getting entirely too complicated for this new piece of information. "Are you casting some sort of spell on them?" I joked.

She gazed at me. "If I said yes, what would you think?"

"Honestly?" I looked out the window before I answered. We were almost to my house. "I'm surprisingly open-minded."

"I don't really know if that's what it is," she confessed. "A spell, or whatever. All I know is that I get these feelings. Like the one tonight, to call you. That, and the fact that plants seem to like me. Maybe I am a little bit witchy."

My house came into sight, and I was completely relieved. Normally I would have been happy to stay and talk to her about the freaky thing she had going on, but right now all I could think about was Caspian.

She pulled into the driveway and put the car into park. I unlocked my door and put one hand on the handle. "If you want to talk about it later, just call me. I'd stay now, but I have . . . something else that needs to be taken care of."

She glanced at the house. It was dark, except for a single light in the kitchen, and then she nodded. I opened the door and got out of the car.

"Thanks for the ride, Cyn," I turned back to say.

She winked at me. "Have fun, Abbey."

I was left standing there with what must have been a confused look on my face as she pulled away. *Does she know about Caspian? There's no way . . .*

I squared my shoulders and turned back to the house. Something told me that even if Cyn *did* have an idea of what was going on, she wasn't going to tell anyone. At least not anytime soon.

I glanced down at my phone again, feeling a pinch of nerves in my stomach. It was 12:13 a.m. November first.

Caspian's death day.

Chapter Twenty-one

NOVEMBER FIRST

❧❀❧

When he entered the house, the conquest of his heart was complete.

—"The Legend of Sleepy Hollow"

My legs were shaky as I walked up the front walkway, and I exhaled. I put one hand on the doorknob, turned it slowly, and then pushed the door open. A trail of red rose petals greeted me, leading the way across the living room and into the kitchen. I followed it and found a piece of paper there that said, *Astrid, come find me upstairs.*

Placing my purse on the counter, I slipped off my shoes, then padded over to the downstairs bathroom. My white dress was hanging on the back of the door there. *Please let him like me in it . . .*

Taking another deep breath, I unzipped the back of my red dress and wiggled my way out of it, draping it across the edge of the tub. I pulled down the white dress and gently removed it from its plastic garment bag. The silky fabric whispered across my skin as I stepped into it, and I could almost hear the soft sighs of another time and place. Of another woman, who had worn this dress before me, to go meet the man she loved before he would be taken from her forever.

The bodice took some extra time to lace because my hands were trembling, but finally, *finally* I was ready.

I turned and looked in the mirror, slightly stunned again by my miracle cleavage. The dress was just as beautiful as the first time I'd tried it on. It was as if it had been made for me.

My makeup, however, was not beautiful anymore. I pulled off the false eyelashes that I'd been wearing, and washed away the mascara stains from under each eye. Luckily, I had a spare cosmetics bag under the counter, so I was able to touch up my blush and lip gloss. I didn't want to overdo it too much. It didn't feel right in this dress.

I debated whether or not to take my hair down, but decided to leave it up. Caspian hardly ever saw me wear it that way and I wanted to surprise him. I did take out the rose that Ben had given me, though, and put it on the sink.

With one final look, I left the bathroom behind and started slowly up the stairs.

I could feel the rough pattern of the carpet runner underneath my bare feet, and I tried to focus on that. My stomach felt all fluttery and nervous, and with every step I took, I came closer and closer to the reality waiting for me just a few short feet away. *Please, please let him like me . . .*

Please . . .

The top of the stairs was lit with candles, and more rose petals were scattered on the floor. They pointed to my bedroom.

I bent to pick one of the rose petals up and rubbed the velvety smoothness between my fingertips. *This is a dream. It has to be.*

My bedroom door was open, and I could see more candles lit inside there. The flower petal path led me to the bed, and I didn't even realize that I'd been holding my breath, until I stepped into the room.

Caspian was sitting there. Head turned. Looking away.

Holding my breath, feeling my chest get tight and my head grow fuzzy, I moved closer to the bed. Closer to him.

He was wearing a tuxedo. Classic black, with a white shirt and dark tie. His hair was swept back, but I could tell that stubborn black streak didn't want to stay in place, and his green eyes were bright and unnaturally shiny in the candlelight. Twin orbs of flame reflected back at me in the irises.

He stood and took a step. Then another.

I held my breath again.

"You," he whispered, bringing his hand to hover by my cheek, "are the most beautiful thing I have ever seen."

And then he touched me.

A shock wave of feeling rolled through me, and I turned my face into his palm, closing my eyes, rubbing my cheek against his hand like a kitten demanding to be nuzzled. *Demanding* to be closer.

Finding it hard to believe it had been a whole year since the last time I'd felt his skin, my fingers were greedy and grasping, sliding onto his coat. Up his shoulder. Into his hair. I reached for him . . . and he was solid.

Caspian reached for me at the same time, and we crashed somewhere in between want and need. His free hand laced with mine, and I *felt*. Everything that was there, everything that made up *him*, I felt. The solid warmth of his fingers. The gentleness of his hand. Even the tiny bumps and ridges that were a part of his knuckles.

He cradled the back of my head, and it was blinding speed, and a mad, sweet rush as a tidal wave of emotion washed over me. The space between us had been there for *so* long, and now I was pressed against him, and laughing and crying, and trying not to let my makeup run all over the place again. . . .

And I could *feel*.

We could feel.

He was real, and I was real, and this was *so real*.

I tipped my face up, blindly searching for his. He pulled away his hands and traced my cheeks, my lips, my eyebrows, my chin. Any part of me he could touch, he touched. Slowly. Achingly. While the whole time I was going mad, burning from a fire within that was tearing me apart.

"Please, please," I heard myself whispering. "Please . . ."

Then he kissed me. And I was lost.

If I'd thought I had been burning before, *this* was drowning. My lips coaxed his apart, and I couldn't get enough. Couldn't feel enough. Wasn't close enough.

I pushed myself against him and ran a searching hand through the inside of his jacket. *Closer.* I wanted to be closer.

A shirt was in my way, and I wanted to howl in outrage. Hurriedly, I unbuttoned the top button, and it gave way to skin.

I had found him, and he was mine.

Caspian groaned, and pulled me against him even tighter. I could feel all of him, even through the bulkiness of my dress. We moved backward, and a wall was suddenly behind me. My hands moved up, twining in his hair, and his hands moved down. Across my collarbone.

I couldn't stop kissing him. Tasting him. Touching him. And my hands roamed freely. I had a lifetime of touch to make up for in such a short period of time.

He broke away and kissed my neck, I shivered. He slowed at a sensitive spot near the bottom of my ear, and my knees almost gave out. "Ummmmmmm," I said.

"What's that?" Caspian whispered. He lifted his head a fraction of an inch.

"Don't stop. That's what I said."

"Oh, really?" He laced his fingers through mine, and pinned my hands against the wall. "Because I thought it sounded more like a moan than actual words."

"Mmm-hmm," I said, moving my head to give him better access. "Same thing."

He returned his attention to my ear, and I barely noticed that he was looking at my dress until he pulled back again. "You wore that to torture me, didn't you?" he said, lifting his head, eyes blazing a dark green.

"What do you mean?" I glanced down.

He freed one of my hands and pulled on the laces. "*This*. Is torture. Do you have any idea how long it's going to take me to undo them?"

A wicked thrill shot through me, and I took a deep breath,

causing the laces to strain. I shook my head. "How long?"

"*Too* long. Much too long. And with your hair up, all sexy like that, and just a couple of these curls teasing me by falling down . . ." He traced a loose curl, and then groaned again. "Torture."

Suddenly he wrapped his arm around me, and we were moving to the bed, falling onto it. He pulled me down on top of him, and my legs wrapped around his as a sea of rose petals and the skirts of my dress billowed up around us. He ran one hand gently down my face.

"I've been waiting a *very* long time to do that," he said. "And I think I need to do it again."

I let him pull me in again for another kiss, and this time we were both lost. I couldn't get enough of his skin. He teased the corner of my lips, and I opened my mouth for him. But he pulled away.

I tried to pull him close again, offering myself in exchange for more, when he moved on to the corner of my eye. He slowly kissed his way down the side of my face, tracing a path to my neck. I freed one hand and reached up to let my hair down. It tumbled around us, and he growled a little as he plunged both hands into it.

My skin was growing warm. Too warm, and I wanted my dress off. *Now.*

I was the one who pulled back then, and he tried to follow. But I held him down with the palm of my hand. Shaking my head, I gave him a coy smile and turned my attention to his shirt. The rest of the buttons were easy, and in no time his chest was laid bare.

I dragged my fingertips across his skin, and he shivered.

"Tease," he whispered.

"Tease? No. This"—I tugged the end of the laces on my bodice, and the top row of strings came free—"is a tease."

Caspian licked his lips. "That's definitely a tease."

"And this, what would you call this?" I tugged the laces again one by one, slowly removing them. Exposing more and more skin.

"A big, big tease?"

I nodded. "Your turn."

He didn't hesitate. He pushed back the sleeves of his shirt and pulled it off. In the glow of the candles, his skin was burnished gold and highlighted copper. He was *beautiful*.

"How does this work?" I said softly, staring down at my palm resting upon his heart. I could feel it beating. "I didn't think we would get the chance—"

He laid one finger against my lips. "I don't know. Just accept it. That's all that matters right now. Stay with me. In the here and now."

I gave him a shaky nod, and then moved his hand to my bodice laces. I wrapped the loose end in his fist. "Why don't you finish the rest?" The top of the dress spilled opened, and he sat up, pulling me closer to him.

"You're beautiful, Abbey," he said. His tone was hushed and reverent.

"Blow out the nearest candles," I said quietly. I was still nervous. "Please."

Within a couple of seconds the candles around the bed were out, and I could just barely make out his face. I reached for him again, already missing the taste of his lips. He touched them to mine, and I pulled him down. On top of me.

We kissed for a long time. He laid one warm hand against my bare leg, and when he touched me, fire ran through my veins. I grasped his face and held him close. Staring into his beautiful eyes, I said clearly, "I want you. Every part of you."

He held very still. "Are you sure?"

"Yes."

"I don't want you to feel like you have to—"

"Yes."

"Or later, regret—"

"Caspian, *yes.*"

"I just wanted to give you a good memory here. Since—"

"Yes, yes, yes," I said desperately, hungrily. "Give me a good memory. Please. I love you, Caspian. Love me."

He cupped my face, and gently pushed aside a curl. "I love you, too, Abbey. More than life. More than death. More than forever."

Then I was drowning again. But this time I wasn't alone. This time he was with me. Guiding me. And we were drowning together. Closer than life, and death, and everything in between.

I cracked open an eyelid, and immediately wondered where I was. My arms and legs felt heavy, like they were still asleep. I moved to roll over onto my side, and felt a twinge of soreness from muscles I didn't even know I had.

My eyes opened all the way, and Caspian came into sight. I realized that I was on my back, my hair spread out around me, my dress not at all where it should be, and I tingled all over. A simultaneous feeling of exhaustion and contentment spread through me.

Caspian was lying next to me, the sheet wrapped around his waist. I could tell that I was blushing even as I looked at him. "That was . . . intense," I said.

He raised an eyebrow. "Mmm-hmm."

"Was it, um, intense for you?"

"Very intense." He leaned forward and ran a finger down the tip of my nose. "And so very worth the wait."

Now I was blushing even harder, a ridiculously happy feeling of satisfaction suffusing me. "How did I manage to keep my dress on?"

"Luck? Skill? Sheer force of will?" he said. "We were a bit too busy to think about it."

I grabbed for the sheets to pull up around me. Suddenly I was feeling exposed.

He gently moved a piece of hair away from my face. "Don't get all shy on me now," he said.

I reached up and took his hand, smiling at him. "I'm not." Then I glanced back down at the sheet I was desperately clinging too. "Okay, maybe I am. A little."

He smiled too.

"Only twenty-one hours left," I whispered, looking at the clock. We were on borrowed time. It was almost three a.m.

"Twenty-one hours *more*," he corrected. "Twenty-one hours to be together." He reached for the white tuxedo shirt on the floor. "I think we should have a dance. Since we didn't get to share your prom."

When he looked away, I took advantage of the moment to gather the top of my own dress together. One of the laces was dangling free, at the end of the bodice, but the other one was missing.

"Have you seen my string?" I asked. "I had two."

He glanced around casually. "Nope. Don't see it. Guess you'll have to make do with just one."

"One won't lace it up all the way."

"And that's a problem?"

I laughed. "I guess if you're not complaining . . ."

He held up both hands. "I'm not complaining."

I grinned, pulling up the lace and tugging it into position. It slipped through the bodice holes easily, but it was definitely not pulled as tightly closed as it could have been. When I looked up again, Caspian had his shirt back on.

"The tux was a nice touch," I said. "How did you pull it off?"

"Uri. He helped me out with a couple of things. The tux, the roses . . . It took me a while to set everything up because I . . ." He looked away.

Gathering up my skirt, I pushed myself to a standing position. My legs and thighs ached, like I'd been running a marathon, and it took me a second to get used to the feeling. Caspian went over to a CD player on top of the fireplace mantel and pushed a button. Jazz filled the air, and when he returned to me, he held out his hand.

We danced through four songs, and I never wanted it to

end. The candles burned lower, most of them were almost gone. I looked up at him, and he was looking down at me. His eyes were wide and focused. "What?" I asked.

"Just you. I'm just happy being with you," he explained.

"Me too." I sighed. "I feel all warm and gooey inside. Like chocolate chip cookies."

"I don't remember what chocolate tastes like."

"You don't?" I stared up at him in disbelief.

"No."

"Then, we need to fix that. Come on. We are going to do some baking." I grabbed his hand and led him to the door, stopping along the way and blowing out the remainder of the lit candles.

He followed me down to the kitchen, and I flipped on a light. It didn't take long to assemble the ingredients, and in no time we were both elbow-deep in cookie dough.

"Taste this," I directed him, after stirring in half a bag of chocolate chips.

I held up a spoon to his lips, and he tasted some and swallowed. A comical look crossed his face. "I don't know if I like it," he said, licking the corner of his lips. "It's . . . weird."

"Weird?" I waved the spoon in front of him. "Weird? What planet are you from?"

He laughed.

"Okay." I pulled my hands out of the dough and dug into the chocolate chip bag. Producing a morsel, I held it out to him. "Try this. Tell me if this is weird."

He bent his head closer and opened his mouth. His lips wrapped around my finger when I pulled away. His eyes caught mine. "Delicious," he said. Then, with a mischievous look on his face, he dug a hand into the bowl of dough and tossed a tiny glob at me. It landed on my cheek.

"What?" I shrieked. "You did not just do that! Are you starting a food fight?"

His eyes said it all, and he taunted me with another handful of dough.

I retaliated with a fistful of flour. It showered down upon his head, coating his eyelashes and eyebrows, and I couldn't stop the eruption of giggles that burst out of me.

He threw sugar next, and I shrieked again as the cold grains ran down the front of my dress. More flour was my only option, and he was laughing too, even as the front of his suit exploded in a blossom of white powder.

Caspian advanced, fingers coated with sticky cookie dough, and I laughed as I retreated. The kitchen was a mess, we were a mess, and I had dough on my face, sugar down my dress, and the threat of more coming my way.

"Truce, truce," I called, throwing my hands up in mock surrender.

"Aye, for there to be a truce, ye will need to pay a bounty," he growled in a terrible fake pirate accent.

I couldn't stop laughing at the sight of his white eyebrows, and I doubled over in a heap of giggles. He pounced, and pinned me down, sticky fingers grabbing mine as he straddled me.

"The bounty," he said. "I think we can come to an agreement."

Pulling one of his hands down to my lips, I licked his finger clean. "Mmmmm," I said. "Chocolate chip cookie dough has never tasted so good."

His eyes went dark and his lips met mine. "You are so right."

Chapter Twenty-two

LOSING TIME

But if there was a pleasure in all this, while snugly cuddling in the chimney corner
of a chamber that was all of a ruddy glow from the crackling wood fire . . .

—"The Legend of Sleepy Hollow"

We left the kitchen behind and stumbled back upstairs.
We were almost to the bed when I realized that we
were still covered in baking supplies. "We're all dirty," I said,
taking my mouth from his. "We're covered in flour and sugar,
and . . ." I wiped my cheek. "Cookie dough."

Caspian pulled back. "You're right. I have an idea. Stay here."

I sat on the edge of the bed as he left me behind and went to
the bathroom. An instant later I heard the sound of bath water
running.

"Wait ten minutes and then come in," he called out.

I sat and waited. An *excruciating* ten-minute wait. Then

I got up and went over to the closet. I had an extra bathrobe in there. After pulling off my dress, I hung it up and put on the robe.

The water stopped. The bath was full.

"Are you ready?" I teased, moving closer. "It isn't big enough for two people, you know."

I stepped into the bathroom. Steam was scorching the mirror. Caspian was waiting by the edge of the tub, his jacket off, shirt sleeves rolled up, hair and face all clean. A matching set of purple towels and a washcloth sat on the counter. Mounds of fluffy bubbles practically overflowed from the water's edge.

He made a short bow. "This bath is for you, milady."

"You made a bath for *me*?" I was impressed. And just a little bit nervous about taking off the robe in front of him. I dug one toe into the bath mat. "Can you . . . ?" I glanced down at my robe.

He gave me a half smile, but turned his back. "Better?"

I slipped off the robe and hurried to the water. "Much." Sinking down into the tub, I let out a groan of satisfaction. It was heavenly. Just the right temperature. I tipped my head back and slid under the water for a second, wetting my hair.

When I surfaced, Caspian had turned back around and was leaning on one knee, settled on the floor beside me. "Good?"

"The best. You're amazing."

His smile was beautiful, and I moved forward to kiss him. My fingers lingered in his hair, and I didn't want to let him go.

But I'll have to . . .

My throat tightened, and I cleared it brusquely. I didn't want thoughts like those to intrude on our time together now.

"So," I said. "Now that we've had our dance and made some cookies—even though we forgot to put them in the oven . . . What should we do next?"

"The moon?" he suggested. "Vegas? Russia? Thailand at midnight?"

"Oooh, you're a romantic. What else?"

He rattled off a list of things to do, and places to see, and I leaned my head back and listened. It didn't matter that we couldn't do any of those things. Just hearing him talk like we had a future was enough for me.

I reached for the orange burlap bag of pumpkin spice bath salts that I always kept on the edge of the tub, and poured a handful in. The salts were rough beneath my fingertips, and I moved my hands through the water to make them disintegrate faster, while a memory from another time and place hit me. Another bath, where I'd put bath salts into the water. But he hadn't been with me then, and all I could do was wonder. Now it was a completely different experience.

A clump of salt caught in my hand, and I lifted it out of the water, staring at it. The little piece of rock salt was slowly falling to pieces, and I realized that all this time I'd used these bath salts like it was just an everyday, normal thing, and I'd had no idea. No idea that I might not have years ahead of me to take more baths. Years to just sit and enjoy the warm comfort of the water on my skin, the scent filling my nose, the silky sensation left behind from the oils . . . *Normal. Everyday. Mundane things. Things I have taken for granted for so long.*

"Astrid?" Caspian's voice broke through my thoughts.

I looked up. "Yeah?"

"What are you thinking?"

I'm thinking about this piece of salt in my hand and musing over the wonders of life. "Just about how great this is," I said with a smile. "Can you hand me that washcloth?"

He picked it up, but instead of handing it to me, he reached over the tub and dunked it into the water. After ringing out the excess water, he dabbed some soap onto it and ran it slowly over my outstretched arm.

Paying careful attention to each finger, he washed my

knuckles, my thumb, my palm. Then he ran the cloth all the way up my arm again.

"I have two," I said.

I brought my other hand out of the water, and he lathered that arm too. Laying the washcloth down, he cupped some water in between his hands and poured it over my arms to rinse off the remaining bubbles. Then he picked up the washcloth again and started on my shoulders.

Slowly he ran it down the front of my neck and then moved to my back. I gathered all of my hair and piled it high on top of my head. He dipped and swirled the cloth across my shoulder blades as I leaned forward and pulled my legs up close.

His hand moved to the front. Traveled down, and I leaned back, giving him even greater access. My knee jutted out of the water, and he followed my thigh up until he crested my kneecap.

Caspian's face was so close that all I had to do was turn my head to kiss him. But I held out. Resisted. I didn't want to distract him from his task . . .

. . . and then I reached for him.

Using both hands, I pulled his shirt close to me, heedless of the water stains I was leaving behind. I offered my lips as his bounty. The room grew hotter, steam from the water drifted up in lazy curls, and I wanted to crawl inside of him. To wrap him around me and never let go. To fuse with his skin.

I must have pulled his shirt a little too hard, because the next thing I knew, he was losing his balance and falling into the water with me.

Water splashed up, hitting both of us in the face, and I choked on my laughter. He laughed too, hair dripping as the water ran down in a steady stream.

Our laughter didn't last for long, though, when I noticed that his hands, which had previously been using the outside of the tub for balance, were now using my thighs for balance.

He noticed too.

"There really isn't enough room for two people in this tub," he said.

"Yeah, I think I'm done with my bath now. Can you hand me a towel?"

Caspian pulled himself out of the water, then reached for one of the purple towels. Spreading it as wide as it would go, he held it out in front of me. I stepped out of the tub. And against him.

He blindly reached a hand for the robe I'd discarded and held it up to me. "Do you want . . ." His words died. He tried again. "Maybe this too?"

I tucked the ends of the towel against myself. "I don't need that."

Caspian stepped back to look at me. "I know I probably shouldn't say this, but you look adorable."

It was the best thing he could have said. The most perfect thing he could have said, because with my hair wet and straggly, the damp towel wrapped around me, and all of my beautiful makeup washed off, I was feeling anything but adorable.

I reached up and undid the towel, letting it drop at our feet. And then . . . well . . . I kind of jumped on him.

He reached for me. Held me. And I wrapped my arms around his neck, my legs around his waist. All I could think about was how much I wanted him again.

Love . . . Mine . . . was running through my head, over and over again in a blurry haze.

He leaned back against the sink, and I pushed myself into him. *Closer. Deeper.* He held me in place with one arm and used his hand to run it up my leg. He skimmed the back of my knee, and I wanted to scream, *Yes,* as he drove me to a fevered pitch. His fingers whispered down my back, caressed my spine, and I arched like a cat in the warm sun, trying to stifle a moan.

I think I did scream then.

We were nothing but touch, and taste, and feel. The towel was beneath us. The floor rushed up to meet us, and afterward I found myself thinking that I'd never known how comfortable tile could really be.

Caspian carried me into the bedroom, and I rested my head on his chest. I could barely think. Could barely move. Could barely keep my eyes open.

The towel was wrapped around me again. I snuggled deeper into it, and deeper into him. My eyelids were heavy but I didn't want to sleep, didn't want to waste a single second of our precious time together.

Twining our fingers together, I moved my head so that I could hear his heartbeat. I'd only get this one chance. "Stay with me," he whispered. "Stay awake for me."

But I was already drifting away.

Sunlight was streaming in through the windows when I woke up again. I propped myself up and just looked at Caspian, lying beside me. He stretched and turned to face me, green eyes glinting in the sun.

I brushed some hair off his face and whispered, "Take him and cut him out in little stars, / And he will make the face of

333

heaven so fine / That all the world will be in love with night /
And pay no worship to the garish sun."

He touched my hand and turned it to his lips, kissing my
palm. "What's that?"

"Just something I found written on a piece of paper.
Shakespeare."

"Mmmmm." He stretched lazily, and I touched the tattoo
on his arm.

"I talked to you, you know," I mused, almost to myself.
"Even though you couldn't hear me, I spoke to you."

"I heard every word," he said. "Every whisper, every plea.
Every heartfelt emotion you poured out to me . . . I heard them
all. And I held them close."

I dragged one finger down his bare chest. "You know, I've
wanted to touch the tattoo on your back ever since you first
showed it to me, and now I get the chance." He rolled, and the
dark outline was suddenly in front of me. His shoulder blades
flexed as he positioned his head on his arms.

I let my finger glide, following the smooth black line as it
angled in and repeated itself. His skin was warm—something
I'd wondered about when I'd thought about what this day would
be like.

"Is it strange?" I asked.

"Is what strange?"

"Living. Being real. Just for one day." Now both of my hands glided across his skin.

"For the first two years, it was strange. Really strange. This year? I don't have any complaints."

"What are we going to do?" I leaned over him and breathed the words onto his skin, coaxed the fine muscles to ripple to life. "How are we ever going to go back to not being able to touch after this?"

He sighed deeply, but didn't answer.

We spent the rest of the day being completely lazy. We headed downstairs and curled up on the couch to watch movies, just enjoying the chance to lie wrapped up in blankets and wrapped up in each other. I made us popcorn and brownies. And for dinner it was just simple spaghetti.

Caspian told me it was the best spaghetti he'd ever had.

As night fell and the shadows came cruelly chasing away the rest of the daylight, a dark cloud settled on me. Our time was slipping away. Already it was eight o'clock. Only four more hours to go. Four more hours left to fit in a year's worth of touching.

It wasn't nearly enough time.

Eventually we got dressed. Him in a pair of jeans and an old T-shirt that had once been Dad's, and me in jeans and a dark blue sweater. I grabbed a large flannel blanket and made us each a steaming mug of hot chocolate, and then we went to the front porch. The swing was out there, and so were the stars.

We cuddled together in the dark, safe in our big, comfy blanket. One of his hands rested securely on my hip, and one of mine rested safely against his heart. He hummed a soft lullaby as I looked up into the night sky and made wish after wish after silent wish.

The hour was fading. And my heart started to hurt.

"Astrid," he said suddenly, shifting his body away from mine. "I have something for you." He reached into his jeans pocket. I could tell by the change in his body language that he was nervous.

I sat up. "What is it?"

He held out his hand, opening his fingers slowly, and there sat a ring.

The stone was oval-shaped, a color somewhere between ruby red and pink grapefruit. Delicate filigreed scrolls of dark metal flared out around it, holding the jewel in place. Eight tiny matching jewels dotted the edges. Even in the dim light, it sparkled.

"It was my grandmother's," he said softly. "My dad gave it to me a long time ago, and I kept it safe in the treasure box that we found back at my old house. I can't exactly ask you to marry me, as much as I want to, since I spend most of my time hidden from the rest of the world." I opened my mouth to interrupt, but he shook his head. "Just let me finish."

I nodded, and he continued. "But I want you to have it as a promise of *my* forever. Whatever that is. Whatever I can give you. You have all of it. All of me."

I held out a shaky left hand, and he slipped the ring onto my hand. It fit perfectly.

I reached out to cup his face, the ring solid on my finger. Like it had always been there. "I promise you forever too," I vowed. "Whatever that is. Whatever I can give you. You have all of it. All of *me*."

"Astrid," he whispered, closing his eyes. "Astrid . . ."

I closed mine too, and our lips met, clung. Frantic words of love and eternity passed between us. Utterances of sacred vows that meant more than anything we'd ever said before. And when I started to taste salt, I knew where it came from.

I didn't bother to wipe the tears off my face.

Chapter Twenty-three

THE DAY AFTER

The hour was as dismal as himself.

—"The Legend of Sleepy Hollow"

My feet were cold, and I wondered why the blankets weren't covering them up all the way. I tried to dig my toes further into the bedsheets, but felt only a hard surface beneath me. Eyes opening, I looked around.

I was outside, on the porch swing. A flannel blanket was sliding off me.

Caspian sat on the front steps, staring out into the yard. He must have heard me moving, because he turned around. "Morning, beautiful."

"Morning." I wrapped the blanket more securely around my shoulders and walked down to sit next to him. "Sorry I fell asleep."

His smile was sad. "It's okay."

Without even thinking, I leaned my head against him. Or at least tried to.

The sensation of falling over hit me, and I jerked upright. Our time was over. It was November second. He couldn't touch me anymore.

I knew I wouldn't be able to hide the tears, so I quickly stood up. "I'm going inside. I need to . . ."

But I couldn't finish. I raced for the safety of the bathroom and sat on the edge of the toilet lid, weeping until my heart couldn't break anymore and I had no tears left to cry.

When I was done, I still didn't feel any better. All I wanted was to be able to talk to someone. Someone who had been through this. Someone who knew exactly what I was feeling. *Katy. Go talk to Katy.*

Katy was the perfect person to talk to! She *had* been in my situation. Exactly.

Stumbling to my feet, I barely managed to remember to run upstairs and get dressed. Caspian was sitting at the window seat, looking out the window. He must have come up while I was in the bathroom.

"I'm going to take a walk," I said.

But he didn't respond.

I threw on a different pair of jeans and a sweatshirt. Grabbing my jacket, I went over to him. "Hey," I said softly. "Are you ignoring me?"

He looked up at me, eyes faraway. "What? No. Sorry. I'm just distracted. Thinking."

I wanted to touch his hand. His face. *Anything.* Instead I stuffed my hands deep into my pockets. "I won't be gone long," I told him.

"Where are you going?" he asked.

"To see Katy."

"Do you want me to come with you?"

I answered carefully, trying to avoid explaining why I wanted to talk to her. "That's okay. I think, after yesterday, I just need . . . I think I just need some time. To deal with this whole not-being-able-to-touch thing again."

I softened my words with a smile, and he smiled back.

"Okay," he said. "Take your phone and be careful. I'll be here."

I gave him a smile again, but I walked out of the bedroom quietly, my head full of questions that didn't have easy answers.

I made my way through the woods that would lead me to Nikolas and Katy's house, and when I got there, Nikolas was working out in the yard again. He saw me approaching and waved excitedly.

 340

"Hi, Nikolas!" I said.

The front door was open, and he called for Katy to join us. She came out with knitting needles in hand. "Abbey!" she said. "I'm so happy to see you."

I ran to her and wrapped her in a hug. She smelled faintly of lavender and tea. "I'm happy to see you, too," I said. "How are you?"

"We are well. And you?"

"Good. I was hoping we could have some tea and catch up on things."

"Absolutely." She gave Nikolas a knowing look.

He just smiled. "I will go back to my task, then," he said. "And leave you ladies to yours."

He turned away from us, and Katy directed me inside. I sat down as she put a kettle of water on to boil over the fire. The room was warm and cozy, and I shrugged out of my coat.

"How are things with Caspian?" she asked, taking the seat beside me.

"November first was the anniversary of his death day," I said, trying not to blush. "We got to spend it together." She nodded, but didn't say anything. "Actually, that's why I'm here. I had some questions for you, if you don't mind. You're the only one I know who was like me."

"I'll do my best," she said. "What do you wish to know?"

"How did you know you were ready to be with Nikolas forever? Were you scared? Worried? Did you ever doubt yourself?"

Katy folded her hands on the table. "My situation was different, Abbey. I was sick. I knew that I had a limited amount of time left. It was not a difficult choice for me." She looked me directly in the eye. "You are having a difficult time, though, yes?"

"Yes. But I know it's going to be soon for me, too. Caspian has been . . . Well, he's been losing his ability to touch things. And he falls into this deep sleep. A dark place that he goes to. Where he can't wake up. Sometimes it's hours, even days, before he comes back to me."

"And you are worried about your future together?" Katy guessed.

I leaned forward. "What if I complete him and eventually we become unhappy?" I told her about Abbey's Hollow and how Mom had paid the rent for my first year. "What if I start to resent the fact that I'll never have the opportunity to own my own business? Or make perfumes again? What if I start to hold it against him that I'm stuck here? Wherever *here* will be."

The teakettle whistled, and she got up to prepare the tea. She returned with two cups, then she went back for the milk and honey. I doctored mine up while I waited for her to sit down again. Eventually she said, "Who has told you that you will never get the chance to make perfumes again?"

"I'll be dead. How am I going to get supplies and stuff?"

She gestured around the cottage, to the bundles of dried flowers decorating the walls. "Supplies are all around you. Oils come from plants, do they not?"

"Well, yeah, but . . ." I took a sip of my tea and thought about it. I *did* have my plant distiller. As long as I had access to that, and fresh flowers or herbs, I could make my own essential oils. "Actually, I guess I *could* still make my perfumes. If everything works out right."

She nodded, a wise smile on her face. "You do not have to give up everything you love for the one you love."

"And how can I be sure of that?" I said desperately.

"You must find that within your own heart," she replied.

I leaned back in my chair, playing with the handle of the delicate teacup. "I *know* that I love Caspian," I said. "I know that without a doubt. But I also love my friends. My family. My future plans for my shop. Why am I going to be forced to choose between them? Why me?"

"Why are children taken before their parents? Why does disease and poverty fill the world?" she said. "It's just the way it is. Some things we must accept."

"Yes, but diseases can be cured. Poverty ended. Those things can be changed with enough man power and enough money."

"But you cannot cure death," she said quietly.

"You're right," I agreed. "That's the one thing there's no getting out of."

As I finished my tea, I didn't want the conversation with Katy to end on such a heavy note, so we switched to talking about knitting and patterns and string. When I realized how long I'd been sitting there, I told her I needed to go. I needed to get back to Caspian.

Saying my good-byes was bittersweet. I didn't know when I'd have a chance to see her again, so I just hugged her and promised that we'd get together soon.

I said good-bye to Nikolas when I got outside, but he offered to walk me to the edge of the woods.

"Have you had any more run-ins with Vincent?" he asked as we walked.

I was partially turned away from him, and I turned to face him fully. "No. I don't know what happened to him. I don't know if he's gone, or what. I like to think he is, but I'm not really sure. Why?"

"Have you talked with the other Revenants?" He asked the question casually, but it felt like there was more behind it.

"Yeah. But why? About what? Uri told me more about their background, and what they really are, but I get the sense that they aren't telling me everything."

"You know that the Revenants are needed to help a Shade and his other half be completed," he said slowly. "Have you ever thought about which ones will help *you* cross over?"

"Is Vincent . . ." Horror filled me, and I felt sick. "Is Vincent one of my Revenants?" I asked. "Is he *supposed* to be the one who helps take me?"

"I cannot be sure, but I have my suspicions," Nikolas said.

I turned blindly from him, waving my hand in some semblance of a good-bye. I couldn't speak. Couldn't think. Could barely breathe. Vincent was one of *my* Revenants? I had to get back to Caspian. I had to tell to him about this.

All this time? All this time, he was supposed to be one of the ones to cross me over? To see me in my final moment and help me get to Caspian? And the other Revenants knew? *Was this what they didn't want to tell me? That I wasn't going to be able to complete Caspian because* my *Revenant didn't want to do his job?*

The trees rushed past me, their dark colors blurring into one another. I couldn't move my legs fast enough. My mind was screaming, *NO, NO, NO.* It couldn't be him. He couldn't be the one . . .

My head was down, trying to watch my feet so I didn't stumble on another rock, when a shadow filled my vision.

I looked up.

"Hello, dear," Vincent said. "Long time, no see."

And then he punched me in the face.

When I woke up, immediately I became aware that my jaw was hurting like hell, and I was lying on the seat of a strange car. The backseat. My legs were stretched out, and I could feel leather beneath my hands.

An engine roared as we picked up speed, and the sick feeling in my gut matched the feeling of pain in my jaw. I couldn't see the driver, but I knew who it was.

I was in Vincent's car. And I had no idea where he was taking me.

Panic started shooting off in my brain, and I lay there for a good ten minutes just letting the fear take over. Finally I told myself that all I had to do was stay calm. If I could get out of the car, I could run. Wherever we were, I had to be able to run to a phone or a house or something.

That calmed me down a bit, and I focused on visualizing myself running down the road, away from *him*. My fingers slowly groped for my pocket. *My phone.*

But it was gone. *Of course.*

The car drove on for what felt like hours, and I had absolutely no clue in which direction we were headed. All I could do was lie still and preserve my strength. And try not to think about the fact that the back molar on the left side of my jaw wiggled a little bit now.

Asshole.

Eventually we came to a stop. The car shut off. "Are you awake back there yet?" Vincent asked.

I ignored him.

"Aaaaaaaaabbeeeey. I said, are you awake?"

My toe started itching. I pictured myself scratching it, but it didn't help and it was driving me crazy. I shifted subtly, trying to relieve the tension.

"You big faker," Vincent said. "I knew it!"

My eyes opened just in time to see Vincent leaning over the seat, and then there was an excruciating pain in my jaw as he pressed down right on the spot he'd hit.

"Aaaaaaaaaammmmmmmmmmppppppphhhh!" I screamed, and he took advantage of the moment to shove a bandanna into my mouth. Before I could do anything, he was tying it around my head. I lifted my hands to rip at him, tear at him, do *anything* to him, and he zip-tied my wrists together.

Tears of humiliation ran down my cheeks. *I'm so stupid!*

I'd been so busy thinking about how I was going to run away from him that I'd never even taken inventory of my own body. If I had, I would have realized that my legs were tied together.

"I got you a new bandanna," he said courteously. "It should taste nice and fresh. You can thank me later."

I rolled my head back and glared.

"Your eyes say you want to kill me, but your tears say you are *such* a baby."

He let go of my hands, and I kicked my legs against the seat out of sheer frustration.

All it did was scuff up the leather a bit.

He noticed it, though. So I did it again.

"Don't." His voice was deadly.

I kicked harder. My legs weren't moving much, but my shoes had black soles on them that left nice rubber marks on what looked like a brand-new leather interior.

"Stop it," he said again. "Do. Not. Do that."

I kicked as hard as I could, and he leaned down and touched my jaw.

Pain like I'd never felt before roiled through me and split my head in two. I screamed again, but it was muffled by the bandanna. He just kept his finger there, pressing on that tender nerve, until all I could do was whimper. And stop kicking.

He moved his hand a fraction of an inch. "Will you stop?"

I nodded.

"Good. Now let's go inside. That's where the party is."

He got out of the car and came around to the back. The door opened, and then he was grabbing the front of my jacket, trying to haul me off the seat. I fell to the ground and took the brunt of it on my knees. The driveway was gravel, and I knew I was going to be sore the next day.

Vincent tried to get me to stand, but I couldn't with my legs tied together. I just kept flopping over. Finally he grunted and lifted me up, swinging me over his shoulder. My head was upside down, my curls flinging back and forth as he walked.

I wiggled a bit, testing to see if I could get free, or maybe hurt him somehow, but a firm hand clamped down on my butt. Immediately I stopped moving.

"Believe me," he said with a note of distaste in his voice, "I don't want to be touching you either. Just stay still. We're almost there."

Upside down the world looked different, but bit by bit I started to place things. When we came to a standstill in front of a wooden door, I already knew where we were. Even from my position.

Vincent had taken me to our cabin. My family's very secluded cabin, way out in the woods.

The cabin where I'd first heard the news about Kristen's death.

He fumbled for a key, then opened the door and stepped in.

With one arm he tossed me across the room, and I landed hard on the couch. He locked the front door and pocketed the key. Turning back to me with an evil smile, he patted his pocket. "That should be safe in there. Are you comfy?"

I glared at him, and mentally promised him a slow, agonizing death.

"What do you think of the place?" He gestured around the room. There was a fire burning in the fireplace, yet all of the windows were completely boarded up. "I made a few upgrades. Took care of the exits and entrances. Cut the phone line, of course. Sure, it's been unbearably shabby to stay here these last couple of weeks, but I've managed to keep myself occupied." His smile turned into a leer. "Oh, the sacrifices I've made for you!"

My hands might have been zip-tied together, but that didn't mean I couldn't flip him off. Which was what I did.

He came over and sat next to me, propping his feet up on the coffee table in front of the couch. "I was going to take the

350

gag out of your mouth, but just for that? I think I'll give it another hour."

I shifted away from him, and he grabbed a nearby magazine. I was starting to lose feeling in my hands when he finally looked up.

"You aren't going to scream, are you?" he said. "No one's going to hear you if you do. I just don't want to have to listen to your caterwauling."

I shook my head.

He reached for the back of my head and undid the knot. I spit out the bandanna and took a deep breath. "What do you *want* from me?" I exploded. "Why did you bring me here?"

Vincent sneered. "I don't want anything *from* you."

"Then, I'm here because . . . ?"

"You're here to stay as far away from Sleepy Hollow and Caspian as possible."

"Why?"

"Why don't you just shut up now? Stop talking. It's annoying."

"Can I have a glass of water? And maybe some Advil?" I said. "My jaw is kind of sore. Must be, oh, I don't know, maybe because you *punched me in the face!*"

Vincent gave a sigh of epic proportions and launched himself off the couch. "Fine."

He went rummaging through a couple of drawers for the Advil and then got me some water.

I swallowed down the pills and gently touched my tender jaw. Then I held my hands out to him. "Can you cut me free?"

He pulled out a pocketknife and sliced through the plastic. I rubbed my hands together, trying to massage some of the life back into them. He pocketed the knife and moved over to the fire, throwing a fresh log onto it.

"Look at me!" he said. "I'm going all mountain man up here."

"What exactly are we supposed to *do* here?" I asked. "Read books? Do crossword puzzles? Oooh, I know! Monopoly by the fire."

"You can do whatever you want. I'm going to be catching up on the latest season of *Supernatural*."

I rolled my eyes at him. "Oh, great."

"Hey!" he said. "I went through a lot of trouble to make sure you would have supplies. I'm not heartless, you know. I bought food, water, even toilet paper. What else do you need?"

"*Supplies?* How long are you planning to keep me here?"

"Today is November second, so . . . it won't be much longer." He looked disappointed. "I guess you won't be needing all of those supplies, after all." Then he brightened. "But we can stay longer if you want."

Chapter Twenty-four

BLOODLINE

❧❀❧

...a worthy wight of the name of Ichabod Crane, who sojourned ... in Sleepy Hollow ... He was tall, but exceedingly lank ... with huge ears, large green glassy eyes ...

—"The Legend of Sleepy Hollow"

B efore I could answer, Vincent went over to the DVD player and grabbed the remote. Returning to me, he propped both of his outstretched feet across my lap. With a grimace I shoved his feet off. "I'm not your footrest. Thanks."

My own feet were starting to ache, and I massaged the skin that was pulled tight at the ankles by the zip tie. "Can you please cut these off me?"

"Let me think about it. . . . No."

He pressed PLAY, and a ball of fire appeared on the screen. Two guys ran out of a building, each one holding a shotgun.

"I saw this one already," he said. "Dean's going straight to hell for this. Or wait. It might be Sam this time. I can't keep them straight."

I didn't want to beg him. But the pain was heading toward unbearable. "Vincent, please," I said. "Cut these off of me?"

"What will you give me?" He cocked his head and slowly slid his eyes down my body. Every nerve ending shrank back, and my skin felt like it wanted to run away screaming. What exactly was I going to have to do to earn my freedom?

"I, uh . . . I . . ." I swallowed loudly.

"Well?"

My feet could fall off. I'd crawl to the door if I had too.

Vincent cocked an ear toward me, waiting.

"I have to use the bathroom," I said instead.

"I'll walk you." He stood up and offered a hand. I ignored it at first.

"You have five seconds to make up your mind," he told me. "Or else you won't be going until tomorrow morning."

Reluctantly I took it and hobbled to my feet. Trying to take a step was virtually impossible, and I wobbled wildly. "I can't do it," I said. "I need my feet."

Vincent gave me a look of disdain.

"I can pee right here on the floor if you want," I offered.

He pulled out his knife again and slit the tie. My feet sprang apart, and I uttered a sigh of relief. That relief was short lived, though, because he clamped an arm down on my wrist and grabbed hold.

Forcefully, he directed me over to the bathroom and shoved me into it. I turned on the water to make him think I was washing my hands, and sized up the small window over the tub.

Too small.

Vincent banged on the door. "Hurry *up*. I'm *waiting*."

"I'm coming, I'm coming," I yelled back.

Gripping the edges of the sink, I stared into the mirror and turned my head to look at my jaw. A faint yellow and pink stain was there, the beginning of a bruise starting to form. I touched it and hissed as pain went screaming through my head again. *Time for plan B, Abbey. You need to get out of here.*

The doorknob rattled. "Open up. Or I'm breaking it down. Then any peeing you want to do really will be in front of me."

I turned the water off and opened the door. Vincent grabbed my arm again and walked me back to the couch. Turning myself completely away from him, I scooted down closer to the other end and curled up into a ball. How long would it take for someone to find me?

"Why did you do it?" I said softly, wondering how much I could get out of him.

"Do what?"

"Stalk me. Leave things in my locker. Visit my parents dressed like a priest. And then . . . just disappear. Why did you do it?"

He looked excited. "Did you like the fingernails? I thought they were a nice touch. And that perfume? *Very* expensive. The priest outfit was my personal favorite. Hard to move in, though. It restricted the blood flow." He grinned at me as I shot him a *You're crazy* look. "Oh, come on. I had to do *something* to keep myself occupied. I was killing time."

"Killing time until what?"

"Until this, of course. You're a little thick, aren't you?"

I sat up. "What do you mean?"

"They didn't tell you? I bet that was Sophiel's idea. She's such a bitch."

"Why don't *you* tell me?"

"Has your lover boy been experiencing any strange symptoms lately? Maybe losing his ability to *touch*?" He held up one finger. "Or he suddenly likes to take extra-long naps?"

I considered lying to him, saying no, those things had never happened. But other than Uri, he seemed to be the only Revenant willing to tell me anything. "Yes. Why?"

"And you." He pointed at me. "You don't react the same way to the Revs anymore, do you? No more burning smell or tasting ash?"

I shook my head. "What does all of that mean?" My voice came out in a whisper.

"It means that your little Revenant buddies have been lying to you. I'd wager from the very beginning." He seemed absolutely delighted. "Do you even know what November third is?"

"No."

"It's the reason why you're here. The reason why your boy toy's been losing his ability to touch and getting trapped in the dark sleep so often. It's why you don't react the same way to the Revenants. Because it's getting closer. It's almost time."

I waited for him to tell me. It was obvious that was what he wanted to do.

"D-day," Vincent said.

"That's not true," I replied. "There is no exact date. The Revenants haven't figured out when or how I'll die."

"Not yours. . . . His." Vincent smirked.

"But how can that be? Caspian already died. I've been to his grave."

"Did you really think that Casper the Friendly Ghost was going to stick around forever? Stay with you, in this world,

 357

so you could bump uglies once a year?" He gave me a look of annoyance.

I tried as hard as I could not to let my cheeks flush, but I don't think I was successful. "How can Caspian die *again*?" I asked, desperate not to let the conversation get sidetracked.

"The short answer is, you."

"I'm going to kill him?"

Vincent roared with laughter, and then his face went completely still. "No, you'll be right here with me. But without you Caspian can't stay. As of midnight November third, he no longer exists."

"How can I stop that from happening? How do I complete him?"

"You die."

"And are you"—I gulped—"going to be the one to kill me?"

"No, no, no." Vincent patted me on the head. "Remember? We already had this conversation. In your bedroom? I want to keep you *alive*."

"But why? I don't understand. Why would you want to keep me alive?"

"Because once you're dead, you can complete him."

This was like a vicious circle without answers. "Why do you care whether or not I complete him?" I said. "If you're a Revenant, then you've helped other Shades before. Why not us?"

He crossed one leg over his knee. "It all goes back to the original Revenants. Rumor has it that God and the devil made a deal and chose six representatives of heaven and six representatives of hell to help them sort out the whole reaping/death business. The representatives were split into teams of two, one angel half, one demon half. Or one light, one dark. One yin, one yang . . . yadda, yadda, yadda. You get the idea. Over time they were designated to help one group of souls in particular cross over—Shades and their other halves. With me so far?"

"Yes."

"Good!" He clapped his hands together. "Eventually the six teams had been around for so long—thousands of years, after all—that they were ready to move on. Shades, the only humans allowed to stay on Earth after their deaths, were chosen to take their place. And these Shades were given a name." He looked at me like he was giving me a hint. "Who do you know that works in teams of two? One good, one bad . . . Well, generally speaking."

"Teams of two . . . The Revenants?"

"And the bonus round goes to . . . !" He touched his nose and pointed to me. "Yes, the Revenants."

"Wait a minute. . . . So you're telling me that Revenants

replaced the original angel-demon teams, and all Revenants were once Shades? As in, human?"

"Ding, ding, ding! Give that girl a prize!" He clapped again.

I stared at him. "*You* were once human!"

"Don't act so shocked. Jesus."

My mind was spinning. "Is that why none of the others knew what to do?" I said. "Because you were supposed to be my Revenant? One of the ones to help me cross over?"

He leaned back and placed both hands behind his head. His smile said it all.

My fingers dug into the couch, and I found myself clenching the fabric. "Why me?" I said through gritted teeth. "What was so special about me and Caspian that you decided you didn't want to do your job anymore? Tell me, Vincent Drake. What was so *goddamned important* that you couldn't just let us alone?"

"Oh, please," he scoffed. "This isn't about you. It's about me. This is *all about me*. Do you know what it's like to be immortal? To not have responsibilities. Or bills. No money problems, or wondering where your next meal is going to come from?" He inhaled deeply, closing his eyes for just a moment. "It's fucking awesome. That's what it is."

He moved in close and put his face inches away from mine.

"I hold the fate of mortals in my hands. Each and every time I come to Earth, *I* am responsible for their lives and their deaths." He smiled at me. A crazy, beautiful smile. "I like that feeling. And I don't want it to end. Simple as that."

"But why would it end? Aren't you guys the new teams, or whatever? Taking the place of the angels and demons?"

"We aren't the original Revenants, you idiot. There haven't been many of us, but there have been others. You get a certain amount of time to do your job, and then you get replaced by the next round of Shades. And those Shades just so happen to be here. Known as Nikolas Degenhart and Katrina Van Tassel, of the Sleepy Hollow Cemetery."

I rubbed my eyelids. Trying to stuff all of this new information into my brain was making my head spin. "So . . . what? You did all of this because you're going to lose your *job*?"

"It's not that simple," he exploded. "It's *never* that simple. While you're a Shade, you live forever, tied to one place. Shades are gatekeepers of sacred spaces. You know, cemeteries, burial grounds, ancient worship mounds?" I nodded, because that seemed to be what he wanted me to do. "When you become a Revenant, you live forever all over the world. When you stop being a Revenant, you move on."

"Where do you go?"

"I don't know. But wherever it is, you don't come back. And that's not going to be me."

"How do you know which Revenants are going to move on?"

"No one knows. That's the problem."

"Then how did *you* know?" I asked.

His voice turned deceptively calm. "Because I'm the oldest. I've been around the longest. And because I had a little help."

Sitting up, he took off the T-shirt he was wearing and exposed his chest. It was covered in a mass of black tattoos. They were small squiggly symbols, repeated over and over again, on top of one another. I couldn't tell where one ended and the next began.

I couldn't help it. I laughed. "You had help from a *tattoo artist?*"

He waited until my laughter died, then tossed his shirt aside. "Done yet?" There was something in his tone that told me to stop.

"Yes," I said meekly.

"These are protection spells." He pointed to one section. "They keep me hidden from the others. The shaman who did these knows what we are, and he told me what would happen in the Hollow. That it was time for two new Revenants, and I'd be the one moving on. I can't let that happen."

"Which is why you don't want me to complete Caspian."

Vincent nodded. "If you two aren't completed, then the other two have to stay. There's a balance to everything. If I can't stop it, then I *will* delay it."

"So how does Kristen play into all of this? How could you think she was Caspian's other half?"

He looked annoyed with himself. "I don't know how I got *that* one wrong. I did all the research on Caspian Vander— raised in West Virginia, moved to White Plains, his mother ran out on him when he was a little baby, he has the connection to Sleepy Hollow . . . blah, blah, blah. Maybe it was my preference for redheads clouding my judgment."

"'Connection to Sleepy Hollow'?" I gave him a confused look. "What do you mean by that?"

"His connection. It's in his blood. Literally. He's a descendant of Ichabod Crane."

"A descendent of . . . ? *What?*"

"The green eyes?" He gestured to his face. "You've read 'The Legend of Sleepy Hollow,' right? Ichabod Crane is described as having green eyes. The legend was true. He was a real person, and he had a bunch of kids. Caspian is one of his great-great-great-great-grandkids. Don't quote me on that number of 'great's, though."

Was it true? *Could* it be true? Caspian did have unusual green eyes, and he'd told me more than once about the pull he'd felt toward Sleepy Hollow. Was this another way we were connected? Me, with my love of the town and Washington Irving, and him through an actual bloodline tie?

What are the odds?

Vincent opened his mouth to say something, but the sound of a car pulling into the driveway interrupted him.

"Damn it." He pointed at me. "*You.* Stay here. I mean it. I'm going to see who that is."

I glanced over at the fireplace as Vincent got up and moved to the front door. There I spotted my opportunity—a half-burned log sticking out of the fire. When he turned his back, I saw my chance.

And I took it.

Chapter Twenty-five

MAKE IT RIGHT

The dominant spirit, however, that haunts this enchanted region, and seems to be commander-in-chief of all the powers of the air, is the apparition of a figure on horseback . . .

—"The Legend of Sleepy Hollow"

I didn't stop to think. I just ran for the log, grabbed it, and headed straight for him. Vincent turned around a second too late, and I drove the hot end right into the top part of his chest—aiming for the section of tattoos that he'd said were his protection spells.

He screamed in outrage as his skin sizzled and split, the raw edges of the wound turning black with soot. A large red burn mark blossomed, and he looked down at it, shock written all over his face.

I held on tightly to the wood, barely even noticing that it was warm to the touch, and pointed it at him, brandishing it as the only weapon I had.

He took a step toward me, but the front door suddenly shuddered open, and the man in the white suit, the man who had been at the insane asylum and who had been watching me in the cemetery, stepped into the cabin.

"Grifyth!" he yelled.

Everything happened at once then, in a blur of motion that left me stunned, as the man tackled Vincent and they went flying past me. The man in the white suit shoved Vincent into the bathroom and slammed the door shut between them. Reaching for a kitchen chair, he wedged it up under the knob. It didn't take long for the pounding on the other side to begin.

I glanced over at him. "Who are you, and what are you doing here?"

"Well, I *was* coming to rescue you," he said in an amused voice. "But it looks like you were taking care of that yourself."

He put out a hand and reached for me. "Come on. We're leaving."

Apparently I didn't have a choice in the matter, because he was already hauling me behind him, and my legs followed.

"What's going to happen with Vincent?" I said.

"He's not going to be happy when he gets out, but we need to get you back to the other Revenants." He directed me to a gray car sitting outside. We both got in.

"What's your name?" I asked.

"You can call me Monty."

"Do you know where Caspian is?"

He nodded. "With the Revenants. But he doesn't have much more time."

He looked sad as he started up the car, but he floored it and we drove away. He was going over the speed limit by a good thirty miles as we headed back to Sleepy Hollow, but something told me we weren't going to be stopped by any cops.

"You were at the asylum, right?" I said. "Gray's Folly?"

"Yes."

"How did Uri know you would be there?"

"I spent a lot of time there when I was human. The place was named for me, actually."

The puzzle pieces were starting to slide into place. But the biggest one, the most obvious one, didn't fit yet, and I wanted to tread delicately. I don't know why, but he struck me as someone with a wounded soul.

"Monty . . . can I ask you something?" I said.

He nodded.

"Are you Vincent's partner? His other half?"

Sorrow crossed his face, along with something else. And I knew the answer was yes.

"How can that be?" I said. "I thought Shades were supposed to be male and female? A love match?"

"Most are. But when Grifyth was a child—I'm sorry, I mean Vincent. When he was a child, he was a student at my school. He died there, but I still kept seeing him everywhere. I thought that I was being punished for not saving him."

"Not saving him? How did he die?"

Monty's expression darkened. "He drowned."

Vincent had drowned? Now it made sense. Shades and their other halves *were* a love match. But for Monty it had been a self-sacrificing love.

"So when you found out you were like me, you completed him out of guilt, right?"

He sighed. "I did. That was many lifetimes ago now."

We passed the enormous covered bridge as we drove through Sleepy Hollow, and I glanced back at it for a moment. It reminded me of what I was rushing toward. If I was going to save Caspian, if I was going to complete him, there was only one thing I was sure of: I had to die first.

Reaching over to touch his hand as we pulled up to the cemetery, I said, "Thank you, Monty. I don't know what would have happened if you hadn't come." Then I got out of the car, unsure if he would follow, but I knowing where I had to go.

To the river. To the spot where Kristen had died.

They were all there, waiting for me, forming a small circle, with Uri and Cacey off to one side and Kame and Sophie on the other. Caspian was standing in the middle, gesturing and speaking loudly.

I went running. Flying. Toward the bridge. Toward *him*.

He met me halfway, and I stumbled, hands reaching out for him. They went through, of course, but I was so happy to see him that I didn't care.

"Where *were* you?" he asked. "Oh, God, Astrid. I was so worried! We didn't know where to look, but I didn't want to leave in case you came here. What happened? Why didn't you—"

"Vincent was here," I said. "He took me, to my family's cabin. He kidnapped me."

Monty came strolling up behind me, and the others welcomed him. He didn't seem very comfortable around them, but Uri slapped him on the back, and I heard him say, "I knew you'd help."

Caspian came closer to me. "He *took* you? Oh, love. Did he hurt you?"

My eyes slid away from his. "He was . . . his usual charming self."

Caspian looked me over, his eyes narrowing. "What did he do?"

"He sort of used his fist to subdue me," I admitted. "In the face."

"Jeez," Cacey said. "He really *has* gone off the deep end."

Caspian glared at her.

"Later," I said. "We don't have much time."

"Why?" Caspian asked suspiciously. "That's what they keep saying. Does someone want to clue me in?"

"At midnight it's November third," I replied. I looked over at Cacey. "Vincent told me everything. About the original Revenants. About the fact that you were once all human. Why didn't you tell me? Why did you lie?"

Kame held up one hand. "There were certain things we *couldn't* tell you, Abbey."

I turned to Uri. "*You* told me practically everything. Why didn't you tell me about what would happen to Caspian? Was it really that hard? I had to find out from *Vincent*."

"This was all new to us, Abbey," Uri replied. "Vincent and Monty were the only ones authorized to tell you anything. We were just here to find Vincent and bring him back, to restore the balance."

"Oh, come *on*. You had to have had some idea. All the signs were there. You might not have known the exact date, but you knew it was getting close."

"Well, now you know, and that's that," Cacey said.

"There is a bigger issue to be dealt with here, Acacia," Kame said. "You know that."

I traded looks with Caspian. "What's the bigger issue?"

"Vincent is your Revenant," Kame replied. "That means he must help you cross over."

"But he doesn't want to do the job. So that means I'll have to do it," Monty said. "And I'm going to need the help of everyone."

"Nothing needs to be done," Caspian said. "We'll just keep things the way they are." He softened his tone. "November first will come around again next year, Astrid."

I closed my eyes briefly, but that didn't stop the tears from coming. "You don't understand," I told him. "All the recent changes lately, you losing your touch, falling into a deep sleep . . . it means something more. If I don't complete you now, you'll move on. Without me."

Caspian looked around for one of the Revenants to tell him I was wrong.

The answer came from Cacey. "Your time is up, sweetie."

He looked down at the ground, stunned disbelief written all over his face, and my tears came harder. I tried to push them away, scrubbed my hands across my face, but the tears just came faster. "Please," I said. "*Please.* Just let me be with him."

"It's not up to us," Cacey said. "That's just the way it goes."

"But you guys have powers. You have to be able to do something."

Uri came over and put his arms around me, wrapping me in a protective embrace. Turning me away from the group, he whispered, "Abbey, you don't understand. You don't have to die. You get to *live*. Doesn't that mean something to you? Anything?"

I gazed at Caspian. "Not without him."

Uri let out a frustrated sigh. "I didn't tell you this before, but my death hurt. It was painful, and I wouldn't wish that on anyone."

I shook my head stubbornly. "I don't care. I don't care if it hurts. Besides, Nikolas told me that his death was easy."

"It's different for everyone, that's true, but don't you see? Why would you want to give up all of this? I don't get it."

I wrapped my hand in his. "Think about Cacey. Acacia. Then tell me you still don't get it." A half smile stretched across his lips, then disappeared. "See?" I said. "You get it."

Straightening my shoulders, I stepped away from him and moved to Caspian. "Love," I whispered. "It's okay. I've decided."

His eyes were filled with anguish, and he put one hand up next to my cheek. "You can't, Abbey. You can't do this. You have to let me go. Just let me go." Very purposefully he stepped away from me and turned his back, moving next to Sophie on the other side of the circle.

"Do it," he said tersely. "Take me with you and let her stay."

"Caspian." I raised my voice. "This is *my* choice. Don't take that away from me."

"You can't think that I'm—"

Cacey held up her hand and interrupted us. "Wait, wait, wait. There's no need for any of this. It still doesn't change the fact that we *can't do it*. It's Vincent and Monty's job, remember?" she said.

"But Monty wants to try. Doesn't that mean anything?" I asked.

Kame leaned over and said something to Sophie. She shook her head, then replied, "I don't know. The chain has been interrupted. We can't be sure—"

The sound of hoofbeats came thundering up from behind us, and we all turned to look. Nikolas was sitting on top of a dark gray horse, with Katy behind him.

"We have searched the other side," he said, "and still no sign of—" As soon as they saw me, they came to a stop.

"Abbey!" Katy said, sliding down from the horse. "We were so worried! We have been looking everywhere for you."

She came toward me, and I gave her a big hug. "I was with Vincent, but I'm okay."

"What did he do to you?" She turned my face and looked at my jaw. "You poor thing."

"I'm okay," I whispered. "Everything's going to be fine now."

"Abbey?" Someone else called my name. From behind me.

The voice was high pitched, but it sounded like . . .

"Cyn?"

She stepped forward hesitantly, and I could see that Vincent was holding her with one hand across her throat. Something glinted, and I knew it was a knife.

Immediately Caspian moved next to me and Nikolas edged his horse closer.

"Did you start without me?" Vincent called. "You know I couldn't stay away. But I have my insurance policy here." He pushed Cyn forward roughly, and she stumbled.

"What are you *doing?*" Cacey asked. "Are you crazy?"

Vincent glared at her.

"Okay, okay, don't answer that," she muttered.

"Let the girl come to us," Kame instructed Vincent, his tone soothing. "We can discuss this."

"There's nothing to discuss." He jerked her head back. The wicked edge of a blade shone against her pale throat. "I'm *not* being replaced."

"Hey, schizo," Cyn said to Vincent, "want to loosen up on the grip? I won't struggle."

Vincent ignored her.

"Why don't you let Cyn go?" I said. "She doesn't have anything to do with me and Caspian being completed."

374

"Can't," he replied. "See, what I need is for you to make the decision *not* to complete him. And the only way I see that happening now is for me to hold on to *her* so you don't do anything stupid."

"Why didn't you just stay away?" I said suddenly. "If you didn't want to do the job, why not just head off to some tropical paradise and stay as far away from me and Sleepy Hollow as possible?"

He sighed heavily. "Radar thing. It's like a time clock on steroids. A real bitch."

"What's the radar thing?"

"A program that's hardwired inside our brains to guarantee we show up and do our job." He shifted the knife away from Cyn and gestured to his head. "See, when a Shade's time is up, we get this little blip that starts beeping in the back of our heads. The more we ignore it? The louder it becomes, until it's this crazy full-on blaring signal that drives you mad and all you can think about is finding your Shade. You have to get within ten feet of your charge to shut it down."

He grimaced, and I could tell that he'd obviously experienced that a time or two.

"Anything else you want to know?" he said. He glanced at his watch. "We have some time to kill."

I saw movement out of the corner of my eye, and realized it was Uri and Caspian edging closer.

Vincent saw it too.

"I will gut her like a fish right here and now if you don't *back the fuck up*," Vincent threatened, moving the knife to Cyn's stomach. "I won't kill her, but I'll make her bleed."

They halted.

"This is getting old," Cyn called out. "One of you want to tell me what his damage is?" She hissed in pain as Vincent dug the edge of the knife in deeper. "Okay, okay. Forget it."

"No! Don't!" I said. "You win, Vincent. End of story."

"Actually . . ." He cocked his head. "That's not the end of the story. Did they tell you the other part? The *best* part? Probably not. Because they're cowards."

"Like you're anything better?" Caspian said.

"I'm lots of things, but I'm no coward," Vincent replied. "I have balls of solid *rock*." Then he turned his attention to me. "You know that friend of yours? The dead one? It was supposed to be you."

I tried to keep my face blank. "You already told me that. You thought she was Caspian's other half and wanted to get her out of the way so they could never find each other."

He shook his head, but grinned gleefully. "It was only a mistake on my part to get *involved* with her. If I'd been more patient, I could have avoided that. When she died"—he looked over at the Crane River—"right over there, I believe, *you* were supposed to be here. It was *your* death day. Not hers. Before I interfered, you would have met Caspian, and then who knows where we'd all be? I just got tired of having a loose end, so I decided to take care of it on my own. Now you're unwritten and none of us know when it's gonna happen."

Shock hit me. I glanced over at Uri. "Is that true?" I asked. "*Tell me.* Is that true?"

Nikolas got down from his horse. "Abbey," he said, "you have been given a chance—"

"Been given a *chance!*" I said hysterically. "I haven't been given a chance! My life was spared because my best friend's was taken in its place."

Vincent grinned. "I was hoping that she'd bring you along with her. Then I would have had a two-for-one."

Suddenly Cyn started whispering something. I thought I caught the word "veil," but she was talking faster and faster and I couldn't hear what she was saying. Her eyes closed and her head slumped forward.

She jerked once, then stood upright. When her eyes opened again, they had changed.

"Abbey," she said, "it's okay."

Blinking rapidly, I tried to clear my vision. Cyn was doing whatever she'd done at the séance. Her smile, her eyes, her expression . . . Except for the longer hair, everything about her was Kristen. *She's really here.*

"Kristen?" I said in a whisper.

Vincent must have been seeing it too, because he looked just as stunned.

Cyn put her hand on my arm. "I've missed you so much." She put her other hand on my face. "I'm sorry I lied to you. I'm sorry I didn't tell you about him. For almost a whole year I kept his secret because I was so ashamed. I didn't want you to think any less of me. I just wanted to get him out of my life without you ever finding out. That's why I didn't ask you to go with me. To the bridge."

My vision blurred again. *Stupid tears.* "I could never think less of you, Kris," I said. "I miss you *so* much. There's so much I want to tell you."

She smiled. "I know about everything now. I know when you come to visit me in the cemetery. I knew when your boy was keeping watch for you, and tending my grave." She glanced back at Caspian. "He's good for you. Very good for you. Do you love him?"

"Yes," I whispered. "More than anything."

Vincent interrupted us. "I don't know what's going on, but this—"

"You know what you need to do." The voice that interrupted came from behind Vincent. Monty was standing there. "Grifyth, you know what you need to do. Let them be together. Let this be over with."

"My name is Vincent!" he said. Rage turned his face purple, and Cyn/Kristen grabbed for my hand. "And *you* should know that!"

He pulled the knife away from Cyn for a split second to point it at Monty, and I pulled Cyn's hand as hard as I could to jerk her away from him. She must have been thinking the same thing, because she propelled herself at me.

Vincent reached out to grab her, but he only got a handful of her hair and it slithered out of his grasp. Uri and Caspian launched themselves at him, and all three of them went down in a tangled heap.

I could hear punches flying and grunts of pain as fists hit flesh, but I couldn't see what was happening.

When the dust finally settled, Uri was sitting on Vincent's chest, pinning his arms down on either side, with Caspian holding his feet. Monty stood by, looking unsure of himself.

He glanced at me, and I could see guilt written all over his face. Guilt that he hadn't done anything to stop his partner.

"Make it right," I told him. "You can still make this right."

He shook his head.

The other Revenants and Nikolas and Katy were still waiting by the riverbank. Grabbing Cyn's hand, I raised my voice. "Vincent interfered. He was supposed to do one job, and he did another. He took a life that wasn't his to take. You need to set the balance right."

"Abbey, we can't just—," Cacey started to say.

But I held up one hand. "Yes. You can. I don't care how you have to do it, but you need to set things right. Bring Kristen back. Take me. Restore the balance."

"Abbey," Caspian pleaded. "Don't. Don't do this for me."

I turned to face him. "I would give up my heart and breath and soul for you. Gladly. But this is bigger than you. And bigger than me. It's my destiny to be your other half, but it's also my destiny to be the best friend that I can. To Kristen. She was robbed of her future, her dreams. Vincent took that away from her when he had no right to."

"I won't stand in the way of your decision," he said. "I'll support you. Always."

My heart almost broke again at the unwavering look of love in his eyes.

Kame spoke up. "You realize what will have to happen if we do this, right, Abbey? What you're asking? We'll have to change time. To change the order of things."

Briefly I thought about Mom and Dad. Uncle Bob and Aunt Marjorie. It wasn't fair that I wouldn't have the chance to say good-bye to them.

But that was life.

"I'm asking you to repair the order," I said. "I'm ready."

He hesitated. "We can't be sure about what will happen, *after*. This is a real mess. It's something entirely different from anything we've done before."

I looked to Monty. "Are you willing to try to help me cross over?"

He glanced at Vincent.

"Don't you fucking do it, Monty!" Vincent yelled, bucking against Uri and trying to throw him off. "It won't work. And if you—"

Uri clamped his hand down over Vincent's mouth. "Enough from you."

"He's burned on his upper shoulder," I called out, gesturing on myself where I'd hurt Vincent. "Just there."

Uri poked Vincent's chest and he made an angry, choked sound.

"He may not be willing, but he's still here," said Monty. "I can try to use that bond." Then he nodded. "Yes. I am willing."

I let out a deep breath. Kame smiled at me. "Now or never, baby girl."

I smiled back, and then I locked eyes with Caspian. "Now. Definitely now."

"We're going to need Uri," Cacey said. "And Caspian."

Nikolas stepped forward. "I can take their place."

Cacey gave him a sideways glance. "Are you sure about that?"

Drawing himself up to his full height, Nikolas scowled at her. "You doubt a Hessian?"

"Okay, okay." She shook her head, and Nikolas went over to where Vincent was lying. He quickly exchanged places with Caspian and Uri, and had no trouble whatsoever subduing Vincent on his own.

Caspian came to join me, and I turned to Cyn. She still looked like Kristen.

"Bye, Kris," I whispered, holding up my hand. "I love you. Don't forget that. Take care of my mom and dad."

She placed her hand against mine, our palms touching, and nodded.

"Bye, Abbey," she said with a sad smile. "I love you, too."

Then she stepped back.

The Revenants moved forward, forming a tight circle around me and Caspian. Their arms were touching. Uri straightened, and said, "Acacia, I call upon you."

Cacey answered. "Uriel, I call upon you."

"Sophiel, I call upon you," Kame said.

"Kame, I call upon you," she replied.

"And I call upon myself," Monty said, "And Grifyth."

Monty picked up my hand, and then picked up Caspian's. Bringing them together, one on top of the other, he placed his hand on mine, directly above the ring Caspian had given me, and then pushed down.

With Monty's hand touching mine, I could touch Caspian. I looked down. "I . . ."

When I glanced up again, Caspian was smiling.

"I promise you forever," I vowed to him, staring into his green eyes. "Whatever that is. Whatever I can give you. You have all of it. All of me."

"I promise you forever," he replied. "Whatever that is. Whatever I can give you. You have all of it. All of me."

"Now," Monty said.

I closed my eyes.

The feeling of water swept over me.

The scene flashed and changed, and the cottage was in front of me. Nikolas and Katy's cottage. But instead of seeing their belongings, I recognized Caspian's art pad. His charcoal. Empty bottles stood along the windowsill, waiting to be filled with new perfumes.

A bowl of fresh peppermint leaves sat on the table beside my flower press and oil distiller, waiting . . . for me and Caspian. The new caretakers of the cemetery.

 383

Nikolas and Katy came walking toward me, leading Nikolas's horse behind.

"Did it work?" I said. "Am I crossing over?"

They just smiled.

"Take good care of Stagmont," Nikolas said, handing me the reins to the horse. "He'll stay with you now. At the cemetery."

I nodded. "And you?"

"On to something new."

As he spoke his face started changing, the wrinkles lessening. His hair turned darker, and so did Katy's. The faded strawberry blond color she used to have became a rich, vibrant shade of red. Color bloomed in her cheeks. She laughed as she held her hands out in front of her. Then she turned to Nikolas.

But Nikolas wasn't the old man I'd once met raking leaves. Now he was young. No more than twenty. Katy was young too. Maybe seventeen.

They stepped back, turning away from me. Katy lifted her hand to wave, and I did the same. But already the scene was changing again. They were dissolving around the edges. Moving on. Becoming the new Revenants.

Everything started to fade. . . .

And the last thing I remembered was feeling a smile on my lips.

Epilogue

The girl walked along the cemetery path, her feet remembering the way. She had been here so many times before that she didn't need to see where she was going. The boy next to her swung her hand in his, to a rhythm only they could hear, his curly brown hair ruffled by the wind.

She clutched the flowers she held tightly. Red ones. *Her favorite color.*

The headstone came into view, the surface smooth and polished. She dropped to her knees, kicking off her sandals in the warm afternoon sun, and Kristen Maxwell laid the roses reverently next to the words that made up the sum of her best friend's life.

She traced the carved name in bold letters, ABIGAIL.

"Hi, Abbey," she said, pulling the graduation cap from her

head and setting it on top of the stone. "Today was the big day. I wish you could have been there."

The boy sat down beside her. "I think she was. There with us in spirit."

"I know, Ben. But still ..."

He took her hand, laced her fingers through his and pulled them up for a quick kiss. "What do you want to do today? To celebrate?"

Kristen looked off into the distance. In the direction of a cottage that she would never know was there. "Let's stay here with her a bit longer. Then I want to go downtown and look at the vacant shops. I had this dream last night about a beautiful little store with perfumes and lotions and creams. That was what Abbey always wanted to do. To open a perfume shop here in the Hollow."

She played absentmindedly with the ribbon in her hair. It came loose and fell free.

She tried to catch it. Stood up, laughing, as she tried to chase it down. But it slipped through her fingers, and she couldn't hold on. The wind carried it away.

I watched them from the edge of the cemetery. Kristen and Ben. She looked so beautiful, in her graduation cap and gown.

And Ben . . . It was obvious that he couldn't have been happier.

Caspian came up from behind me, wrapped his arms around me, and kissed the side of my neck. I leaned into him.

"I'm so glad she's happy," I said.

"Me too," he replied. "Are you happy?"

I thought about all that I'd lost. And then I thought about all that I'd gained. I threaded my fingers through his and watched my friends holding tightly to each other.

"Yes," I answered. "I am."

Something touched my bare feet, and I looked down. A green ribbon was lying there.

I bent to pick it up, and smiled.

Tucking it into my pocket, I turned to Caspian. His lips met mine, and the world faded away. The stars came out. And the sun shone brighter than the moon.

ACKNOWLEDGMENTS

Special thanks go to Washington Irving, of course. I hope you don't mind that I've added my own pinch of salt to the soup mix. To my editor, Anica Rissi. Thank you for all your hard work, enthusiasm, and patience, especially when I wrote and chopped, and chopped and wrote, and chopped and chopped and chopped some more. "THE END" seemed so very far away, but I finally found it. To my agent, Michael Bourret. Thank you for working so hard on my behalf and championing this book through the many levels of the publishing process. To the Simon Pulse team: I am so thankful for all of you!

Thank you, Lee and Lucy Miller, for your unconditional love and support. I know I don't say it enough, but you really are Mom and Dad to me. To all of my friends and family members who came to signings, posted messages on my Facebook page, and spread the word: "Thanks" seems so inadequate, but I'll say it anyway. Thanks.

The Hollow trilogy started with best friends and ended with best friends, so I'd like to thank all the best friends who have been a part of my life: Steph Batchelor, Rachel Hall, Nicole Sandt, and

Lee Miller. Some of you I talk to more frequently than others, but I love you all. Thanks, besties!

To Mrs. Vincenty for her encouragement, Mrs. Carson for always knowing when to read another chapter, and to Mr. Welch: I didn't become a rocket scientist, but at least now I'll have the chance to write about them! P.S. You were a great teacher.

To Johnny Cash: The journey almost ended before it began, and you helped me make it through. See you in September. Thanks to the people, places, and things that have inspired me along the way, including the Jack Daniel's distillery, the Buffalo Trace distillery, and the George Dickel distillery. Not just for the fruits of your labor, but for teaching me that sometimes the best words come slowly and steadily, aged with time.

Thanks to Michelle Zink for being a confidante along the way, and for being willing to put up with me when I e-mailed to say, "So, how about going on this crazy book tour that we put together *ourselves*?" You are an amazing person, and I'm honored to call you my friend. To all the bookstore owners, booksellers, libraries, librarians, and store employees who were a part of the Ghosts and Graves tour: Thank you for your enthusiasm and graciousness; thank you for welcoming us. We couldn't have done it without you. Thanks also to Jim Logan at the Sleepy Hollow Cemetery for the walking tour and arranging the bell ringing at the Old Dutch Church! Best. Moment. Ever.

To Erin and Keith: Here's to a happy and healthy future for both of you, always. I love you guys. To Ephraim: You inspire me with your adorableness and never-ending spirit. I am *so* incredibly proud to be your auntie. As soon as Mom says it's

okay, I'm buying you that puppy. To Lauren, Matthew, Caitlin, Connor, and Samantha: You guys make me feel old, but that's okay, because I am completely amazed by how gorgeous, talented, smart, and beautiful you all are. (I get bonus points for putting you in a book, right?) And to Aunt Debbie and Uncle Albert, thanks for showing me just how cool the garbage biz can be.

And now, thank you, dear reader. Thank you for investing your time in this story. Thank you for coming to see me at my book signings. Thank you for e-mailing me to tell me how much you loved the story and how much you loved Caspian and how much you want to be BFFs with Abbey. Thank you for telling me what my words meant to *you*.

Last but not least, my eternal thanks go to Lee. I could fill a whole page, but you already know all the thank-yous that should come your way—from the very big to the very small. Lots and lots and *lots* of 'em. I'll keep trying. Maybe one day I'll get thru them all.